WINDS OF THE OLD DAYS

Betsy Aswad

WINDS *of the* OLD DAYS

The Dial Press

New York

Published by The Dial Press
1 Dag Hammarskjold Plaza
New York, New York 10017

Manufactured in the United States of America

First printing

Design by Francesca Belanger

Library of Congress Cataloging in Publication Data

Aswad, Betsy.
  Winds of the old days.

  I. Title.
PZ4.A845Wi   [PS3551.S9]   813'.54   80-17446
ISBN 0-8037-9638-2

*Grateful acknowledgment is made for permission to reprint the following copyrighted
material:*

Lyrics from "Diamonds and Rust" and "Winds of the Old Days" by Joan
Baez: copyright © 1975 Chandos Music (ASCAP). Reprinted by permission.
All rights reserved throughout the world.

Excerpt from "Apostle" in *Encyclopaedia Britannica,* 15th edition (1974).
Used by permission.

You strayed into my arms.
And there you stayed, temporarily lost at sea;
The madonna was yours for free.
Yes, the girl on the half-shell
Could keep you unharmed.

Joan Baez, "Diamonds and Rust"

Why do I sit, the autumnal judge?
Years of self-righteousness will not budge.
Singer or savior, it was his to choose;
Which of us knows what was his to lose?

'Cause idols are best when they're made of stone;
Savior's a nuisance to live with at home.
Stars often fall, heroes go unsung
And martyrs most certainly die too young.

Joan Baez, "Winds of the Old Days"

Part One

Super Bowl Sunday
January 15, 1978

11:00 A.M.

"Where? Where've they gone?"

Rosalind's own words woke her, and she twisted sideways, kicking out a futile foot for her husband, Will. Panic turned her body to a shambles; she nearly fell out of bed, then fumbled hands and head into the ancient football jersey crumpled on the floor where she'd shucked it the night before (her father's jersey with his retired number: Barney Chase's revered 33). She sat on the floor, breathing hard. The jersey felt old and familiar, a cocoon. Absurd, she mocked herself, absurd that, with a houseful of people—a husband, three children, her visiting parents—she could imagine everything beyond her bedroom door had vanished. Ben, she thought then without willing it, Super Bowl Sunday, your obelisk, a comic dagger on the calender. Who'll Barney pick in the Super Bowl tonight? She willed her mind to focus that, but the periphery intruded frayed edges of hoarfrost and fear.

Rosalind rolled back and stood up fast, took the three stairs to the bedroom door with one flamboyant stride. In the hall the other bedroom doors were closed. Moving, she touched knobs, ran a finger along the wall; and her legs, watery and boneless at first, as if fear had liquefied the marrow, seemed to resume bodily connection on the spiral stairs down, then moved fast and sure and part of her again around the rampant Ficus benjamina, across the front hall, and up another flight of stairs into the kitchen. Rakish and improbable, the house—completed just three months before—was all ups and downs, a controlled adventure (Rosalind was impatient, easily bored); there were sudden, whimsical stairs, rooms on different levels, ceilings that were peaks and trapezoids, the entire jagged cedar construction designed and built to Rosalind's ethereal specifications by an old student of hers, Andy Grimshaw, whose brains, according to Andy's tough little wife, Flo, were "in his hands, not his head. I mean," she'd told them, waving exasperated, pudgy hands, "Andy loves wood. Can you imagine loving wood?" "I'm fond of red oak myself," Will had said deadpan, and Rosalind, a helpless slave to cerebration, had murmured, "How peaceful really, Flo."

Now, holding onto Andy's stair rail (it alternated wooden spheres with metal rivets and was surprisingly pleasant to hold), Rosalind achieved the kitchen, and in the kitchen was Will. I will Will, she thought, and grinned. The panic dropped from her like a shrugged garment. Through the window over the sink she saw snowflakes, lazy but dogged, a speckled backdrop to the warm setting. In a woolly white turtleneck and patched jeans aged soft as suede, Will stood with a paring knife cutting intricate, tiny morsels—salami, green pepper, onion, cheese—for his famous Sunday omelets. Smiling, he turned towards her, his fine copper hair a halo against the darker copper hood of the stove.

"You look about ten," he said. Rosalind looked down at herself. Barney's football jersey hung to her thighs. She flirted it like a can-can skirt, did a little bump and grind, and lunged to hug him from behind, her hands fists on his flat middle. She pounded him lightly. She could feel his sperm, glazed and tacky, on her legs from the night before, and the restless, rocking hours of love they'd made as a charm against the nightmare that hit every year, seven years now, like a ceremony. "You think you can ravish me out of a dream?" she'd asked, panting. "I can sure as hell try."

"Sleep well?" he asked now, conversationally, a pretty little leer at the corner of his mouth. Peacock, she thought. She watched the paring knife in his hand, briefly fantasied sticking it into the soft flesh under his ribs, then trailed her fingers across his rib cage and released him.

"I didn't have the traditional nightmare," she said, being honest, being fair. She pivoted away, dipped down the two stairs round the counter, and sat on a bentwood chair at the table on the other side. Lacing her fingers lightly together and resting her chin on them, she watched Will preen masculine feathers about the night before as he sliced, chopped, dissected. "Seven years," she said. "Our cells have changed. Our skins have all sloughed off like snakeskin." Ah, tara-diddle. She touched the narrow slice through her left eyebrow, souvenir of Chicago in 1968; she studied Will's bony, broad shoulder, where the old gunshot wound lurked under his turtleneck, its scar like a blowsy rose, one petal detached and floating over the collarbone. The bullet had just grazed his shoulder. A dumdum bullet, Rosalind thought idly, refusing to focus on what the other dumdum bullet had done.

"You don't slough off the brain," Will said.

"And there's no statute of limitations on murder," Rosalind retorted sharply, her eyes on the gaudy geraniums in the center of the round table. She closed her eyes, and the old nightmare lurched across her mind's eye, her first husband's dead and frozen body, Ben Roth's body, immobile but seeming to lurch, for she had doubled up and vomited, remembered the scene as if someone had dropped the camera. . . .

"Roz?" She opened her eyes. Will's gray eyes regarded her with a look soft as velvet, serious and concerned. His temple muscles tightened; she could see them. She let herself admire the articulation of hard and elegant bone under that skin.

"I had a different nightmare, a new one," she said laughing a little, but nervously. "It was almost funny; it was even boring." She heard her voice go singsong. "I dreamed that you and I were making a list, a list of suspects and their motives, like Lord Peter Wimsey and Harriet Vane at Wilvercombe." Again she heard her nervous laugh raddle the air. "You were wearing your trooper's uniform."

Rosalind pulled a forelock of blond hair across half her face to picture Will Eddy as she'd first met him, a disarmingly sincere and handsome state trooper. I've polished Will's life, she thought, and oh, God, should I have? He'd had a scatty B.A. when she'd met him—an appalling B.A. actually—courses he'd picked up at disparate, random Pennsylvania colleges, such courses as were encouraged by the Pennsylvania State Police, for whom he'd worked, and his degree was awarded by a jerkwater institution that folded a year later, a "degree in criminology." Shockingly criminal indeed Rosalind had found it that he confessed only one English course (that in Jacobean drama, of all things) and no art or music at all. So, when they were married, she'd set up a cozy study for herself and inveigled him into it; there were books all around—"Oh, try this!"—she had talked, talked, talked. It was child's play. With sheer razzle-dazzle and infectious chatter, she'd enticed him through five years of law school at night, working them both hard, no piker she, teaching her own full load of English courses at Caliban

College, writing her dissertation, pregnant, exemplary. They'd worked, the Ph.D. candidate and the cop, at adjoining desks until they were no longer an anomaly. Now, at thirty-seven, Will was a lawyer, just recently appointed an assistant district attorney, the only registered Democrat in the history of the county to be so appointed, and both he and Rosalind suspected the white-haired D.A. had simply assumed that any local lawyer had to be a Republican—certainly any former cop.

Poor Will, Rosalind thought, saddled with difficult, mad me and my frayed and fragmented past. She raked her fingers through her hair. High-handedly she'd appropriated Will's sweet innocence without shame and molded it to her convenience, because she needed him—at her side and in her bed. Was Will happier? She didn't know. How could she know? "You look like Lord Peter Wimsey," she'd murmured to him the first time he'd stopped her speeding car. She'd been crying wildly, shouting and cursing at him, and then softly she'd laughed and called him Lord Peter Wimsey. Now Will was well-read and articulate, knew his wines and his Mozart. Ah, big deal, she thought, big deal. Patiently he was waiting for her to tell him the rest of her dream, holding the paring knife between two fingers like a cigarette, his other hand lightly on the edge of the counter. He can stand so still, Rosalind thought. How can he stand so still?

"You were writing the list," she went on, "in a loose-leaf leather notebook, and you wouldn't let me look at it. I said, 'Will, I know you're putting my name on it,' and you said, 'No, I'm not,' but you kept what you were writing covered with your hand, and finally I got mad and said, 'All right, I want your name on the list too. You're a suspect too.'" Rosalind and Will stared at each other for a long moment.

"Whew," Will finally said. He resumed his chopping. Rosalind fiddled with the clay pots of geraniums and let her mind's eye block-print a name on the list of suspects Will's hand had hidden in her dream: MUFFY. She remembered the FBI man's raised eyebrows, his mouth like a dainty rosebud in his loutish, jowly face. The TV wrap-up of Super Bowl V had flickered soundless on the right, while his mocking repetition of that coy, foolish name jabbed from the left. "Muffy? Muffy?" "I hadn't seen Ben in over a year," Rosalind had tried to explain. She'd looked to Will for support. "I just didn't pay much attention to the girl. I didn't say, 'Muffy who?' if that's what you mean." The FBI man hooted his incredulity. She tried again. "Ben and Muffy turned up here at the cottage late in the afternoon of New Year's Eve, and Ben said, sort of offhand, 'This is Muffy,' and I said, 'Hello,' nodded, oh, something, and she, Muffy, just said, 'Fuck you,' casually, like a greeting." The FBI man banged his fist hard against his palm. "What'd she look like, this Muffy?" Flinching back, Rosalind had groped, "She had bad skin and an awful cold sore. She was really rather amusing—" "Height? Weight? Hair color?" "I don't remember." "This girl arrived with your husband; you were jealous, weren't you? Furious." "No, no!"

She could no longer focus on Muffy's face; it floated away, a mottled blur around a cold sore. Still, the pressure to identify stayed on intact and immediate in Rosalind's mind; just a week ago, she'd stared at hot-eyed faces in *Time* magazine, some haggard relics of Weatherman the FBI had flushed out in Los Angeles, and she'd found herself dutifully scrutinizing the photographs of the two women. Was either Muffy? Ah, she didn't think so. Someday might Muffy yet emerge from the woodwork fingering her cold sore and toss off casually, "Oh, by the way, I shot that wimp, Ben Roth." Not likely, Rosalind wryly thought: except in stylish mystery novels like her onetime lover Paul Damian wrote on the pseudonymous, academic sly, the *deus ex machina* was quite out of fashion.

Still, it often seemed to Rosalind that a merciful *deus ex machina* must have killed Ben, some god with a bizarre sense of grace. She contemplated the grain of the table, the whorls and scallops of red oak like giant fingerprints, and slid back in her chair, hunching her knees against the table's edge. What if Ben hadn't died? she'd thought, examining the *Time* photos of the captured men (there were three, and one was damnably handsome): what if seven years later Ben had been caught? I'd've still been stupidly, stubbornly waiting. She'd ripped the article from the magazine, crumpled and thrown it in the fireplace. It was better Ben got murdered, she thought now harshly. Cleaner. She tipped her head and caught the scarlet geraniums against the white of the wall, fresh blood on the snow. "It was so cold," the medical examiner had testified in a burst of enthusiasm that proved the high point of the inquest, "Roth's blood must have frozen *immediately*. It was bright red. I never saw anything to beat it."

Remembering the medical examiner's childlike excitement, Rosalind felt the perverse and irresistible flicker of a smile. Ben's arms had wrapped around him; his frozen eyes had beamed on the grim gathering. "Never saw anything to beat it," the medical examiner had repeated. "It was that cold." He'd gone on to establish that Ben Roth's last meal had been a bowl of Lucky Charms cereal. Comedy impinged on tragedy; a harlequin darted across the somber stage of Rosalind's memory. Over the counter she looked at Will, her lovely, living husband, and thought: Once it was cold, now it's not.

"Say," she asked, "where's everybody? I can't believe my father's still asleep the day of the Super Bowl."

Will smiled, and Rosalind could feel his relief wrap

around her, warm as his arms. One-handed, he cracked eggs. "Barney couldn't sit still," he said. "He was supposed to go to New Orleans, you know, but elected to stay with Annabelle." They smiled at each other with conspiratorial glee. "But Barney," Will continued, "was like a caged beast. He kept worrying how the players could wait until six o'clock for the game. *He* couldn't have waited, he said."

"As if Barney ever played in the Super Bowl."

"Barney plays in every Super Bowl."

Rosalind laughed.

"So Barney rousted Kit out of bed, and they went for the papers. Annabelle"—Will looked into space, grinning—"took Joe and Daisy into bed with her." Rosalind stared. A little tentative about it, for he wasn't to theatrics born, Will tipped his head and mimicked the fluted tones of Rosalind's outlandish, queenly mother: " 'You must learn to sleep *in,* as ladies and gentlemen do.' "

Rosalind laughed out loud, so preposterous did it strike her, the juxtaposition of wriggling small bodies with her mother's artful distribution of poised limbs, her proud unpillowed head held primly straight to thwart sleep wrinkles. "She must be trying to impress Barney with these belated motherly gestures," Rosalind decided. "Just once as a child I tried to get in bed with Annabelle," she, laughing, reminisced for Will. "Annabelle had this brass bed with a canopy that jingled just a little when I got in; and Annabelle sat bolt upright out of a sound sleep and announced"—Rosalind mimicked too; it was irresistible—" 'No one, my dear, wishes to be encroached by a small, hot body that veers to the perpendicular.' "

"You still turn sideways," Will said, laughing.

"My small, hot body. . . ." Rosalind giggled.

"Didn't I tell you I heard conversation?" Annabelle

Chase's dramatic delivery projected up the stairs. "All these staircases really are a jot disagreeable. Daisy, don't clutch!" Rosalind's mother, a Shakespearean actress recently retired ("I mean, my dear, they wanted me to play Juliet's nurse! A sail, a sail! I'd sooner attend a prizefight with your father") climbed into the kitchen like a benevolent Medea into her chariot. Clinging to Annabelle's robe were three-year-old Daisy in a floral nightgown and five-year-old Joe in an old Barney Chase football jersey like his mother's. Joe's dragged on the floor, the *33* on a level with his navel. Red-gold-haired and fair-skinned like Will, the children peered mischievously at their parents, as if to say, Look at us. Applause, please.

Will beckoned and Rosalind held out her arms, but Daisy and Joe hung on, a pair of charming stage-props, a part of Annabelle's tableau. Annabelle's poised glance wafted across the kitchen; her shoulders shifted gracefully where the green velvet robe was caught with golden clips shaped like snakes; her eyes finally settled to confront Rosalind's over the geraniums. Her face was like Rosalind's, bony and elegant, with honed cheekbones and a strong jaw ("We'll never suffer double chins, my dear, not with these jaws"), but her body was smaller, tighter, disciplined to hold together better. Annabelle had presence. Even her hair had a decorum about it, while Rosalind's grew baby-fine and lank, and blew in the wind. Always, Annabelle made her feel floppy and attenuated; now, automatically, as if directed by her mother's eyes, Rosalind straightened up in the bentwood chair, pulled her sprawled limbs into an improvisation of integrity, crossed her ankles, and smoothed the ridiculous football jersey.

"How many of those garments *have* you, Rosalind?" Annabelle asked with droll displeasure. "I caught a glimpse of

Kit wearing one too. I feel surrounded by *Barneys*." She rolled her eyes. "Not," she said then with a lascivious smile, "that Barney wears anything to bed when he's with me." And pat as if it had been staged for her, Barney Chase, Rosalind's father, burst into the kitchen through the back door, slamming it back so hard it hit the wall, and his big shoulders, his bluster, his lined, smiling face under the curly helmet of iron-gray hair filled the room completely. His feet stamped, scattering snow; his shoulders wheeled and dipped; his overcoat landed on the floor.

"Barney, you are larger than life," Annabelle caroled, clasping her hands. Like a maiden to her swain, she glided to him.

"It's colder than the proverbial witch's you-know-what out there!" Around Barney's knees Joe and Daisy bobbed, as ineffectual as tacklers used to be when "The Chase" was on the move; and through the open door, into the rollick and whirl, Kit, Rosalind's firstborn, Ben Roth's son, fourteen years old, entered with the newspapers, a huge stack of them. Grinning slyly, he tossed the car keys on the counter. Barney let him drive! Rosalind suddenly thought. As Kit bent to retrieve Barney's overcoat from the floor, Barney gave his behind a smart athlete's slap, and Kit, pantomiming a snap from center, darted past Rosalind. "We're starved!" Barney's gravelly voice boomed. Out of the corner of her eye Rosalind saw Will slide two skillets onto the stove, and quickly rising from the table, she feinted left, tried to slip around her father, but was caught. "Rozzy, I like your costume!" Barney gripped her upper arms and shook her lightly. "Too skinny though, babe." Squeezing, then releasing Rosalind, Barney swooped Daisy from the floor to his shoulders, and as Daisy, squealing, one small frantic hand clutching his hair, the other momentarily his nose, settled precariously, Barney grabbed Annabelle with his other arm to hold her tight while Joe stepped both feet onto one of Barney's big feet and hugged Barney's thigh with wiry, dogged arms.

It's an Elizabethan circus, Rosalind thought, a bear dance; then thought, I should make coffee, but over the counter Will and Kit were already collaborating on it, Kit running water into the pot, Will spooning coffee into the basket. Rosalind watched intently as if her eyes could assist; she counted the spoonfuls silently; she felt as left out and shivery as if she were backstage, invisible as a shadow.

"I talked to Barney's New Orleans bookie on the phone," Kit was telling Will with pardonable pride. "His name's Raoul."

"Who'd Barney bet on?" Will asked.

"Don't tell him!" Barney said quickly. "It's bad luck. Raoul thinks he can get a couple of hundred for my ticket. By vamping me into staying here, Annabelle's saving me money, for a change." Annabelle's contralto laugh mingled with his rumbly bass, and, exuberantly, they kissed.

"I love you," Will said quietly to Rosalind. Present again, she smiled, leaned back against the counter to watch her—well —necking parents, and felt her smile grow broader. She was entranced by their unexpected and almost magical reunion, this coming together under her new roof of Barney and Annabelle, who'd diverged (without, however, divorcing) thirty years before, Barney to broadcast-booths over baseball stadiums, Annabelle to the Shakespearean stage. Rosalind's youth from the age of four had been a breathless seesaw of linguistic shifts and costume changes, although, in fact, the day-to-day rhythms remained the same whether she was with Barney or Annabelle, Annabelle or Barney: the casual schooling, buses and planes, hotel rooms, *As You Like It* in the winter, the Yankees in the summer, audiences real or imagined. . . .

"We saw Cynnie and Walter at the drugstore," Kit said.

"Mom?" Rosalind turned. Kit was rotating a frying pan, melting butter, helping Will prepare for the omelets.

"What can I do?" Rosalind asked. "I'll set the table," she said. She stood on tiptoe to get plates out of the cabinet and started ranging them around the table.

"Cynnie and Walter said they'll be here at five," Kit went on. "Cynnie said to tell you they'll bring a stew. Mom?"

"Great," Rosalind said. She'd forgotten Cynnie and Walter were even coming. Will had invited them: crowd the house this year, push out the ghosts. Counting people's heads, she took silverware from a drawer. Ah, Cynnie knows what day it is, Rosalind thought. ("Ben's dead?" She saw Cynnie's hazy Pre-Raphaelite face focus into sharp, exultant horror.) A stew. God, I'm being nurtured to death.

"You know what Barney called Walter?" Kit asked, laughing a bit uncertainly. "He hasn't seen Walter in years, and he said, 'Hi, Walter, you crazy nigger stud.' I couldn't believe it, but Walter just laughed. Barney can get away with anything."

"Walter Pettinger *is* a crazy nigger stud," Barney said. "He was a potentially superb wide receiver, and he gave it all up to marry a chicken-hearted white woman."

"Barney, you know Cynnie doesn't approve of blood sports," Will said deadpan. Kit grinned at him.

"Blood sports!" Barney guffawed appreciatively. "Blood sports." He dropped Daisy, kicked off Joe, let go of Annabelle, and leaving the three of them scattered and comically bereft, strode up the two steps around the counter.

"What's a nigger stud?" Rosalind heard Joe ask Annabelle.

"Football *is* a blood sport," Annabelle told him, as if it were an answer.

"Oh," Joe said.

"Hold it." Barney stood at the counter. "No mushrooms?"

he asked Will. He opened the refrigerator. "Mushrooms! I thought I saw them. Pass me a knife, Kit."

Rosalind leaned her elbows on the counter and regarded her father as, unceremoniously, he dumped Will's peppers and onions from the chopping block and started slicing mushrooms. She was suddenly angry at him. "I'm surprised you didn't call Cynnie a nigger-lover," she said, her voice shaking a little. She steadied it. "Or an ex-lesbian," she said without thinking, trying to be breezy. Barney gave a hiss of real anger. "Not that Cynnie ever really was," Rosalind hastily added as Kit looked at her, shocked, and she thought, What's the matter with me? "Cynnie just talked a good game," she reassured Kit, who adored Cynnie. "You remember," and Kit tried to carry it off, tried to look sophisticated, and, oh, God, didn't he look like Ben? Kit was blond like Rosalind and he would be taller than Ben, maybe he already was—she couldn't remember Ben next to her (on top of her, inside of her, not next to her)—but there was something occasionally in Kit's expression, a wise-guy Brooklynese look that caught his face sometimes, skewed it cocky, raised a corner of his mouth and an eyebrow, dimpled his cheek, and he was Ben Roth to the life, as if just one stubborn gene had survived the violence to make its mark, a gene for bravado. . . .

"How's Morton's hip pointer?" Will asked Barney in a voice earnestly concerned, changing the subject, Rosalind knew, to give her time to compose herself; and she sat back at the table, letting the ensuing animated discussion of Craig Morton's hip pointer fade, letting fade, too, the incongruous and amusing spectacle of Annabelle on the floor with the children, newspapers spread out, reading Doonesbury aloud with an arch, warbling lilt. The FBI man's voice perforated her memory again:

"About this Muffy, Miss Chase, Mrs. Roth. . . . Now, I suppose you're, *ahem*, bisexual, like your friend Cynthia Talleyrand?"

"I'm not," Rosalind said. "Neither's Cynnie, really."

"She sure talks a good game."

He'd talked to Cynnie, to Paul Damian and Luke DiLorenzo, and each time he'd come back to Rosalind again. She'd quoted him just now, quoted that unspeakable man to Kit. Rosalind felt a gutteral growl rasp the back of her throat at this FBI invasion of her language. She coughed. She thought of Kit, only five, six, seven—those serrated years after Ben had so abruptly left: could Kit go back in his memory and now see Cynnie's house as a prologue to his father's murder? A replica of Kit's (presumed) memory spread before her mind's eye as one of the intricate two-sided jigsaw puzzles Andy Grimshaw was crafting and painting and trying to market: he called them "allegories." He'd given them one for Christmas. That puzzle Rosalind had spent hours on, throwing up her hands, laughing, for you had no clues to which side a piece belonged. The puzzle pictured on one side a lovely, bosky wood, sunlit and dappled, where rabbits and fawns, raccoons, bear cubs, and smiling foxes peeped coy and innocent out of the bushes. On the other side the point of view jolted; the same landscape bristled with menace. A Roman temple crumbled. In the center a hunter held a minutely detailed rifle, its shaft hyperbolically dripping with blood. The little animals' faces were contorted with fear; some cowered, some bled; and grotesque, darkening shapes loomed over them, Tolkienesque wraiths, gargoyles, mushroom-shaped clouds. . . .

They'd lived for a year, Kit and Rosalind, in the house Cynnie'd inherited from a maiden great-aunt (Cynnie still lived there, with black, beautiful Walter, to the chagrin of her neighbors), a charming little white-painted, green-shuttered house furnished with spindly antiques and flaunting a fanciful round front porch, the curve of the porch repeated in the flowering front garden, and even the shape of the sidewalk: three parallel ellipses of mathematical precision. Foxglove grew along the gingerbreaded porch, and red-orange impatiens covered the front yard like a carpet.

It was, in short, delightful, and Rosalind and Kit had been extraordinarily fortunate to wend their way to Cynnie's house. Rosalind had paced the Caliban College housing office in despair over the "housing" available, for it seemed that the radical left of Caliban, Pa., was composed of those landlords and ladies who answered *Would you consider a foreign student?* with *Yes, European.* Most just said *No!* with actual exclamation points. She really didn't want to live where a foreign student couldn't, and Ben would say she absolutely shouldn't; but in the slender FURNISHED notebook, the sole detractor on the foreign student issue was a spiky backhand that said a vehement *No!* to children. Rosalind still had Kit, but all the stuff she and Ben had accumulated during graduate school she'd given away when she left New York and Columbia, all but Kit, and she required a place tentative and furnished, a place she could (should Ben come), unencumbered, leave. Or a place that Ben would deign to *stay.* Musing and fuming, Rosalind was coming to the obvious conclusion that mother love had to outweigh political conviction (and where the hell was Ben anyway?), when the girl at the desk pointed to the spiky backhand and said, "I think that one's worth a try. I doubt Cynnie's ever met a child before."

Like Rosalind, the housing office girl was a graduate student in English; unlike Rosalind, she was terrified to teach— "You're going to *teach*?" she asked, as if "You're going to

kill?" The girl had been visibly enchanted with, had positively coveted golden-haired Kit, who sat in quiet amusement while Rosalind strode impatiently about. "It's just
across the Square. You can even walk there," the girl said,
gesturing vaguely towards the window. "Walking distance,"
she repeated, for Rosalind didn't have a car yet. "You ought
to meet Cynnie Talleyrand anyhow." The girl looked Rosalind over. "I think you'd hit it off. Yes, I'm sure you would.
Cynnie teaches math here; she's an assistant professor and
specializes in computers, but Cynnie looks like"—the girl bit
her lip and let her English major's eyes consult the ceiling
for inspiration—"like Tess of the D'Urbervilles."

"Really?" Rosalind had laughed, been intrigued, and she
and Cynnie had indeed hit it off, and Kit and Cynnie had hit
it off, and when Barney came in for his fly-by-night visits,
even Barney and Cynnie had hit it off. The house was
charming, and Rosalind and Cynnie together had a kind of
magnetism, Rosalind the "flame," Cynnie the "halo round
the flame," as a budding poet-sociologist murmured dreamily once, then capped it off: "Two knockout chicks in a little
house with a little boy. Irresistible!"

The house rollicked with poets and guitar players and
crack bridge players from the math department. After a
while, Rosalind found herself quite recklessly involved with
Paul Damian, her professor, and getting involved with Luke
DiLorenzo, her student, but Kit wasn't neglected, she kept
telling herself. Luke shot baskets with him, and Cynnie was
always there if Rosalind wasn't; for a time it seemed as if Kit
were blessed with two mothers, or two big sisters, Rosalind
amended, recalling with a wince his second-grade teacher's
stern scolding of her: "You're his mother, not his big sister.
And cut his hair; he looks like a girl." That was early October, 1970. Rosalind came home and found a student of Cyn-

nie's teaching Kit how to roll joints on a little machine that
looked like a card shuffler. The cigarette papers were a
shocking pink. Kit's hair was to his shoulders. The next day,
Paul Damian's wife, Sarah, had pitched a considerable
number of heavy books at Rosalind in the office of the
Chairman of the English Department. "It was a symbolic
protest," Sarah Damian said, to defend her actions, and ran
out the door. Shaken, Rosalind had come home and re-
counted the ordeal for Cynnie. "Let me think about it, Roz."
A day or so later Cynnie'd blithely propositioned her; Cynnie, who'd somewhere along the way, unbeknownst to Rosalind, come to fancy herself a lesbian and also to fancy
Rosalind, had wheedled in that soft breathy voice that belied
her brilliance as mathematician, "It's all so simple, Roz. Look
how badly Paul Damian has behaved, letting you and Sarah
fight it out. Poor Sarah! Poor you. And where, I ask you, is
that prick, Ben Roth?" Cynnie fluttered her delicate hands
in the air to pantomime the fecklessness of men.

Within the week Rosalind had bolted, had cut not only
Kit's hair but her own, and having cut their hair, she'd cut
their losses; she'd moved them out so fast, she could still feel
the whirl of that day, the steaming energy of her body as
she'd gathered her notes on the zeugma for the paper she
owed Paul Damian, her quilting frame, her Anglo-Saxon
dictionary, her color TV, her typewriter, her son, and fled
from Cynnie's house to a laughably more "wholesome" atmosphere, a borrowed cottage at a lake with the improbable
name of Mud Lake, a serene setting for Ben Roth to be murdered in. . . .

Enough, her mind decreed: I am calm now, my hands are
folded, and Cynnie's bringing a stew. In detached wonder,
Rosalind looked down at her still arms on the table and back
on the anger she'd lived with daily the two years after Ben

left her, a fierce physical anger that burned along her arms
like an electrical charge; she'd hit people then, had slapped
Cynnie once, had bashed Paul Damian in the nose; and that
memory made her grin, then laugh, as she sat at her cozy
kitchen table with its centerpiece of geraniums, laugh out
loud, and voices converged on her: "What's so funny?"

"I just remembered," Rosalind said, flinging both hands
back in a fine flourish and clasping them on top of her head.
"Golden-hearted Will has also invited the Damians over to
watch the Super Bowl. Sarah told Paul who told Will that
she'll bring *bœuf bourguignon.* We'll have Cynnie's stew and
Sarah's *bourguignon,* and I won't have to cook a thing."

"A crowd for the game. That's how to do it, if you can't be
there," Barney approved, letting Rosalind know he'd excused her earlier outburst; but Annabelle's voice cut an uncomfortable swath through the camaraderie just beginning
to settle again on the kitchen:

"The Damians? But isn't that . . . ? Rosalind, has that
woman actually forgiven you for, well, you know. . . ." Annabelle touched a hand to her throat and rose from the
floor. She spread her other hand over the children's heads,
as if they couldn't hear above a certain level.

"Oh, Annabelle, we're colleagues now, Paul and I. That's
ancient history," Rosalind said airily, thinking: forgiven? I'd
better not let Sarah Damian wield the bread knife. And how,
she wondered, does Annabelle know so much about that
anyhow? Frowning, she glanced speculatively at her mother.

"Strange bedfellows," Annabelle was musing to the air.
"Academia makes the theater appear positively puritanical."
In brisk non sequitur, she concluded, "I must write some
letters. I adore the postmark Caliban, Pa."

Strange bedfellows. Rosalind appropriated Annabelle's cliché and pondered it. She'd hurled her zeugma paper at Paul

Damian, and he'd given her an A+, even helped her to get it published. He and Will were good friends now (unaccountably, Rosalind privately thought, for Will was a natural gentleman and Paul a born boor). Rosalind cocked a sudden suspicious look at Will, flushed and busy with the spatula over what must be the two largest, slowest omelets in history. Why had he invited the Damians? It was shaping up like the end of one of Paul Damian's murder mysteries, this Super Bowl gathering. Where, my pet, she asked Will silently, is Luke DiLorenzo?

("Just how many men were you 'sleeping with,' Miss Chase, Mrs. Roth, last, ah, semester?"

"Just two," Rosalind retorted, stung, idiotically embarrassed because Will Eddy was in the cottage near the fireplace, angel-faced and apologetic in his Confederate-gray trooper's uniform. "And it wasn't . . . simultaneous. Or not for long. In October Paul Damian and I broke it off completely; his wife had found out, and the thing with Luke DiLorenzo was just nothing, a lark."

"A lark. All right, you've indicated that you also 'slept with' Ben Roth when he visited you here on New Year's Eve. With his, ah, traveling companion, this woman you call 'Muffy.' I suppose you all three slept together?"

"No," Rosalind wearily said.

"But you did sleep with Ben Roth?"

"Ben was my *husband*."

But he'd shifted the tack; she saw it too late to keep her balance. "There was no trace of any such, ah, activity, on Roth's body." Activity! The FBI man watched her face; the crabbed parentheses around his mouth moved back and forth like barbed wire; his rosebud mouth flattened, then pursed.

"Ben took a shower." It sounded inane, but it was true,

and she persisted. "I heard him take a shower. He sang. He hadn't washed in weeks; he was filthy."

"A shower before or after?"

"After."

"And was it for another 'lark' that you slept with a filthy man?" He slapped his notebook shut. "Ah, never mind!")

The omelets materialized on the table; figures bustled about, sat down. Daisy loomed, bouncing up and down, on a tall stool beside Rosalind. The omelets roiled in her vision, all yellow and white and wet and clotted with pink, green, brown. Rosalind's stomach churned. She got up. "I'm sending myself to the showers," she quipped, catching both hands at the back of her chair, pushing off from it. She tasted dry brass at the back of her throat, like dragon's breath. As Daisy scrambled precipitately off her stool and climbed into Rosalind's chair, Rosalind hastened up the stairs to the kitchen proper, down the stairs into the hall. At the bottom she stopped next to a renegade branch of the Ficus benjamina and heard Annabelle proclaim: "Hold your tongue, Barney Chase. Just hold your tongue."

"It's a rough day for Rosalind," Will said. Don't *apologize* for me, Rosalind thought angrily.

"It's been seven God damned years!" Barney exploded. "Why couldn't you guys have found Ben Roth's body on Good Friday or Yom Kippur? Why on Super Bowl Sunday?"

· I

"I think he wanted to lose his men, that's what I think. He falls asleep at the wheel pretty conveniently, wouldn't you say?" From the back of the room under the clock, the student's voice came at her, a whizzing shaft of aggression or an unexpected fastball; Rosalind pretended to duck, to fend his words off with her hand, and then she stretched up like a bush-league pitcher and pantomimed throwing his words back at him. The rest of the class laughed. She grinned at them.

"And his men have been a real pain in the ass, and all his bitching and moaning sounds kind of, you know, *phony* . . ." The student (she ran an imaginary pencil down the class list in her mind), Jay Seiden his name was, had his scruffy bearded face thrust forward; his eyes flashed with the excitement of an impending critical epiphany. He's on to something, she suddenly thought.

"Rhetorical?" She gave him the word.

"Yeah. Yeah. Rhetorical. He doesn't mean it." Jay Seiden was holding his hands clawed in the air in front of him, bouncing them as he struggled to hold his ideas together. "Well, listen, first he falls asleep at the wheel, and his men let out the winds. Then, all of a sudden, when they want to land on that forbidden idlans, he just gives up. Without hesitation, he says, 'I am alone, outmatched.' Now, that's bullshit, wouldn't you say, Miss Chase? He can talk them out of anything; he's a master of the pep talk; he could've cheered them up. But, no, he falls asleep *again*—"

Rosalind held up a hand. "Wait a minute." She folded her right elbow on the lectern before her, cradled her head as if she were all alone and very weary, watched her hair drift over her sleeve onto the lectern, a composition in swirls, dark-gold hair, cable-knit scarlet sweater, burled oak. Odysseus goes off to pray, she thought, for Odysseus an act not exactly in character, and it is very, very defensively that he recounts this particular act. He blames the gods (she closed her eyes to see the words): the gods "only closed my eyes/under slow drops of sleep." Yes! Still draped on the lectern, Rosalind let her voice ring out: "You have a stunning paper topic. And for Tuesday, I want the rest of you to be able to document for me the stages by which Odysseus so conveniently"—she rolled her eyes on "conveniently" and slid her hands on her hips—"manages to disencumber himself of his men." (*Disencumber:* is that a word? she wondered momentarily. Unencumber?) "And I do mean *document,*" she rode over the possible faux pas of "disencumber." "None of this"—she made her voice breathless and girlish, mimicking— "'Oh, Odysseus is too nice a man to do this; he's a *hero.*' Odysseus is not a nice man in our terms. Wait'll you see what he does to the suitors."

She watched as seven students dutifully wrote down what she had said. Were they writing, "Wait'll you see what he does to the suitors"? She felt an ironic smile lift one corner of her mouth. Rosalind had an amused (and outspoken) contempt for the students who took down every word and consequently never lived the wildly kinetic classroom experience. "Does Odysseus subconsciously want to lose his men? Is that why he keeps falling asleep? Does he protest too much, as the man says," she elaborated, smiling at Jay Seiden who made a manful effort not to appear pleased. Random points of hostility seemed to sharpen. Were they jealous of Jay Seiden? "Reread the episode, it won't kill you." She went on, flipping out her hand in automatic staccato thrusts, "Document, quote, gather examples, prove. Do Odysseus's actions always jibe with his words?" and while she was talking the period to its close, she allowed herself, in a fit of momentary masochism, to search out the three recalcitrant students who'd stubbornly resisted her flamboyance all semester. Not won over yet, huh? Why didn't they drop, or at least cut once in a while? The Hostile Three were scattered today, not sitting together in awful glowering concentration as they sometimes did, two female students, one male, all dark-haired: Did they resent her fair hair? she wondered idly. "Don't forget your brilliant *Odyssey* papers due two weeks from today," she concluded with a winsome smile as the clock clicked to one. "Well, one o'clock."

No one moved. Rosalind swept her hands at them impatiently, at them all, over the lectern, whisking them off, the adoring faces as well as the hostile. "That's it, all. Shoo, scram." In reflex she grabbed the lectern as the class rose, braced herself against the ones who would always insist on talking to her. It was one o'clock; she had a lot to do. As the students converged she faked a move right, towards the windows, then veered abruptly left, gathering her books and briefcase expeditiously in the process, tossing her scarlet-lined glen-plaid jacket over her shoulder in adroit, shifting progress to the door. The students followed, bumping into each other, and just outside the door, Rosalind saw Mrs. Ritter from her Chaucer class and stopped in alarm. Had something gone wrong about the cottage? The students piled up behind her.

"Rosalind." Maisie Ritter stepped quickly to confront her, a small, dark, motherly woman in a tightly belted trench coat. She was an IBM executive's wife, a shy housewife gleefully back in school for her B.A., an unlikely savior and provider of refuge, but there it was. Maisie's dark hair swirled backward as if in agitation; she had a tight-skinned face with long eyes that pulled around the sides, like sunglasses. Maisie nudged her small hand at Rosalind's free hand. The gesture was deliciously secretive; Rosalind instinctively opened her hand and grabbed, felt a key. She fingered it.

"I told the Maunciple," Maisie glimmered at her. Rosalind looked at her blankly. Oho, we're talking in code, she realized. Chaucerian code. How enterprising of Maisie. *Maunciple*; Rosalind's mind glossed it: *purchasing agent*. Well, Maisie's husband, whose wrath Maisie inexplicably feared, was a high-level executive for IBM—when had Maisie mentioned that, and whyever?—hence, at any rate, Maisie had apparently "told" her husband she'd rented their posh summer cottage to Rosalind, and what? What had "the Maunciple" said?

"And?" Rosalind prodded with gentle urgency.

"He said you should have both keys. So you won't be afraid. He says he's delighted to be of assistance to the girl who made me get the sexy little dress."

Grinning with relief, Rosalind leaned against the doorway, and some of her appendant students, among them Jay Seiden, who smiled at her self-consciously, went around her, away. About five remained to clutter the doorway, listening intently, she could feel them, an over-the-shoulder audience. "I'm glad you told the Maunciple," Rosalind said to Maisie. "I'd've hated to be ousted in the middle of some dark night by an irate Maunciple." She laughed a wild little laugh.

"Oh," Maisie Ritter demurred, "he never goes there except in summer. Still, I'm glad I told him. He was so nice!"

"Do not fear the Maunciple," Rosalind said. This is crazy, she thought, as she and Maisie beamed surreptitious, brimming smiles at each other.

"I told you about the mail."

"Yes, I got a box. The postmark's terrific." Wary-eyed, they both laughed. Who would hunt one down to Mud Lake, Pa.?

"I swore the Maunciple to secrecy. He hopes the *Squyer*"—Maisie raised her eyebrows—"will enjoy the fishing there."

Rosalind, delighted, laughed at this Chaucerian rendition of golden seven-year-old Kit, the Squyer indeed; then, feeling heaved sighs and joggling impatience from her waiting students, knew she had somehow to bring this scatty game to a close. (The coda is up to me, her mind winced at the irrepressible pun: the coda of the code.) Impulsively she leaned forward and kissed Maisie's cheek. "Maisie, I'm eternally grateful; I mean that." Juggling books, she shrugged into her jacket.

"Ah," Maisie deprecated, "it was nothing." Then, as if it had been prearranged, they said in sprightly unison, "I must dash," laughed, waved, and turned in opposite directions down the hallway.

"Miss Chase, may I handwrite my paper? I write very neatly." The students walked along after her; she walked very fast; she had to mail the change-of-address cards, had to pick up the paychecks she'd forgotten, for clean out of her head they'd gone in last week's fiasco, with Sarah Damian flailing and furious in the Chairman's office—oh, God, the startled Chairman's harrowing, paternalistic lecture!—had to clear the rest of her stuff out of Cynnie's house before Cynnie got home (God, she thought, spare me another encounter with Cynnie), pack it in the Firebird, collect Kit from school, get his hair cut. Oh, I wish I could go un-derground like Ben, she thought despairingly; Ben, oh hell, but the cottage will help, a refuge for Squyer Kit and me, a refuge from lusty professors and their deceived, demented wives, a refuge from sudden, importunate lesbians—what is the matter with Cynnie anyhow? She's no more a lesbian than Maisie Ritter . . . probably. Rosalind slid the key into her jacket pocket.

The students were still following as she went out the door of the Humanities Building into the afternoon sunlight. She could feel them but refused to look at them, flipped answers over her shoulders, used her long hair to fend them off like a celebrity eluding a pack of reporters.

She dipped at a sudden right angle into the colonnade that led to the Administration Building—two students turned away, disappointed, shaken off. Three persisted, scrambling to keep up. Just a few yellow leaves clung to the colonnade; it was only the second week in October, but it had already been a fierce, gusty autumn. "Yellow leaves or none or few," Rosalind's mind muttered, and she felt a pang at Kit's impending haircut.

"Miss Chase!" She heard a high-pitched voice behind her, noted peripherally baby-faced Andy Grimshaw next to her now, her attendant angel who always escorted her from class, laconic and companionable and unaccountably de-voted, and on her other side, bright-eyed Susan Jasper; and who was that clipping at her heels, piping her name in a little voice? Oh, no, that silly, plump, whey-faced girl who'd once said in class that a critic with a name like Lionel *Trilling* had no right to comment on the name of a literary character—a truly astonishing declaration, Rosalind had to admit, and one she was sure would remain in the clutter of her own mind for the rest of her life. "Miss Chase, if you were Penelope, would you just sit around and wait for Odysseus?" the little voice piped.

Rosalind stopped in her tracks. Behind her the Trilling girl—what was her name?—got her toes stepped on; she was breathing hard, clutching her books to her prodigious bosom, but she smiled hazily around. "I mean," she said, blinking her eyes as Rosalind looked at her with intense, piercing interest, "don't you think Penelope's a little lamebrained? Odysseus *cheats* on her. And what if he never came back at all?"

"I think Penelope's the real hero of the *Odyssey*," Rosalind said, helplessly honest. She felt her eyes ache with sudden, rising tears.

" 'Penelope, the Hero of the *Odyssey*,' " Susan Jasper repeated in a rapt voice. "I love that, calling a woman a hero."

Diverted and grateful, Rosalind smiled at her. The tears receded. "Samuel Butler was convinced," Rosalind, peripatetic again, told them, "that a woman must have written the *Odyssey*. A sort of prehistoric Jane Austen, he called her."

"How neat!" Susan Jasper said.

"Prehistoric? You mean, like *cave*men?" the Trilling girl asked.

Andy Grimshaw and Susan Jasper rolled eyes at each other and started most rudely and infectiously to laugh. Rosalind heard her own laugh ripple out to join theirs, and she felt the warmth of the sun through the lattices and flickering yellow leaves of the brick-pillared colonnade, kicked with sudden jauntiness the crepey fallen leaves before her, and, as Andy Grimshaw broke into a warbling whistle, was happy for a moment. The campus exuded bucolic peace. The yellow wisteria leaves and gnarled branches reticulated across the arch of the colonnade like crewelwork. What a perfect day to move to a lake. Into the gaudy mailbox at the end of

the dappled, lacy tunnel, casually she tossed two change-of-
address cards, one to Barney in New York, the other to Annabelle in London: to her parents, both of whom were fully
capable of rousting out the local police—long-distance or
transatlantic from Scotland Yard—if they couldn't locate her
and feared fugitive Ben might have kidnapped her and
Kit—oh, that he would—two change-of-address cards with
the terse, typed R. CHASE, BOX 47, MUD LAKE, PA., then her
scrawled and cryptic appendix: "No phone, don't worry, will
write." Feeling her fate somehow sealed as the iron flap of
the mailbox clanged shut, Rosalind moved swiftly up the
brick steps to the Administration Building, eyes fixed downward on her striding legs in scarlet tights, like the Wyf of
Bathe's. She had her hand on the doorknob when she heard
a jangling scream from the Trilling girl: "Don't go in there!"

Rosalind's hand jerked away from the doorknob as if it
were hot. She turned, and from the step below, in a row,
they regarded her: the Trilling girl, her mouth agape, Andy
and Susan with comically alert and eager faces.

"She thinks they'll eat you," Susan said to Rosalind.

"You can go in," Andy encouraged. "It isn't like a picket
line."

"If she goes in, she'll condone what they're doing," the
Trilling girl self-righteously said. "The faculty doesn't condone it." Feistily she stuck her plump chin out. "The faculty
voted *not* to condone it."

Andy Grimshaw turned on her, his usually bland baby-
face contorted and angry. His soft pink upper lip curled,
revealing a chipped canine tooth. "You really are a scab, you
know that, Bratty?"

Bratty? Rosalind thought, looking from face to face.

"Our Bircher-in-residence," Andy taunted. The girl's
hand moved slowly out and encroached upon Andy's cheek

with a slap that seemed to float out of a thirties movie, soft-handed and halfhearted, a Claudette Colbert slap, Rosalind's mind registered on an idle, frivolous level. She watched Andy's face as if it were in a movie. Infuriatingly he turned his other cheek. The Trilling girl's face went desperate, crumpled; she burst into tears (no other phrase for it, Rosalind dizzily thought), and crossing her arms over her books, turned awkwardly and ran back through the colonnade.

"Andy, you can be a bastard, you know that?" Susan Jasper told him without anger, fondly. "And a shithead." She said to Rosalind, "Bratty's father's a brigadier general," as if in explanation, "and of course Bratty's an idiot, but still—"

"All right, Susan," Rosalind interjected, "what's in there?" She flicked a thumb at the door of the Administration Building and tried to arrange her face into a stern, no-nonsense expression, but couldn't hold it. "I've been sort of out of touch," she explained lamely.

Andy and Susan looked at her as if she were an infant or in her dotage. "The hunger strike," Susan wonderingly said, fanning out her hands. "The strikers want the administration to call off the Marine recruiters next month. They've been striking for a week now. They're protesting the war in Vietnam."

Rosalind leaned her shoulders back against the door, and started helplessly to laugh. The Revolution! Her hair fell over her face like feathers tickling. It was October of 1970, and the Revolution had finally come to Caliban. The small, sequestered campus that had made no fuss, no fuss at all last May over Cambodia and Kent State was finally rushing into the breach. And I almost missed it, she wildly thought, almost missed it skulking hangdog around the campus because Sarah Damian threw a few books at me. Ah, Ben, she

thought, you should have stuck with me, kid. You could
have ruled this charming, dilatory campus instead of slaving
underground, wherever that is. "Well, better late than
never," she managed finally to quip for Andy's and Susan's
startled faces. She hoisted her books. "See you Tuesday."

As she pulled open the door, squinting ahead into the dim
lobby, she heard Andy mutter, "This isn't Columbia,
y'know," and Susan retort, "Oh, shut up, Andy," and she
thought, Dear God, can that poor girl's name really be
Bratty?

On the verso of the door, the air felt hushed and thick,
and it was nearly dark, slatted wooden blinds having been
lowered on the French windows that opened to the terrace
and formal commemorative gardens behind. With exaggerated care Rosalind pulled the door to, winced at the noise
the latch made, and paused a minute, letting her senses adjust to the palpable change in atmosphere. In her sensory
recollection the scene just enacted on the steps (for scene it
had been; Annabelle would have loved the slap) glittered:
the light sharp; her laughter boldly ringing; the glints and
scents of fall, clean and whistling. In here the only light
came from round clerestory windows high up. The Administration Building, all rose-colored brick and white pillars, a
graceful stately Georgian mansion on the outside, had been
gutted two years before and modernized, but amazingly, not
emasculated. Well endowed, Caliban College had taken time
and money not to botch the interior. Exposed brick and
warm, golden wood-beams soaring to arches lifted one's
eyes; and a cantilevered staircase rose, airy and geometric,
from the center of the polished floor and bifurcated halfway
up into a wide V, where one floating tributary veered to
Payroll, the other to the Dean of Students' office. Rosalind,

peering, could dimly make out a sawhorse blocking the dean's staircase at the landing, a sawhorse flaunting a rakish red flag, the flag tipped askew and seeming to wave like a pennant on a stadium. Whatever did it mean, the flag? The students boycotting the dean or vice versa? Knowing the priggish dean, Rosalind decided it was probably the latter. The left-hand staircase to her destination, Payroll, appeared clear.

A muzzy, unwashed smell crept insidiously into her nostrils. In the darkness under the cantilevered stairs, she gradually discerned lumpy forms, bodies ranged, crumpled, piled. Her senses began sluggishly to adjust, to register the odor of sweat, of unwholesome sleep, the gutteral sounds of breathing, the plangent, almost imperceptible quaver of a guitar. How many days have they been here? she wondered, beginning gingerly to walk towards the stairs. Tread lightly in the netherworld, her mind cautioned. A poster, crooked on the far wall, sported a large number 7. Mickey Mantle's number, Rosalind automatically thought. She put her foot up the stairs; something came through the treads and grabbed her ankle. She stifled a scream; it was eerie, melodramatic; why weren't the lights on? "Chase!" came a triumphant voice from the floor under the stairs.

"Luke." She backed down and ducked quickly round, banging her head on the underside of the staircase. Bending to locate him, she tried to arrange her long, scarlet-clad legs into a semblance of decorum, but her glen-plaid skirt hung only seventeen inches from the waist and barely reached the middle of her thighs: a literal cutty sark. She felt stupid and exhibitionist, standing above the prone, exemplary bodies. An idle corner of her mind flicked a picture of Maisie Ritter's "sexy little dress," a shiny green affair. Rosalind had been at the counter in a dress shop, protesting a bill as histrionically as Annabelle might have if someone had stolen *her* charge card, when Maisie's dark head had poked out of a dressing room. "I knew the *voice*. Would you come in? Would you tell me what you think?" "It's darling," Rosalind had tipped her head judiciously to say into the mirror, appraising Maisie's self-conscious, compact little body, her staunch, shapely legs. The miniscale was perfect on her. "Oh, I don't know! I'm thirty-eight years old! What will my husband's IBM colleagues think? What will Marshall, my husband, say?"

And Rosalind now, her knees together, cursed the miniskirt as, awkwardly, she maneuvered herself under the staircase, holding on to the graduated overhead steps as to monkey bars. Scattered protesters started to stir, to protest her invasion as they protested the Marine recruiters, nonviolently. Their yellow armbands moved, contracted, flickered like lightning bugs. She knelt among them, and it was like going into a cave or a jail cell, dim bars of light filtering through the stairs. He let her grope around for him, the bastard, Rosalind thought, crawling on her hands and knees, but when she found him, the epithet faded; her eyes went soft and warm. Luke DiLorenzo, once her student, once her lover (one time, that was all, in her *car*), his head leaned back on an elbow and a rolled olive-drab blanket, regarded her with an endearingly weary version of his cocksure grin.

After their mutual madness last month in her car, she'd reluctantly severed their relations and now, looking about her, felt belatedly uneasy to be so close to him under the stairs. Ah, nobody knows, Luke wouldn't tell, she reassured herself, hating the idea of her one hasty, unexpected romp with him being made public, like the Damian affair. ("You're involved with a *student* as well as a married professor?" she hypothesized the white-haired Chairman's incredulous ques-

tion. "Who do you think you are, an Iris Murdoch character?" She'd be out on her ear, and, ah, how much more
humiliating, somehow, to be caught with a younger than an
older man.) Luke looked, however, almost ageless now, she
somberly observed, looked not at all boyish, was fully
bearded, wore a heroic denim headband slightly askew over
his forehead. His face was very gaunt; he'd been lean as a
rake to begin with, and now he was emaciated. She smiled at
him, shaking her head mock-ruefully. "Hey, boy," she said,
"what's all this, what's all this?" On his chest, he held a bottle
of orange juice, sipping it through a crimped hospital straw.
"Poor baby," she said, touching his shoulder. There was a
cozy smell about him, like rumpled bedcovers or a laundry
bag, a comforting, sleepy smell; she had a passing impulse to
lie down with him. Despite the lean, loose length of him, his
bones were light, almost fragile, and she felt protective of
him, wanted to hold him. He was twenty-one, she was
twenty-seven; a misalliance, a lovely misalliance.

He offered the orange juice bottle to her. She shook her
head; they both laughed.

"How's Kit?" he asked. "I miss him."

"He misses you," she whispered.

"I can't come? Not ever?"

"Not ever. I've enough trouble."

His eyes gleamed. "I heard about that," he said. "How's it
going?" Luke was always tactful, had never approved of her
more public misalliance, but he treated it noncommittally, as
if he were the adult, she the unruly student. I'm on *your* side,
he always said.

"It'll be all right, I think. The wronged wife has calmed
down since the grand disclosure." Rosalind's tone was flip,
but in her mind she saw Sarah Damian's towheaded Dutch
bob whirl against the bookcases, saw her rosy, round-

cheeked face go hysterical and blind, as she pulled books, hurled them. "And, of course, the renunciation."

"It was really something to see, I heard," Luke said. "She threw stuff at you?"

"Books," Rosalind said. "All over the Chairman's office." They both laughed a little.

"Chase," Luke said speculatively after a minute. "I miss you." He always called her that; couldn't first-name a former teacher, an older woman, so he last-named her. She ruffled his hair.

"You're just hungry. Why you, by the way? Why not some fat students? There're an awful lot of fat students." She wrinkled her nose fastidiously; she scorned fat people.

Languidly Luke pointed his orange juice bottle at her. "The fat ones didn't last. They don't utilize food well. The doctors, well, the premeds, they won't get us doctors"—he twisted his mouth—"told us with no food at all the fat ones would last longer. But we have milk once a day, all the orange juice we want. God, I'm sick of orange juice."

"You all must be." Rosalind glanced curiously around at the other students, perhaps fifteen of them, limp and torpid, some in, some on their sleeping bags. They didn't look too bad. Up close, the sloped space under the stairs was homey and intimate, a fusty cocoon. Some students slept, but one had *Ulysses* propped on his stomach, and two others were whispering. Back against the wall, a boy and a frizzly-haired girl with a guitar sang softly, fitfully, a tune she couldn't quite make out, then could, the guitar fretting the air with the edge of a song, a fragment of "Joe Hill."

"The girls are best," Luke said. "They last best."

"Really?" Rosalind was diverted. "Why, I wonder?"

"More fat," he said. She looked down at herself, startled. "Not you."

"The women in the Donner Party," she said reflectively, "survived the men two to one."

He raised mocking eyebrows. "Schoolteacher."

"How much longer, Luke?" She waved her hands ambivalently in the air, one hand to applaud, the other gently to mock his hunger strike. He saw only the applauding hand.

"Who knows?" Luke rested his head back on the rolled blanket, a tired hero. "We need a big speaker, we need a rally, but we can't seem to get any support at all from the national SDS in Chicago. We've—"

Rosalind interrupted. "Is there still a national SDS?" He looked blank.

"Well, yeah, I think so. The one letter we got had SDS for a letterhead. Great letter." He laughed shortly. "You know, 'Sorry and right on, up against the wall.' A form letter. It seems our timing's a little off."

"You didn't exactly jump the gun," said Rosalind, and he grinned at her.

"Yeah. By now, all the movement leaders are on trial in Chicago, or else underground." He raised himself up on his elbows and shook his head. "Underground!" he repeated. His denim headband slipped over one eyebrow.

"Where is Mark Rudd?" Rosalind uttered rhetorically. She reached over and adjusted his headband. "Where is Bernardine Dohrn?"

"Where is Ben Roth?" Luke picked up the litany. Rosalind felt her body clench, then go weak. She studied his face, but found it innocent.

"Yeah, where?" she asked. "Hey, I've got to dash." Gathering books and briefcase with one hand, reaching up the other to grab a step, she pulled herself into a crouch and smiled down at him, supine on his sleeping bag, his head

tilted towards her like Michelangelo's Adam. He swooped
his eyes suggestively up her legs. "I wish you luck," she said.
"I've got to get to Payroll before it closes." She gestured up,
through the stairs. "I've missed two paychecks."

"Well, you have to eat," said Luke with a lovely, slow, ironic
smile.

· II

After she had the two paychecks safe in her briefcase, Rosalind, walking fast across campus towards the far parking lot
where she'd stashed her half-packed Firebird, began to find
the melodrama of her headlong flight a bit preposterous,
comic even. What, after all, was she running from? The FBI,
whose Ten Most Wanted List Ben had so fleetingly adorned,
had never shown the slightest curiosity about Ben Roth's
abandoned wife. Still, she felt an uncontrollable identification with Ben's plight, a mad loyalty: if Ben is harrassed, I
should be. If Ben runs, I should run. So I ascribe murder-
ous intentions to a Dutch-bobbed faculty wife, weave lavender menace around poor Cynnie: I invent an enemy so I can
flee.

Across the rolling mounds of earth, heaped fill from the
parking lot that some imaginative student had dubbed
"Hobbiton," Rosalind climbed the low brick wall of the back
campus and started up the road leading to the raw, new sup-
plementary parking lot. They'd razed woods to make it, but
no one had protested. No students had thrown themselves in
front of the bulldozers. "I protest," Sarah Damian had stood
up and proclaimed when Rosalind came through the Chairman's door. "I protest my husband's mistress." She'd started
to chuck books then. "She and Paul, they're fucking all over

the place! Everybody knew, and nobody told me." The Chairman had sat at his desk, amazed. "And you," Sarah'd whirled on him, "you half-assed English professors, oh, you're so *civilized*!"

The damned parking lot was as far away as Cynnie's house. What had she thought Cynnie would do if she spied books and clothing in the Firebird, steal the distributor cap? Well, Cynnie did know engines. Cynnie had a soldering iron and an electric drill. Walking along, toting up visually the things she'd left in the house to allay Cynnie's suspicion, conspicuous things—the color TV Barney'd brought on his last visit, her typewriter with the Bosworth-Toller artfully open next to it, her quilting frame, its unfinished quilt impaled by embroidery needles flamboyantly at the ready—plotting the prodigious enterprise of getting everything out fast, Rosalind was startled, and jumped when a car scudded noisily to a stop beside her.

"Christ!" Paul Damian shouted. "I recognized you across the campus by your legs. I'd know those legs anywhere!"

With loathing, Rosalind looked down at the gaudy red Alfa Romeo he flaunted like a codpiece, at his big face looming momentarily in the passenger's window next to her. The gears ground, and he twisted back to the driver's side. Rosalind choreographed in her mind a stylized dancer's kick, a scarlet leg kicking the red car away, like a toy. Paul Damian shoved the gear stick into park, his head out of the window. "Rosalinda, don'ta look at me like that," he wheedled. "You are gonna miss me. Admit it." His head tipped up at her, a large head set low on his shoulders by a coarse, truck driver's neck. "I've got a bull neck," he'd told her once, proudly, in bed, as if it were a sign of virility. "Sixteen inches." His face was craggy, ruddy, and dissipated; his eyes were a pure, disarming blue. His springy brass-colored hair was fashionably long, but he whacked it straight back, like a sideburned fifties hood. In bed (and in vain), Rosalind had once tried to comb it for him, but the hair had protested, almost standing on end to manipulate itself into its defiant backward shock. "This ain't a beauty parlor, sister." He'd put his big hands around her neck, gathered her long hair into a hank, and yanked her down. "This here's a *bed*."

"Rosalinda," he said now from the window, grinning enticingly up. His eyes went wide and innocent. "What'd *I* do? Sarah has these hysterical fits, I told you," shrugging hugely as if, Look what a cross *I* have to bear, so, baby, don't blame *me*.

Her eyes narrowed with scorn. How dare he? She'd had to shoulder all the responsibility as if she'd seduced him, this burly, arrogant, forty-five-year-old professor who wrote such dapper, elegant prose and talked like a gangster. When Sarah had appeared at the Chairman's office with her "compleynt"—"The Compleynt of Sarah Damian," Rosalind dubbed it, wryly, in her mind—it had been Rosalind who'd been summoned peremptorily out of class, not Paul Damian, "our eighteenth-century man," the wild man of the department with his amusing *sotto voce* sideline: lucrative mystery novels. Secretly Rosalind preferred his tongue-in-cheek mystery novels to his criticism, which was arch and prissy; and searching for a retort, considered telling him right now, "Your criticism is arch and prissy," then rejected it as a low blow. (An academic mistress, she'd been heaped with signed copies of his books and offprints, a bounty she was obliged to study with attention, for he demanded intelligent, liberally documented praise—oh, he was impossible! "Well, what'd you think?" He'd leaned back against the pillows. "The Pope book is brilliant," she'd obediently begun, cross-legged among the sheets. . . .)

"Go to hell," she said now, in a tight voice. "Nobody threw books at *you*."

"Oh, snappy comeback." She started walking then, head high and defiant. His gleeful mocking laugh followed her. Furious, she kept moving, furious but remembering despite herself what a thwacking great lover he was, lusty and uninhibited—he could make love so fast, so hard that she (caught up, pounded, mastered) fancied her own thudding responses were thrust into her from without, orgasms that dispensed with the charted preliminaries and simply *were*, whole and stark and elemental. Paul Damian could drive Ben clean out of her consciousness. Oh, she'd miss him all right. . . .

With jagged stops and starts he followed her, the Alfa Romeo urgent and mischievous, like a nasty Dodgem. "Rosalind," he called, swerving close, "you're being childish."

That tore it. Hounding her with his stupid little car, and *she* was being childish. She started to run up the exit ramp to the parking lot, noting with satisfaction that two cars were on their way down. He'd have to go all the way to the entrance up the road.

Of course, the Alfa Romeo was waiting at the foot of the exit ramp when Rosalind came down in her Firebird; the Alfa was waiting and Paul was waiting, a triumphant leer on his face, she could see it through her windshield and his, so flagrant was his triumph, so florid was his face. She cursed her stupidity. For a moment, their two cars confronted each other slantwise like wary dogs, and then Rosalind, with sudden grim exhilaration, gunned her accelerator, swerved around the Alfa, and headed in the direction it was not pointing. Oho, he'd have to turn around to pursue her. Her year-old Firebird, which she drove like a Jeep, was a splendid, peppy car, and the speedometer went all the way to 160, surely a sign of potentially heroic velocity. She could outrun Paul Damian; she could and she would.

She was winding up and around the new dirt road that cut a spiral through the back-campus woods before her mind separated from her car and asked abruptly, Why? Why outrun Paul Damian? And why should Paul Damian pursue her? What possible motive could he have? If he wanted to talk—did he want to talk? to seduce again?—he'd do better to wait for her at Cynnie's house, just as he'd so cannily waited at the exit ramp. His fictional detective, Percival Dane, never followed people, Rosalind recollected; the elegant, surpassingly lazy Percival Dane simply waited where he knew they'd turn up eventually. He never damaged property or snagged a thread of his embroidered waistcoat; casually and easily he broke into suspects' homes and lounged in their drawing rooms, drinking their twelve-year-old Scotch until they returned, crying, Egad! Percival Dane is *beastly*, Rosalind thought now, childishly, letting her brain revert to the driver's seat as, damn him and egad, there was Paul following her; she could see the red car through a stand of tall pines.

Her world contracted to the space of her car. For an instant Rosalind recognized and relished the single-minded concentration her actress mother and her athlete father could achieve at will; then she became all poised, exultant driver, pure function. Leaning forward, pushing the car to seventy up the winding dirt road, she tried to focus her mind's eye on Paul Damian's speedometer—how fast could *he* go? *Amps*. She could see, but the numbers blurred. God knows, she ought to have his speedometer by heart, all the time she'd spent on the leather seat of the Alfa, her knees jammed under the dashboard, so no one would see her with

Paul and tell Sarah. For almost a year, almost weekly, she'd sat like that till they were out of town, and still she couldn't visualize his speedometer. Probably it was in kilometers or something Italian—Roman numerals?—and anyhow she had an uncomfortable suspicion that Alfa Romeo was a famous racing line; only a suspicion, that portion of her prodigious sporting education being sketchy, for Barney considered the Grand Prix beneath his notice, a diversion for "rich sissies."

Barney lisped "sissies," but never said "fags," Rosalind recollected idly, looping round, leaning with the car, watching the angles of her body—knuckles, glen-plaid elbows, splayed scarlet knees—her jolted vantage catching sporadic views of the indefatigable red Alfa. Fleetingly she remembered Cynnie saying she should see how fast the Firebird would really go—"It would do this darling car good," as if the Firebird were a coddled child who needed more exercise. "It'll go a hundred and sixty miles an hour," Rosalind had said. "Look at the speedometer," and Cynnie had laughed her delicious, tinkling laugh.

At sixty Rosalind skittered through the chain-link back-campus gates, open, thank heaven, these gates utilitarian enough for a concentration camp, while the front gates were vaulted brick and ivy-twined, and, scattering dirt and stones and leaves, she turned and headed straight and mindless for the Interstate. Chase, she thought, with wild, sudden energy. " 'The Chase' is on the move," radio sportscasters used to exult in the forties whenever Barney barrelled through the line. "Here's 'The Chase,' " his baseball co-announcer still said, before Barney's gravelly voice came on the TV. What would Lionel Trilling say about *that* name? she proudly wondered. The red Alfa followed her up the ramp to the Interstate; the fall color whipped by; the Interstate went up and down with the mountains; her scarlet leg moved deftly from

brake to accelerator. Quilting frame, Kit at four, barber
shop: fragments of her list nattered away, as Paul Damian
hurtled along next to her in the passing lane, turning occasionally to show her he was laughing his fool head off,
looking for all the world as if they were making love, and
they drove for a time neck and neck, and at ninety Rosalind
found she dared not go any faster; still, she kept her arm
straight and sure to the top of the steering wheel while her
mind clicked movie images of chase scenes, Robert Mitchum
and Jane Greer in Mexico, that awful scene at the end of
Butterfield 8 where Elizabeth Taylor's red Sunbeam-Alpine
goes flipping in slow motion through the air, and she felt
balanced with Paul, suspended in slow motion, when suddenly he tooted his horn, thrust his bull neck forward, and
surged ahead so fast, Rosalind dazedly thought, He must be
going a hundred and twenty at least. In her rearview mirror
she saw a flashing red light. A Pennsylvania State Police car
replaced the Alfa in the passing lane, and it very, very gently
nudged her over to the shoulder. Damian's car vanished into
the distance ahead.

Heart   pounding,   adrenaline   racing—did   adrenaline
race?—her hair wild and tangled, she could see it, on the
edges of her face, Rosalind sat watching the tall trooper get
out of his car and amble over. Violently she rolled down her
window, turned to fumble through her briefcase for her
wallet, and then hurled the wallet through the window into
the road. The trooper bent over all in one casual, graceful
motion and retrieved it. If he said, "You dropped something," she'd spit in his face. She actually sucked her mouth
to gather saliva, but he simply flipped lightly through the
wallet till he got to her license and stood reading it, as if he
had all the time in the world. He was bareheaded, she noticed sidelong; could a bareheaded policeman give a ticket, a

bareheaded, red-headed policeman? If a bareheaded, red-headed, woodchuck chuck.

He leaned down to the window. Peripherally she registered white skin, chiseled cheekbones, impossibly aristocratic nose, but she stared straight ahead.

"Are you all right?" he asked her.

"All right?" She heard her own angry scream, and she was crying wildly all of a sudden. "Why don't you get *him,* you unutterable *fool,*" she ranted, fluttering fingers, flailing arms towards the distance ahead. "He was chasing me, hounding me, running me to earth, and now he's off, scot-free, that unspeakable parody of an eighteenth-century rake, with his prissy criticism and his stupid phallic car and his crazy wife who threw the entire *OED* at me—" She paused for breath and heard as if by instant replay her mad recital. God, he'd have her committed. "Go get him," she nonetheless imperiously repeated. "Go after *him.*"

The trooper had one arm folded across his chest; he rested his elbow on it and lightly tapped his cheekbone with a finger. He was looking fascinated. Slowly he smiled, and then he said, "If you mean the guy in the red Alfa, well, I couldn't possibly have caught *him.*"

His smile was perfectly beautiful. Rosalind, her head leaned back on the seat now, felt a lazy irrepressible laugh begin deep in her throat. She tipped her head sideways towards him and asked softly, "Do you know who you look like? You look exactly like Lord Peter Wimsey. . . ."

"Oh, foolish, stiff-necked quilting frame!"

Rosalind kicked savagely a wooden leg of her quilting frame, but nothing happened. You could fold the frame without removing the quilt, but only Cynnie knew how to perform that particular sleight of hand, Cynnie having set the frame up. Rosalind paced around the perimeter of the frame. She wondered if removing the braces would help. Into the quilt, under the embroidered rainbow that dominated the center portion, Rosalind had sewn the manila envelope that held Ben Roth's paper and plastic identity—birth certificate to BankAmericard—her last communication from him. She'd received the envelope in March, soon after a Greenwich Village town-house explosion had yielded up blown bits of bodies and a finger, this elliptical carnage eventually traced to Weatherman. Rosalind, who'd fortunately not known how radical Ben's politics had become in a very short time (on hearing of the explosion, it had not occurred to her to wonder if the finger might be Ben's), had nonetheless felt a lurch in her vitals at the penned warning in Ben's comic southpaw handwriting on the manila envelope. Doubly sinister, she'd tried to pun in her mind, but her hands were shaking. TO BE OPENED IN THE EVENT OF MY DEATH, BEN ROTH. She'd ignored the superstitious pang (you could not kill someone by opening an envelope) and carefully unsealed the flap. The paper and plastic spilled out, a mystifying array: library and credit cards, driver's license, bookmarks, a senior lifesaving badge, a letter from her, draft card, myriad nonsense till she found Ben's hasty note: "Roz, I knew you'd open it. I'm not dead, I'm underground. I love you." Ah, cloak-and-dagger, and she'd participated, sewing the damned envelope into her quilt.

How to get it out of Cynnie's house and into the Firebird? She glanced at the mantel clock. It was amazingly, blessedly not yet three o'clock; she couldn't believe it, felt caught in a benevolent timewarp or the ship scene in *Othello* where time so obligingly contracts. Bratty's slap, the hunger strike, Luke and Paul, the chase through the mountains, the beautiful trooper blurred in her mind like so much fiction remembered. She'd already lugged Barney's color TV to the car, checked out Kit's room and her own, and even paused a moment to be sad. She'd miss the graceful four-poster and the yellow-sprigged dimity curtains, miss seeing her face framed in the fanciful rococo mirror over the dressing table. During the year she'd been in Cynnie's house, through such relics, Rosalind had carried on a dreamy romance with the ghost of Cynnie's maiden aunt, who'd lovingly gathered the furnishings, planned the gardens; she'd have adored Cynnie's aunt, she was quite sure.

The aunt would have approved Rosalind's quilt, Rosalind thought, admiring it extravagantly on its frame. It was the only thing in her life she'd ever made with her hands. About a year before, she'd started idly piecing denim scraps together—she and Kit seemed to exude denim like an essence—for a poncho, she thought, but she found the patchwork process so soothing to mind and body that the modest effort had gradually turned ambitious. "I might make it into a quilt," she'd raised her head one winter evening to remark. "Piecing is peaceful." Cynnie had groaned. Kit, however, laughed, a born punster like his mother. "Well, Roz," Cynnie had said, "as long as you're doing it, why don't you do it right? Get a quilting frame. Look at you." The *œuvre* had by that time reached unwieldy proportions. While Rosalind sewed at it, bordering seams with daisy chains and peace signs and snakes playing Follow the Leader, it spread out round her chair like an enormous skirt, warm and comfortable, but rather awkward for sewing. "Make a crazy quilt. It would have to be a crazy quilt." Cynnie winked at Kit.

So the quilting frame was purchased, puzzled over by Rosalind and set up by skillful Cynnie; and once the quilt was affixed, Rosalind's imagination, hitherto entirely verbal, had

run rampant with pictures to embroider and appliqué. In
the center, a free-form rainbow sprawled, flanked by four
large panels: Shakespeare's Rosalind in purple doublet and
hose in the Forest of Arden; Nathan Hale, bareheaded on
the scaffold; a spouting Moby Dick attacked by tiny stick figures with harpoons; a botched and knotty attempt at Leda
and the Swan, badly botched; Rosalind frowned at it now.
Kit, pointing to the swan, had asked if it were Donald Duck.
She'd take the stitching out and try again, she decided.

Maybe she could fit the frame through the door without
folding it. Speculatively Rosalind eyed the recalcitrant object.
She could turn it on its side and angle it through. Cross the
bridge of the car door when she came to it—perhaps open
the windows? She wrestled the frame over on its side; it
wasn't heavy, ah, fit nicely through the front door. On the
round front porch, she stood holding it by a leg and, looking
down the rather steep steps, closed her eyes, gave a push,
and the frame flopped over on its back and lay down
the steps like a giant rectangular insect, six stiff legs in the
air.

"Roz, you ought to fold it. You're going to snag the embroidery." Cynnie Talleyrand, looking lovely in a scalloped
blouse the color of willow leaves in fall and a pale-blue suede
skirt, appeared between the two lower legs of the capsized
quilting frame. Hell, Rosalind thought, oh hell, bloody hell.
Cynnie put her books and her slide rule on the ground. "I
know you're leaving, Roz." Cynnie did something to the
lower legs of the frame and they folded like magic. Oho,
they fold vertically, Rosalind thought, watching Cynnie with
fascination as Cynnie edged up the stairs around the quilt
and folded the middle legs. "I told Billy off for teaching Kit
how to roll joints, by the way," Cynnie said. "Kit was really
super at rolling, Billy said."

Cynnie joined Rosalind at the top of the stairs and bent to fold the top legs. Rosalind watched her with helpless admiration—for her skill, and for her beauty, which never bored or became banal. As tall as Rosalind, Cynnie was lighter of bone, softer of flesh. She had ash-brown hair as soft as a cloud, which she wore in a wispy pompadour around her face and a fall of soft ringlets in the back. In her soft fabrics—the challis blouse, the suede skirt—she looked as if she'd just arrived from another century, the near past, the distant future. "What on earth are you thinking about?" Rosalind had once asked her, drawn by a look of rapt reverie on Cynnie's face. "I'm thinking about Riemann's Zeta Function," Cynnie had breathed. At times Cynnie seemed to Rosalind to be surrounded by Riemann's Sphere, a topological heaven that Rosalind, after Cynnie's explanation, visualized as a dreamy ellipse much like the round front porch, where people disdainful of Euclid sat around whispering that parallel lines do not exist. "How can they not?" Rosalind had demanded. Cynnie had sighed. Now Cynnie did something to the quilting frame's edge, and a portion folded over. Patiently she manipulated until it had contracted, accordion-pleated, into the size of a card table. "There," Cynnie said. "I'll put it in the car for you, Roz." Rosalind stood at the top of the stairs thinking, This is the Riemann Sphere. . . .

Cynnie came back, smiling an enchanting smile. "Well, come on," she invited. "Let's go in. You've got a few minutes, Roz." Rosalind followed her into the parlor. "Sit," Cynnie said. They sat in spindly yellow-painted rockers to the left of the fireplace with the Adam mantel. Cynnie rocked gently, and her gathered suede skirt spread gracefully out, shadows in the folds. She wore boots of fine glove-leather. Rosalind watched her own scarlet knees tense as she rocked, too, but vigorously, faster than Cynnie. She studied Cynnie's

face, her sad, down-tilted gray-blue eyes, as she waited for
Cynnie to speak. A brilliant mathematician, Cynnie was
charmingly inarticulate, almost inept at ordinary conversation. One learned to wait.

"How'll Ben know where to find you?" Cynnie stared at
Rosalind with some menace. Rosalind was puzzled. Cynnie
had met Ben once, last winter, on his way to Flint, Michigan,
for something he called a War Council, and she'd loathed
him on sight. The last thing she'd do would be tell Ben
where to find Rosalind. Still, she was the only Caliban friend
of Rosalind's who'd been told about Ben, the sole key to the
secrecy surrounding the identity of Rosalind's husband.
Luke DiLorenzo, bless his heart, seemed casually to assume
Rosalind was an unwed mother, and she'd told Paul Damian
she was "separated." He'd of course evinced a persistent,
prurient curiosity, even tried to trick her occasionally: "Did
what's-his-name like oral sex? What's-his-name, uh—" "I
never asked him." Cynnie's asking for my address, Rosalind
finally managed to interpret her question. She's afraid I
won't tell her where I'm going.

"Cynnie," she said, "I'll give you the address. I was going
to anyway." Rosalind tore a page off the phone pad on the
table between them, wrote, Box 47, Mud Lake, Pa., handed
it to Cynnie, who read it, wadded it up, and put it in her
mouth, chewing soberly. Rosalind laughed.

Cynnie didn't laugh. She took the wad of paper out of her
mouth and pitched it towards the fireplace. Sadly she gestured at the corner. "You took Barney's TV."

"Cynnie, you have a bigger TV. You can bring it down."

"I know." She fixed Rosalind with the menacing gaze
again. "Roz, did you tell Barney?"

"Tell him what? I sent him a change-of-address—"

"Did you tell him about my, um, suggestion?" Rosalind
stared. Cynnie must mean her "proposition."

"Cynnie, of course not."

"Will you promise you won't?"

"I wouldn't anyway."

"Promise."

"I promise. Listen, Cynnie, I have to go."

Cynnie looked at her watch. "You've got half an hour."

"Cynnie, you're cutting a class, aren't you?" The telephone between them, yellow like the rockers, rang. Cynnie picked it up.

"Hello. . . . Yes, hello, Paul." She made a face and then raised a quizzical eyebrow at Rosalind. Vehemently Rosalind shook her head.

"No, she's not. . . . You're where? . . . Oh, you're all the way to the New York State Line? Indeed." Cynnie rolled her eyes at Rosalind. "You're going to throttle her. Paul, let me get a pencil." Cynnie mimed uncontrollable laughter, holding her stomach. "Okay, go on. . . . You hope she got a fifty dollar ticket; you hope they threw the book at her. . ."

At that unfortunate metaphor Rosalind glowered. Oh, may the dogs eat her by the wall of Jezreel, and people throw books at her forever.

"She still owes you a paper," Cynnie went slowly on, "a paper on the what? The zeugma?" Cynnie wrinkled her nose and shrugged at Rosalind. "Spell it, please, Paul. . . . Z-E-U-G-M-A. Thank you. . . . You'll give her an F, you really will . . . you don't give A's for—. Listen, Paul, don't say that into *my* phone. Fuck *you,* Paul." Cynnie hung up. "What'd you *do* to him?" she asked Rosalind.

Rosalind, laughing, flopped her hand in spirals to show it was too long a story. Cynnie stared at Rosalind's moving hand as if it were drawing a diagram of infinity. "Roz," she said after a bit, "don't you ever get tired of being, um"—she made a circle of her thumb and forefinger and jammed two fingers through—"fucked?"

Eyes drawn irresistibly to Cynnie's poised fingers, Rosalind said, "No, I guess I don't."

"Pity," Cynnie said. She whisked both hands at Rosalind as if disposing of dust. "Well, bye-bye, Roz." She waved her hand. After a minute Rosalind got up and went for her final bit of impedimenta, her typewriter on the desk near the windows. An old electric, it was damnably heavy. Cynnie got up, too, but not to help it turned out, rather to put a record on the stereo. The Rolling Stones blared forth horribly loud, causing Rosalind to drop her typewriter back on the desk, but Cynnie didn't turn the volume down. She fell into her rocker, leaned her head back, and closed her eyes, looking for all the world as if "Honky Tonk Woman" were a difficult late Beethoven quartet. Thinking *Kit, barber shop,* Rosalind finally managed to maneuver the bulky typewriter into her arms and, hugging it to her bosom, staggered to the front door. The staccato rhythms of Mick Jagger's murky voice followed her across the porch and down the steps.

As she opened the car door, wrestling the typewriter onto her hip like an intractable baby, she heard Keith Richards join his voice to Jagger's, and the lyrics became intelligible: "She blew my *nose* and then she blew my *mind.*"

A wonderful zeugma! Rosalind thought, heaving the typewriter into the backseat.

Amid the Dizygotheca elegantissima that flourished there,
Rosalind sat on the terra-cotta tiled counter of her bathroom
blow-drying her hair. The slender dark-green leaves of the
spiky plants blew with her flying hair. Rosalind's bare legs
dangled aimlessly. She hated being confined to a length of
electrical cord. With the hand that wasn't holding the dryer
(pointed at her head, like a large yellow gun), she tidied the
counter and watered the plants. One-handed, she scrubbed
the sink. She emptied the pockets of her terry-cloth robe.
Encountering her hip bone, she brooded a moment about
Craig Morton's hip pointer, for she very much wanted the
Broncos to win the Super Bowl. She was quite sure Barney
had bet on Dallas.

In the mirror she checked the length of her hair. She
could pull it to her shoulder blades, but it had been that long
for over a year now, would never again achieve the waist-
length glory she'd so perversely sacrificed seven and a half
years ago, a tangled heap of gold, a mess of shadows on the
barber shop floor. Cynnie had a theory that if a woman cut
her hair for any reason but vanity, the hair became outraged
and stunted, would never grow back. "You spited it, Roz."
Cynnie knew a woman who, with drastic pragmatism—"I

mean, Roz, she could have put it *up*"—had had her long hair
cut the day before a job interview at a conservative corpora-
tion; the woman had gotten the job, but not her hair back.
"Not one inch. You were lucky yours grew back at all, Roz."
Complacently Cynnie'd touched her own luxuriant ash-
brown tresses.

Rosalind ruefully pounded her head with the blow-dryer;
she still couldn't figure out why she'd done it. What had pos-
sessed her? She'd even been in a tearing hurry. Impatiently
she'd paced the barber shop while Kit (all seven-year-old resignation and baleful eyes in the mirror) was shorn. He'd
never been much on haircuts. (When Kit was two, a barber
had taken one look at his violent little body, twisting and
frantic in Ben's arms, and shuddered away: "Oh, no. Out! I
have bursitis in my shoulder." Barney had recommended
force, Annabelle, Valium.) This time the protest on his face
suddenly struck her as a bit, well, rhetorical. Maybe, it had
dawned on her, shuffling through the fallen hair on the
tessellated floor of the barber shop, just maybe, Kit was tired
of being mistaken for a girl. The haircut was charming, not
short, just above his collar, and she could see his eyebrows,
the shape of his neck, and just a hint of ears. His head
looked poised, alert, free.

"Could you cut my hair like that?" she'd suddenly asked
the barber. The barber blanched and demurred, and Kit
cried out in honest horror, but the deed was eventually
done, the barber cluck-clucking and tsk-tsking infuriatingly
with every snip. He'd charged her ten dollars to Kit's five,
which struck her as unfair. She and Kit were to the door
when the barber called, "You could have a fall made. I could
do it for you. Say, fifty dollars." Rosalind had turned. "Victorian women used hair to stuff pillows. Why don't you?" she'd
countered pleasantly enough.

Now, sitting up straight on the counter in her bathroom,

Rosalind yanked the plug and put down the blow-dryer. Absently she combed her hair, her eyes fixed on the past, jolting through some skewed association. On an impulse her mind did not define—an instinct almost—she went to the dressing area off the bathroom and carefully removed from the top shelf of her end of the closet a large bundle wrapped in tissue paper and plastic. She carried it into the bedroom proper: her *magnum opus,* her *œuvre,* her quilt. She'd packed it up when she and Kit left Mud Lake to move in with Will, transported it personally, like an escort to a coffin, in her car on Halloween when she and Will and Kit and Joe and Daisy had moved finally and triumphantly into the new house; and never once had she unwrapped it. A smell of cedar from the closet wafted forth as she unswaddled and spread the quilt on the bed. She fancied she could smell My Sin from Cynnie's house, the rich odor of Mud Lake in thaw.

Feeling warm aesthetic pleasure, she let her eyes follow the flamboyant arc of the rainbow over the center of the quilt and range to the intricate, colorful side panels—Shakespeare's Rosalind, Nathan Hale, the spouting Moby Dick. Leda and the Swan were still unfinished. With a finger she touched the perforations left where she'd picked out her first draft of the reluctant maiden, the importunate swan. She flipped the quilt over; it was heavy, the padding thick, and the denim verso spread plumply before her, stitched by hand, her hand, using red number 60 thread for the extravagant loops and ellipses. With the flat of her hand, she searched, pummeled, and finally located Ben's envelope under the rainbow. She found the subtle, hidden seam that masqueraded as part of the quilting stitch and, with nail scissors, carefully cut the threads behind the rainbow. In the cotton wadding the manila envelope nestled inviolate, the pot of gold. . . .

She hadn't told the FBI or the police about Ben's envelope, hadn't told even Will. Her one pathetic holdout. Violate my home, scrutinize my sexual behavior, probe my memory, cut Ben's body into sections and extrapolate his organs; but do not plunder a woman's handicraft. While the FBI man had questioned and policemen had dusted for fingerprints, riffled through books, rummaged through drawers, the quilt had been in full view in the living room of the cottage, mitered on its frame, a monolith.

Rosalind sat down cross-legged on the exposed underside of the quilt and opened the manila envelope. The contents spilled out across the bed like tarot cards. Rosalind picked up items at random, whimsically, as if selecting photographs. Again and again, she read the name BEN ROTH, its perfect spondee embossed, printed, typed, scrawled. "Ben Roth, age eleven" on his senior lifesaving badge made her smile. A splendid swimmer, Ben. She found details that hadn't registered her first time through, so alarmed had she been by the implications of the envelope, so frantic to conceal the evidence in her conveniently waiting quilt. His draft card had an almost imperceptible burned fret along one edge: Lose your nerve, old boy? The top left corner of the Columbia ID card showed a tiny photograph of Ben with a comic Ché Guevara mustache that he'd sported for exactly one week. Rosalind smiled. There was an illuminated card, like something you might pick up in the back of a Catholic church near the holy water, of the Apostles' Creed in fancy, tiny letters, almost unreadable. The renegade Jew disowned by his parents turns revolutionary, Rosalind thought, picturing shadowy figures in fatigue jackets and blue jeans skulking in the backs of churches, passing rifles and dope. . . .

Stuck in the envelope, she found a letter she'd written to him postmarked CALIBAN, JANUARY 10, 1970, a much handled envelope addressed to an anonymous post-office box in

Chicago, the only address that seemed to work (although she suspected Ben actually lived in San Francisco), and early in 1970, even the Chicago address had started spewing mail back: WHEREABOUTS UNKNOWN. This would have been, she calculated, the last letter he got from her before he went "underground." Why the hell didn't he keep it? She opened the envelope and felt her face flush. It was one thing to read an old letter from someone else, quite another to read an old letter from oneself. Her identity juggled, her mind twisted backward into an almost forgotten attitude of wounded flippancy, and she held the letter at arm's length as if it were radioactive, a palimpsest X ray of a changed mind:

> January 10, 1970
> Saturday night

Dearest Ché,

Yeah, yeah, yeah, we're all right. I got an A in Victorian poetry despite yr snorting, panting interruption of my last-minute cramming. (There is cramming and cramming, yes, as you so delicately put it.) I don't know how Kit took your flying visit; he hasn't mentioned it, not once. Barney was here over New Year's and all Kit can talk about is the Super Bowl tomorrow.

Ah, Ben, you swaggering cad, you rag-tag bounder, can't you at least write me a decent letter? What *is* all this circular revolutionary jargon? No, I will not read Mao, I will not read Fanon, or that Brazilian guy whose name mercifully escapes me. I have enough to read. I even skipped parts of your letter. I couldn't hear yr voice *once* in it, or maybe just a tinge at the end in that tender, Byronic, "Can still feel your ———, yes!" which my prim Victorian fingers can't quite bring themselves to spell out.

Cynnie absolutely loathed you, by the way. Same old winsome Ben. Those cloak-and-dagger phone calls were too much. Gee, I hadn't realized Weatherman had a chapter in Caliban. How reassuring in the dark of the night. I love you, but one day I won't.

R

Super Bowl IV that would have been, Rosalind registered
with desperate irrelevance, hoping Ben had caught the game
in whatever "safe house" of whatever collective he was helping toe the line. "Okay, put down your rifles, quit putting
down the collective, and break out the acid: it's time for the
Super Bowl!" Ben didn't live to see Super Bowl V. Now it
was Super Bowl XII. Rosalind bowed her head and started
to cry. The "flying visit" when Ben was on his way to Flint
came back like an assault: the one time Ben had been to
Cynnie's house, the last time but one Rosalind had seen him
alive. . . .

It was after midnight, and she'd been sitting up in her
four-poster wearing a demure batiste nightgown (purchased
for the four-poster and the ghost of Cynnie's maiden aunt),
reading "The Wreck of the Deutschland" for her final in
Victorian poetry the next day. Blue exam-books for the Melville course she was teaching that semester surrounded her
in little piles, their grades also due the next day. A popular
class, the Melville—she'd taught it again in the spring. That
night, in between "Deutschland" stanzas, she would read a
blue book, scribble a grade, economically using the same red
pen for grading and jotting marginal comments in her Hopkins book; the balance was precarious and her lap was full
when the doorbell rang, so she didn't even try to get up.
After a bit she heard Cynnie grumbling, swearing, go downstairs to answer the persistent ring.

The next thing Rosalind knew, there was Ben in her
room, bearded, noisy, and grimy in a fatigue jacket, unzip-
ping his jeans. "Oh, babe, these bouncing country roads!
Roz, spread your legs," and he'd ravished her amongst the
blue books. She could remember crumpled blue against the
olive drab of his jacket, remember how red ink had gotten
all over her nightgown, remember how her body had ob-

liged him, not her, for she'd "spread" without her conscious
volition, angry but all slick and ready, pulling him in despite
herself, her insides wild and hungry, spiraling. "Ah, Roz,
there's no cunt like yours, Roz." Ben had fallen asleep immediately, half-dressed and heavy, all over the blue books. . . .

"The Wreck of the Deutschland": she still hated it. A
vastly overrated poem. Stop crying, one corner of her mind
ordered; your eyes will redden and swell, and all those people are coming and Cynnie will look gorgeous; but when
Will came into the bedroom, Rosalind was rocking back and
forth, keening softly. "Honey, what's the matter?" Helplessly
she gestured around her, at all Ben's junk on the quilt. "I
always wondered what happened to that quilt," Will said. He
squeezed her shoulder. "What's all this?" He riffled a finger
through the mess of cards and picked up the manila envelope. "My God, Roz!" Will sat down on the bed next to her
and started picking up cards to look at them.

"I sewed it all into the quilt," Rosalind said.

"You sewed it into the quilt?" He started to laugh. They
both laughed, slightly manic laughter. Will held the illuminated Apostles' Creed up to the light. "He must have sent
along everything in his wallet," he said. "I'm surprised there
isn't a condom."

You son of a bitch, Rosalind thought, almost with admiration. She held out the letter. "Read that," she said casually.

Will cocked a quizzical eyebrow at her, then soberly read
the letter through, caught his breath, and leaned his head
back against the pillows. With the heels of his hands he covered his eyes, rubbed, then traced his cheekbones down, finally folding his hands on his chest as if to keep them still.
Rosalind could see white strain on the edges of his knuckles.
Why'd I make him read it? she ranted internally. What kind
of sadist am I? yet she waited with eager fascination for his

reaction. Will coughed and cleared his throat; when he finally spoke, his voice was husky.

"I always knew you loved him," he said, not looking at her. "But this—it's so damned *alive*." Rosalind curled her body next to his, put a hand over his folded hands.

"It was rotten of me to show it to you," she murmured. "I seem still to have all this anger. You sounded like a policeman. . . ." Will took hold of her hand. She laid her head on his chest and listened to his heartbeat.

"Say," he said after a while, "Barney's making a pitcher of Bloody Marys that appear to be half Tabasco and half vodka. Why don't I bring you one?"

"What time is it?" Rosalind, startled, raised her head from his chest to ask. Her eyes were already swollen from her brief but fierce indulgence of tears: she could feel them, feel torpor in the corners, impairment of upward peripheral vision. Ah, hell, she thought, envying her three-year-old Daisy who could cry for hours and not alter her flowery face one whit: tears, such a glorious luxury for children.

"It isn't two yet," Will said. "The Humphrey memorial service is still on." He got up from the bed and stood looking down at her.

"Could you bring me some teabags too?" she asked, feeling forlorn.

"Honey, do you want me to make you some tea?"

She laughed, embarrassed. "It's Cynnie's new remedy." Gingerly she touched her eyelids. "If you cry, you put cold wet teabags on your eyes."

"I see," Will said. He smiled at her with wry, warm amusement.

"I don't love Ben anymore," Rosalind said. "Only you."

"Cold wet teabags," Will said, "coming up."

· Onsundran*

November 1970

I

"Are you ready for me to pour your milk?" long-suffering
Kit called from the galley kitchen of the Mud Lake cottage.
Rosalind wouldn't touch milk unless it was ice cold. "Mom?"

"Five minutes," Rosalind, over her shoulder, absently re-
sponded, feeling her newly shorn hair bounce rather than
fly: a peculiar sensation, as if one were light-headed. She sat
at her makeshift desk, a long pale-ash parson's table that
she'd pushed up against the front windows to overlook the
lake. It was eight o'clock at night, and she'd just pulled the
scarlet monk's-cloth curtains against the encroaching darkness, an absolute, almost palpable darkness here in the country. She and Kit, city-bred, wondered at it, the darkness, and
also the silence. *Wine-dark lake,* Rosalind's mind muttered,
mud-dark lake, as she sorted through the student papers on
the *Odyssey.* In November Mud Lake was glittering, crystal
clear; but Maisie Ritter had told her the lake "worked" during the spring thaw, hence its pejorative name.

Rosalind gathered the three best papers. She would read
them aloud in class tomorrow. That and subtly coerced discussion ought to take up most of the hour and a quarter

*Old English for "separated one from the other, apart; alone."

period, and she'd still have time tonight to go over her homework for the Old English Poetry seminar in the morning. The Chairman, who taught the seminar—it was his baby—called on his Ph.D. candidates to translate, like high school students. She wanted to impress him, had been maniacally punctilious about preparation ever since "The Compleynt of Sarah Damian." In class Rosalind fancied that the white-haired Chairman watched her guardedly, with pity and fear, as if she were a grenade that might explode any minute, blowing the delicate Old English elegies all over the seminar table.

Quickly Rosalind leafed through the three *Odyssey* papers. "Cutting His Losses: Odysseus and His Men," by Jay Seiden, a brilliant piece of original criticism, perhaps even publishable; she'd have to prod him into some research. "Penelope, the Hero of the *Odyssey*," by Susan Jasper, a charming, gracefully written performance, and Susan had even looked up the Samuel Butler essay on "The Authoress of the *Odyssey*." Rosalind felt proud to have (albeit inadvertently) inspired Susan's splendid paper. And finally—she grinned, looking at the botched typing and smudges—baby-faced Andy Grimshaw had come through. He'd been in her classes for two semesters now, took his D's and C's cheerfully, and she'd decided he must have a shy crush on her: why else take courses he clearly had no knack for? They weren't required. But this, this was something else: "Encrimsoned Odysseus, the Killing of the Suitors, Cold Corpses at the Gate." Unwieldy title; he probably couldn't make up his mind, and the paper was awkwardly written; nonetheless it was superb. In five laconic pages Andy had managed a lusty examination of the entire blood-spattered killing-of-the-suitors chapter; he gave a careful account of who killed whom, showed an almost military appreciation of Odysseus's underdog strategy, and even discerned the complicity of Athene, Telemachus, Eumaeus, and Eurycleia in the bloodbath. Good for Andy, Rosalind thought, with her red pen impulsively changing the tentative minus after his A to a plus. Then she felt duty-bound to give pluses to Jay Seiden and Susan Jasper. "Kit!" she called suddenly. "Where's my milk?"

Rosalind pushed back her chair and stood up. Her bare feet revelled in the extravagantly soft umber-and-scarlet rya rug that covered almost the entire living room floor. Maisie Ritter's cottage surrounded her, warm and ruddy and open, comfortably rustic and rough-timbered for all it looked to have been furnished out of Sloan's or Bloomingdale's with scattered parson's tables in red lacquer and ash wood and a big soft couch like a double L in front of the fieldstone fireplace. The nightly fire, built by Kit, burned now, throwing undulating, contracting shadows. In the firelight scarlet pillows heaped willy-nilly glowed against the muddy umber of the burlap couch. Rosalind's quilt, which had appeared quaint and old-fashioned in Cynnie's house, here, mitered on its frame behind the couch, became a Kandinsky, as if some sorcery of cryptic coloration had transformed it from folk to modern art.

Halfway up the fireplace wall a narrow catwalk reached by a ship's ladder hovered, its flimsy railing of barn-siding making a shadowy lattice across the cottage. The three tiny bedrooms that opened onto it were rough wood, and their ceilings sloped to the floor. Between Rosalind's room and Kit's room, the fieldstone chimney rose, a pillar of warmth in the cold of the night. The cottage's oil furnace was adequate, but the chimney was comforting in the unfamiliar dark, and both she and Kit kept their beds shoved close to the chimney wall.

Kit, in a black turtleneck and blue jeans like his mother,

brought milk and cookies on a tray. Rosalind sat down with Kit at the big red parson's table near the kitchen pass-through, hungry suddenly, stoking up for the night and the midnight oil over "The Wife's Lament."

"To Morpheus," Rosalind toasted. "To bed," Kit resign-edly countered. Red milk glasses in midair, both she and Kit jumped, spilled milk on the table when a knock came at the kitchen door. "Good God," Rosalind said. She laughed at Kit's comically widened eyes. There'd been knocks at all hours at Cynnie's house, but this was their first knock here. She'd felt their refuge inviolate. Who could be out there in that awesome enveloping darkness? "Well, this is crazy," Ro-salind finally said. "Come on, let's answer it." She waited for Kit to get up, too, took him by the shoulder. "Come on, maybe we have a neighbor." She knew people lived up on the main road near the Mud Lake Post Office and the Mud Lake Tavern, but she and Kit had barely ventured forth during their three-week residence except to town and school, the weather had been so dreadful. Rosalind was still waiting for Pennsylvania's much-touted Indian summer. It hadn't come last year at all.

Rosalind opened the back door a crack and slanted her head so she could see out. "Rosalind Chase?" a man's voice asked.

"Yes?" Rosalind could feel Kit hide behind her, like a guilty urchin.

"You cut your hair," the voice said. Rosalind pulled the door open farther. A tall man with red-gold hair stood on the stoop, holding out some envelopes like an apology. The oil bill? He wore a loden coat and jeans, high-laced leather boots. As the light caught his face she saw that damned aris-tocratic nose.

"The fuzz," she, laughing, said. "Lord Peter. Come in," she

beckoned, bowing low with a swashbuckler's flourish. He came in. They stood grinning self-consciously at each other. "Kit," Rosalind said, "remember the policeman who didn't give me a ticket? Here he is, in the flesh. My son, Kit."

"Will Eddy." He and Kit shook hands.

"I brought your mail," Will Eddy said. "The state police barracks isn't far from Mud Lake, and we got this angry call from the Mud Lake postmistress—" Rosalind giggled at "postmistress," and Will Eddy's fair skin flushed, but he went on. "Your mail's been piling up." He flicked his thumb over his shoulder. "I've got three boxes for you in the car, and these"—he pressed the envelopes on her—"are telegrams that were forwarded." Rosalind grabbed, her fingers suddenly vague and terrified. "I'll bring in the boxes," Will Eddy said. "You want to give me a hand, Kit?"

"Sure."

In a frenzy Rosalind tore open both envelopes at once. One was a cablegram from Edinburgh. Annabelle. Rosalind caught her breath, and her body sagged with relief. The telegram was also from Annabelle. Ben isn't dead, she thought, he isn't dead. Feeling her knees like water, she leaned against the counter and read the cable: MY LADY MACBETH STUNNING TRIUMPH EVEN EDINBURGH. RETURN STATES POSTHASTE. PLAN VISIT YOU KIT IMMEDIATELY. AN- NABELLE. The cable was dated November 6, addressed to Cynnie's house, and had been forwarded from the Caliban Post Office. Didn't Annabelle get my change of address? Rosalind wondered. No, not if she left from Edinburgh rather than London. For a moment, Rosalind glowered: weren't cablegrams and telegrams supposed to be *delivered*? then she had an uncomfortable mental image of Cynnie eloquently shrugging at a Western Union boy. "Ask for her at Mud Lake." Annabelle's telegram was from New York:

ARRIVE SOMETIME TWELFTH. DONT MEET. MUST RETURN POST-
HASTE FIFTEENTH. HAMLET REHEARSALS IMPEND. BEAUTYSLEEP
FOR GERTRUDE. ANNABELLE. Rosalind counted the words.
Fifteen. Economical Annabelle, making one word out of
BEAUTY SLEEP.

Kit and Will Eddy came through the door, bearing boxes.
"Everything all right?" Will Eddy asked. Blithely Rosalind
nodded. She felt positively euphoric from relief. "I'm glad,"
he said. He smiled at her. "Where do you want these boxes?"
He and Kit followed Rosalind's jaunty progress into the living room. Will Eddy put a large carton on the parson's table,
a case of J&B, Rosalind saw. She started to laugh. He must
think I'm a lush, this Will Eddy, she thought.

"That's my father's standard housewarming gift," she explained. "Hey, now I can offer you a drink for your
trouble." She tried to wrest open the carton.

Kit stood impatiently behind her, holding two other boxes.
"Mom, can I open these?" Rosalind let Will Eddy break the
nylon-threaded tape on the carton of Scotch. "Mom?" Kit
repeated.

"Go ahead," she said.

"This one's from Barney." Kit tackled the larger box first.
Rosalind, catching the shucked wrapping, noted that Barney
at least had gotten her change-of-address card. Kit pulled
out football jerseys, a silky tumble of them.

"Good heavens!" Rosalind said. Grinning like idiots, she
and Kit rummaged luxuriously through the booty. "Kit,
they're *his*!" She held a jersey up to her, long as a minidress,
slightly tattered and embossed with a large *33*. "I told you
he'd give us some eventually. Aren't you glad you didn't ask
him?"

Will Eddy extracted a bottle of Scotch, and out of the
corner of her eye Rosalind became aware of him watching
the two of them with their long-coveted jerseys. "They'll be

super nightshirts," she said to Kit, like a British ingenue.
"Kit, is there a note?"

" 'The Chase,' " Will Eddy said. They both looked at him.
"Barney Chase," he said. "One of the greatest running backs
of all time. Number Thirty-three."

"Right!" both Rosalind and Kit exulted. "He's my grandfa-
ther," Kit said.

"And *my* father," Rosalind said.

"I'm in distinguished company," Will Eddy said. Rosalind
gave him a quick smile. She dove her hand into the box in
search of a note. Peripherally she noticed Kit holding the
other box, Will Eddy the bottle of Scotch.

"Kit," she said, "get some ice. And some glasses. You can
open that when we all have a drink. *You* have milk," she
added. At Cynnie's house people had given him beer and
God only knew what else. Heaving an exaggerated sigh, Kit
put down the box and went to the kitchen. Rosalind found a
note from Barney inside one of the jerseys:

November 4, 1970

Dear Rozzy,

Another housewarming present. I finally cleaned out my closet.
They make great nightshirts, also advertising. Wear them in health,
also bed. Give a couple to Cynnie.

Roz, I'm counting on you and Kit (and Cynnie, too, if she'd like)
spending the Christmas holidays with me. We'll have a week in
Florida, then come back and take in some Philadelphia hockey. The
Flyers are hot, and Mac Rich is going to let me try a night with him
in the broadcast booth. A little late to start hockey, yeah, I know,
your dad's old eyes are used to baseball, but it should be fun. I'll try
to finagle Kit into the booth. Write! One more measly postcard, and
I'll have you shot for filial ingratitude.

Love,

Barney

Kit brought out a tray of ice cubes and more red milk-glasses. Rosalind poured generous dollops of Scotch for Will Eddy and herself, and grimaced automatically as Kit downed the milk still on the table. It would be room temperature by now. How loathsome. She turned to toast Will Eddy. "Hermes, messenger of the gods," she teased. He countered with alacrity: "Diana, barefoot goddess of the hunt." Rosalind flexed her toes and laughed with surprise. Though he'd juxtaposed a Roman goddess to her Greek god, for a quick comeback it wasn't bad. Well, policemen can *read*, her mind rebuked her. Don't be such a snob. She moved closer to Will Eddy to watch Kit open the remaining package—from Edinburgh, Rosalind read upside-down—and became warmly conscious of the man next to her, a sidelong consciousness both visual and tactile. Ah, it's been over a month, she thought.

Kit slowly unfolded a long tartan kilt, MacLaren clan, green and yellow and red. "For you, Mom," he said, disappointed.

"It's gorgeous." Rosalind put down her drink and held the kilt up in front of her jeans. She felt Will Eddy's gray eyes on her. She twirled the skirt. Kit extracted another kilt, smaller, from the box.

Rosalind got laughing. "Kit, babe," she said, "I'm awfully afraid that's for *you*. My mother's a wonderful purist," she told Will Eddy, who was laughing, too, at the expression on Kit's face. "Oh, my God," Rosalind said then. "What's the date?"

"Wednesday, November . . . eleventh," Will Eddy said. Rosalind plucked Annabelle's telegram from the clutter on the parson's table.

"Hell," she said. "Annabelle's coming tomorrow. Kit, I'll have to call her from town in the morning: don't let me forget. Can't you just see Annabelle stranded with all her luggage on Cynnie's doorstep?" Cynnie and Annabelle had never met. Would Cynnie slam the door in Rosalind's mother's face? Cynnie had been full of unvoiced wrath, Rosalind reluctantly acknowledged to herself, hearing again the Rolling Stones speed her own ignoble departure from Cynnie's house. Cynnie had even left her books and her slide rule on the lawn. Still, Cynnie wasn't spiteful. . . . To Will Eddy, Rosalind explained, "My mother's coming, and she doesn't know I've moved, and we don't have a phone."

"I know." He grinned at her. "I scoured the county. I remembered your name from your license, so I knew there had to be such a person somewhere near. Finally I called Marsh Ritter, whose cottage"—he raised his glass of Scotch around—"the postmistress had heard rumors you might be in. People had reported lights, she said." In a more serious voice he added, "You really should have a phone."

"Ah!" Rosalind scoffed. "I love not having a phone." She felt suddenly marvelous; let Cynnie and Annabelle, nonplussed, confront each other on the round front porch. She poured Will Eddy some more Scotch. "You went to a lot of trouble," she told him, "to do a favor for a scofflaw. Just look," she glimmered at him, "all the happiness you've brought—an authentic kilt for Kit." She seized the little kilt and waved it in the air. "Oh, Kit, put it on, please put it on. Kit, what *do* you highland lairds wear under your kilts?"

Kit's look was priceless.

"Do you two live here alone?" Will Eddy asked her.

She smiled sideways up at him. I'm flirting, she noticed with interest. I'm showing off. My, but he *is* lovely. What an unexpected boon on the Interstate. Thank you, Paul Damian, you rakehell bastard. "Just us," Rosalind said, deciding to let it go at that, keep it mysterious. She flaunted an arrogant hand over Kit's head. "My son and I."

"What do you do?"

"I teach at the college." He looked impressed, also a trifle alarmed. "I'm a grad student," she added hastily. Will Eddy's fine-etched face relaxed.

"What do you teach?"

"English," she said. With that one word, she could see him retract, start to pick through his vocabulary to muster more conversation. Oh, hell, how to put him at ease? "Say," she said, "what do people at Mud Lake do in November? Do they cavort at the post office and chat up the postmistress? I've never lived in the country before."

He seemed to ponder her question seriously. "Have you seen the Barrager ruins?" he asked.

"You have ruins? How grand. Kit, do you hear that? We can go sight-seeing. My mother might even like to see some ruins," she said. "Where are these ruins?"

He gestured with his head. You can be a pretentious pain in the ass, she read in his gray eyes. His voice, however, was even. "You go across the barley field and up a hill, just into the edge of the woods. Maybe half a mile. There's a road, but it's a nice walk from here. Do you walk?"

"I walk," Rosalind said. She glowered at him.

"Well," Will Eddy went on, "in 1816, Dr. Eben Barrager, a medical doctor *and* a doctor of philosophy, built a villa to overlook Mud Lake. It was pseudo-Roman, and there were nine marble statues and a hundred peacocks and forty tame deer on the lawns. He called his villa 'Calypso'—"

"Calypso!" Rosalind stared.

"Yes. Calypso. It's all crumbled now, covered with moss and pine needles . . . Calypso." He looked her full in the face, then looked away. "Well, I think you might like it there," he lamely concluded. Ah, she'd put him off, and she hadn't really meant to.

"I'm here all Monday afternoon," she said straightforwardly. "Just my Chaucer class in the morning. Um, do you troopers get any day time off?"

"I could come by for you," he said, putting his glass on the parson's table. "Kit, would you like to come too?"

"He has school," Rosalind said hastily. "His bus driver dawdles quite unconscionably. He can go another time."

"All right," Will Eddy said. "About two?" She smiled and nodded, quite delighted and wondering why: whatever was she up to? Damn your eyes, she said to herself, you've taken a vow of celibacy. Besides, he's a *policeman*. Who do you think you are, an Iris Murdoch character? "Wear boots," Will Eddy said, looking at her bare feet. Self-consciously, she put one foot on top of the other. "I've got to push off. Nice meeting you, Kit." He and Kit shook hands. Rosalind walked with him to the door.

"Bye, Hermes," she said. "Thank you."

"See you Monday." He vanished into the darkness, Will Eddy of the flaming hair.

II

"Well, I don't know what I'd have done without Cynnie," Annabelle Chase dramatically exclaimed. Rosalind and Kit, both in school clothes, listened to her in the lobby of the Caliban College Theatre, where a visiting Philadelphia string quartet was about to perform. "There I was, with all my luggage, in this quaint little town with that most confusing Square in the middle, and the taxi driver actually said, 'Make up your mind, lady,' so I repaired to Cynnie's porch, almost in tears, and then this dear child came home." Annabelle wafted a graceful finger to tap Cynnie's shoulder. Both Annabelle and Cynnie wore long gowns; Annabelle's was gold faille, Cynnie's flowered challis. Rosalind was in a rumpled wool safari pantsuit. She was out of breath from racing to collect Kit from the cottage, then racing back to meet Cynnie and Annabelle here at the theater.

"And Cynnie said, 'Why you must be Annabelle Chase; how lovely to meet you; let me make you some tea.' Eventually, we tracked you down, Rosalind, to your English Department and left the message for you to meet us here. My dear, whatever are you doing at a cottage? Cynnie's little town house is exquisite. But never mind; you always were your father's child. Rosalind can actually get excited about football, but I expect you've gleaned that, Cynnie."

"Yes," Cynnie said. She rolled her eyes at Rosalind, looking frightfully amused at the whole encounter. "Roz and Kit both yell at the TV."

"Well," Annabelle said, "shall we go in? They're playing all Haydn. I adore Haydn. He's so joyous. Come along." Annabelle took Cynnie's hand and Kit's hand and shepherded the two of them through the crowd as if the Caliban College Theatre were her own personal reception hall. Trailing behind, Rosalind found herself abruptly, horribly, face-to-face with Sarah Damian. Sarah Damian's Dutch bob seemed to stand on end.

"Come along, Rosalind," Annabelle turned imperiously to demand, then watched with great fascination as Sarah gasped, "Oh, no," and turned away, grabbing onto Paul's burly arm. "Hi," Rosalind and Paul Damian muttered embarrassedly to each other. His twelve-year-old daughter, Belinda, said, "Hi, Rosalind," with obvious pleasure, but Paul said, "Move your ass, Belinda."

"Did you see how that woman looked at you, Rosalind?" Annabelle demanded. "She hates you, my dear. How interesting." Annabelle stopped walking to mull it. "Rosalind, you've been having an affair!" Her voice carried. Mortified, Rosalind looked around her at the crowded lobby. "My dear," Annabelle stage-whispered then, "I'm *delighted.* Well, now, you are having a *life,* after all." Annabelle squeezed Rosalind's arm in an effusion of approbation. "My, didn't she look daggers at you?"

Rosalind could feel Cynnie's silent hilarity next to her. "Say, Kit," Cynnie said, "I'll buy you a soda." Cynnie led Kit off, leaving Rosalind to tender girlish chitchat with her mother.

· III

"Nu ic onsundran þe   secgan wille . . . treocyn . . . ?" At one thirty Monday afternoon Rosalind sat at the picnic table behind the Mud Lake cottage, laboring over the Anglo-Saxon poetic records in the *Exeter Book.* Her Bosworth-Toller Anglo-Saxon dictionary loomed at her elbow and the ready. With the simultaneous arrival of Annabelle and Indian summer Rosalind's entire weekend had been plundered of time, time to prepare . . . anything, and the Chairman would most definitely call on her tomorrow. At least she and Cynnie were friends again, thanks to Annabelle, and, God, wasn't it a glorious day? Mud Lake glittered. Rosalind, feeling the sun through her fisherman's-knit sweater, kicked up her booted heels. Speculatively she eyed the basketball hoop affixed to a backboard on the giant oak that dominated the Ritter property. Had she a basketball, she'd shoot baskets. Idly she pictured herself shooting baskets with the impending Will Eddy. Ah, back to the elegies.

Nu ic onsundran. Now I alone, separated. *Þe secgan wille.* Will tell thee. Ellipses spattered "The Husband's Message."

How maddening. Rosalind wondered what the fragmentary original must look like. *treocyn ic tudre aweox*. Rosalind consulted the Bosworth-Toller. "I am the offspring of the *tree-kind*"? Good God, the narrator of "The Husband's Message" must be a tree. How cute. Rosalind thought of Tolkien's long-winded, ponderous Ents and grinned. She closed both books and sat looking at the nearly naked oak tree. How'd it be to be married to a tree?

She heard the car before she saw it. From the lake road a khaki-colored Thunderbird pulled into the drive and parked next to her hunter-green Firebird. The two cars, about the same size, looked companionable and friendly together. Can you mate a Thunderbird with a Firebird? her mind irrepressibly asked. She giggled. I'm getting positively loopy in this sunshine, she thought, as if I drank the wind. Will Eddy got out of the Thunderbird and came towards her. "I wasn't sure you'd be here," he said. "After I left, I was sure you'd been putting me on." He was dressed *perfectly*, Rosalind noted, pouncing with her eyes; he looked as if his valet had laid out just the proper clothes for a ramble in the woods: a tweed hacking-jacket with suede patches on the elbows, brown corduroy trousers tucked into polished boots: the dandy of the Pennsylvania State Police. She felt suddenly grubby in her baggy old sweater and jeans.

"You look positively resplendent, Lord Peter," she told him. "Bunter has done you proud."

He looked down at himself. "Thank you, I *think*. I'm afraid I only follow about half of what you say. I'm over my head," he blurted, laughing a little. "What the hell am I doing here? When I left the other night, my head was going in circles. I drove home trying to reconstruct the conversation, and it seemed to have been totally crazy—"

Rosalind laughed. "It probably was," she allowed, "and I

apologize. This living in the country seems to have gone to my head." She shook her head wildly, to demonstrate. "My mother—who has fortunately repaired to New York and her *Hamlet* rehearsals—looked askance at me every time I opened my mouth. Next thing I know, she'll be hauling me off to her analyst again." She grimaced. Oh, hell. "Anyhow, Will Eddy, I've not been putting you on. Not much, at any rate. Let's go. Let's go off to see the ruins of Calypso. . . ." She took his arm, letting her breast graze it just a little, as she started them walking, the two of them. She found herself quite liking his stride.

They crossed the road and entered a field of waist-high dried grasses and desultory foliage in clumps. "What's all this lovely stuff?" Rosalind asked, picking a tall stalk with a spiky, stiff tassel.

"That's barley," he said.

"Barley!" Rosalind shredded the golden tassel, felt fine kernels in her fingers. She laughed delightedly and started shredding more, throwing the grains about. "The ancient Greeks," she told him, "scattered barley grains before a sacrifice." She threw some at him, watched as the airy flecks settled in his red-gold hair. "Are you married, Will Eddy?" she asked.

"No, I'm not," he said. They started walking again.

"Were you ever?"

"No."

"How old are you?" That question, for some reason, made him laugh.

"I'll be thirty in exactly two weeks."

Rosalind computed. "A Sagittarius," she said. "I'm Aquarian. We ought to get along."

"I announce I'm going to be thirty, and you cast my horoscope."

She laughed. She found a stick on the ground and used it to ripple the dried grasses around them. "My ash plant," she said.

"That's an oak branch," he said.

"Poetic license," she said. "Thirty's pretty old not to be married," she said then. "Have you got a girl?"

He laughed self-consciously. "Two," he admitted.

She pointed her stick at him. "Why, you egregious cad. Who are they? What do they do?"

"One's a nurse, and the other teaches kindergarten."

"Which one's prettier?"

He stopped walking and considered. "They're different," he said.

"But pretty?"

"Pretty." He started walking again. "Are you?" he asked.

"Why, I'm bloody gorgeous," she said. "Hadn't you noticed?"

"I meant, are you married?"

She took a deep breath. "I'm separated," she said.

"I'm sorry."

"Why sorry?"

"Because you look like you are."

Rosalind bowed her head and with her stick chastised the dried barley vehemently. "Yes, I'm sorry," she said. They climbed a steep, rocky slope and reached the edge of the woods where a dirt road ran. Across the road the woods loomed dark-green and mysterious, fringed round with the dull tans and umbers of November. Dappling sunlight made the evergreens duskily, shiftingly glow. Rosalind could see white shapes through the trees. "I see it," she said. "I see Calypso!" She started to run, and he caught up with her. He appeared delighted with her delight.

"Sometimes you see deer," he said. Among the tall forest

pines and spruces, a crumbling white marble wall jagged up and down, unevenly crenulate, marking out the shape of a circular house. One section stood twenty feet high; in some places, the marble was buried in the ground. The area the wall delineated was covered with pine needles, slick and whispery under their boots.

"Oh, my God, it is so beautiful." Rosalind started to cry. She felt like a fool and she couldn't stop. Will Eddy put his arm around her and sat her down on a level part of the marble foundation.

"I'm sorry," she said. "Sorry. Sorry! You asked me if I was sorry. I'm desperate. I'm abandoned. I'm the victim of a savage abuse. Do you know where he is, my husband?" The question was rhetorical, but she confronted his eyes anyway, like Kit waiting for an answer to "Do you know what happened in school today?"

"No," Will Eddy said, finally. "Where?"

"He's *underground*. He's a fugitive. He's a revolutionary. He's a total unmitigated *idiot*, Ben Roth!"

"Ben Roth," Will Eddy, startled, said. Rosalind looked at him with suspicion, suddenly wary. Two years of silence, and now she was going to spill it all out to a *policeman*, as she had, at the beginning, to Annabelle's analyst. ("I'll give you therapy," he'd said sternly. "You need practical advice," he'd said. "Not analysis, not yet.")

"There was a Wanted poster about, oh, six months ago," Will Eddy said. "I remembered the name."

"He's off the list now," Rosalind said. "They caught the real saboteurs. No longer is Ben one of our Ten Most Wanted. I'm sure his ego suffered quite a blow at that." She shut her mouth hard as if to stop herself from talking. "Please forget what I said. I'm terrified of being flushed out and questioned."

"Rosalind," Will said, "I'm not stalking him, if that's what you're afraid of. Ben Roth belongs to the FBI. I am just a lowly state trooper."

"Why?" she asked him suddenly.

"Why?"

"Why are you a lowly state trooper?"

"I like being a lowly state trooper."

"Okay," she allowed. "Ah," she said, "I expect Ben likes being what he is too. A fugitive. An outlaw. People do what they like: why can't I learn that? And I'm a forlorn, abandoned wife because I want to be. I could have divorced him, couldn't I? I mean, I am *deserted.* Do you know how many times I've seen him since the stupid 1968 Chicago Convention, when he just suddenly said, 'Roz, I want you to leave. Take Kit, take all my money, and leave. This is no place for a family.' I was the one who'd been Maced." She touched the scar through her left eyebrow. "See that? I'm the one who got hit with a billy club." Rosalind started to cry again, feeling Grant Park and the milling thrum of the crowd, the sudden, terrifying surges of policemen. A bloody shirt had just been run up the flagpole. She saw herself and Ben and Kit, just five, silhouetted against the bandshell, arguing. They'd only been back two weeks from Ben's Fulbright year—he'd been researching the Spanish Civil War for his dissertation—and after the clear colors and hushed cathedrals of Spain, the new American violence had Rosalind shrieking like a fishwife. "You come too," she'd demanded. "I'm not leaving without you. This is no place for a *father.* Why'd I let you talk me into coming and bringing Kit?" She'd grabbed Kit and held him to her. "You talked as if it would be a vacation, a *lark*—"

"It isn't a lark. I see that now," Ben said. "I'm so ashamed, Roz. Get out, Roz, get out. My life is changing, can't you see

that? I've been struck by lightning. This is the road to Damascus." Ben's head slanted against the trees and the sky-
scrapers.

"Ben, you're a *Jew*. What do you know about the road to
Damascus?"

He'd smiled at her with soft irony. "Ah, Roz, in any crisis,
why do you always go for my fucking *imagery*?"

"Do you know how many times?" Rosalind asked Will
Eddy again. "How many times since Chicago?"

"No, I don't," he said.

"Four times, and I just sit around waiting. I haven't seen
him since last December. I haven't heard from him since
March, but still I sit around. What's the matter with me?"
The question rose to the arch of the trees like a disembodied
cry.

"Rosalind," said Will, looking at her, then away, "have you
ever talked to anyone about this? Maybe you're waiting because you love him or maybe you're just stubborn or lazy or
you want an excuse not to get involved with anyone else; but
'What's the matter with me?' is a pretty dumb question,
you've got to admit."

Rosalind was diverted. "I never thought of that," she said.
"You're right," she said. "Do you know, I must ask myself
that dumb question ten times a day. What's the matter with
me? Ah, Will Eddy. . . ." She smiled at him. Dear God, he
looked so *concerned*.

"Would you mind," she asked him, feeling a little shy, "if I
told you a long, sad story?"

"Not if you want to tell it."

"Off the record?" He frowned. "I mean, you won't turn
me in or tell anybody about Ben."

"No," he said, "I won't."

"I did see someone," she said. "My mother made me see

her analyst. He gave me therapy, not analysis—your Renaissance man." She laughed shortly. "After Chicago I'd taken Kit back to New York, to our apartment in Morningside Heights—I was getting my Master's at Columbia at the time, or trying to, because Columbia was a god-awful mess in the fall of sixty-eight. We'd been in Spain for a year, so we'd missed all of Mark Rudd's springtime theatrics, and by fall Columbia was like an armed camp. Finally my mother made Kit and me move in with her." Rosalind laughed, heard it sound brittle, like dried oak leaves in the wind. "Her Park Avenue apartment, all very sedate and posh, and the doorman walked Kit to kindergarten. Kit was the only child in the building. I took a cab to classes at Columbia every morning—I *did* finally get my Master's there, by the way, and that bodes well for the future, anyway—my future, my career— and every afternoon, I saw this psychiatrist. A cram course." Rosalind slid off the wall and sat on the pine needles, her back resting against the smooth, warm marble. Will Eddy slid down with her.

"The psychiatrist was fascinated by what had happened in Chicago. I mean, Ben became like another person. He became . . . tragic. Headed for disaster. He'd always had a comic sensibility—oh, Lord, he was funny, I was always laughing, and he kept everything light, sort of sailed through life. I mean, it isn't easy to be a father at twenty-two, and it isn't easy to be disowned by your parents—"

"Disowned?" Will Eddy asked.

"Ben's Jewish. Or he was. The last time I saw him, he was talking about repudiating Israel. But then—we were still undergraduates, at Cornell—he took me home to Brooklyn from Ithaca to meet his parents. I was pregnant, of course, well, not of course—oh, that's another story! We didn't mind my being pregnant; we were kind of proud. I was only nine-

teen and he was only twenty-one, and we were terribly, terribly in love, and my getting pregnant seemed to sanction
that. Well, his mother took one look at me and burst into
tears. At first I thought she could tell I was two months
pregnant, but after a while it didn't seem to be that. I
couldn't figure it out; I was such an innocent. The theatre
people my mother knew were all 'mixed' marriages, and
while my dad can sound like a bigot, it's like a joke, he
doesn't mean it, well, you know how football players talk.
'There's someone not Jewish in her family,' Ben's mother
said to Ben in this awful, accusing tone. I was amazed. And
Ben just cocked his head at her and said defiantly, 'Yes, all
of them,' and she cried harder, wouldn't even look at me. I
never saw anything like it. It was as if I were a *thing*. They
argued about me, and his father said he'd pay for an abortion, and I kept saying, I won't have an abortion, but nobody
paid any attention. It was a battleground on which I was just
a symbol, the flag. Finally Ben said, 'All right, we're leaving,'
and his mother chanted something in Yiddish, I think, and
Ben blanched and said, 'Mama, if that's the way you want it,
fine with me.' He wouldn't tell me what she'd said, but we
never saw them again.

   "Anyhow, the psychiatrist postulated that act of Ben's as a
prelude to what happened in Chicago. In Chicago, the psychiatrist said, Ben became 'radicalized' in an instant." Rosalind snapped her fingers. "Usually it takes much longer.
With normal people it doesn't happen at all. Ben was unusually suggestible and drastic, he said. Revolution was in his
blood. Why look, he said, how fast he appropriated and
impregnated you and provoked his parents into disowning
him. According to him, I became a symbol of rebellion for
Ben. Ben's parents would have come round, the psychiatrist
said (he was Jewish). They'd have come round; the most

caricatural Jewish mamas do when they see the grandchild. The Roths *did* want to see Kit; they tried, but Ben said no, they insulted my wife, they can't see my son. Kit's name is even Christopher," Rosalind said with a little wince. "I suggested it; I didn't realize how Christian a name it is—who thinks like that? 'Well, Christopher!' Ben said with a kind of glee. 'Perfect!' It was a slap in his parents' face. He'd in fact disowned *them,* the psychiatrist said, had cut them like losses, and then he'd tried to do the same thing to me, but he whipped it around so we'd appear the disowners. A friend of ours who saw Ben in Chicago after I left told me Ben said, 'Rosalind has left me.'

"Anyhow," Rosalind went on, picking up a chunk of white marble and hurling it, "it was all Ben. I spent more than a thousand dollars of Annabelle's money to have Ben psycho-analyzed. The psychiatrist said there was nothing wrong with me, not yet, but if I just sat around waiting for Ben, there would be. 'Get out of New York,' he said. 'Make a life for yourself and your son. You were always too much the pretty echo anyway. This is your chance to make yourself into a person. Take your maiden name back: that's a good first step. Be Rosalind Chase, not Ben Roth's self-effacing wife.' "

Will Eddy was looking at her in wonder. "Self-effacing. You? You're the least self-effacing woman I've ever met."

"I'm new," she said. "Hell, Will, I breast-fed, I baked bread, I let my hair grow long. I hovered in the background while Ben talked. He had tons of friends, and I fed them, smiled at them, and every once in a while I'd hear someone ask him, 'What's your wife's name again, Ben?' If people asked me what I thought about anything, I'd smile at Ben, and he'd tell them."

"Whew." Will Eddy shook his head.

They sat quietly on the pine-needle floor, shoulders touching, knees raised and parallel in an easy obtuse angle. The silence and the arch of the trees conjured a sense of the past: one drifted backward. Closing her eyes, Rosalind remembered the day she'd first caught Ben Roth's eye. They'd both been in a history class provocatively titled "Revolutions," and Rosalind, a sophomore, honored to be allowed in the upper-level course with the famous professor, had sat among the juniors and seniors, wrapped in considerable awe. Early in the semester, the professor had cited the figure of Nathan Hale as the prototypical "new" revolutionary soldier, the man who thinks, the man who isn't afraid of dishonor, if dishonor gets the job done. "Nathan Hale may have been single-handedly responsible for the burning of New York City in 1776," the professor had gone on to say. "There's a school of thought," he said, "a theory, that the young Captain Nathan Hale was in fact an arsonist"—he paused—"a regular firebrand in more ways than one!" The class had laughed politely. "This—don't you see?—would explain why the British so peremptorily, so unceremoniously, executed him."

Rosalind had leaned to the boy next to her, a senior with a bold profile who often spoke up in class, and confided, "When I was eleven years old, I was in love with Nathan Hale."

"You're kidding," he said. He had a wonderful lazy, deep voice. "Nathan Hale was the hero of *my* childhood. I was born on his birthday." He'd looked her over. Full face, he wasn't handsome, but there was something attractive about his crooked features, something sleepy-eyed but paradoxically alert. He had an unruly mop of dark-brown hair that looked like it would be fun to play with. "Who was Cunningham?" he asked her.

"The jailer who refused to give Nathan Hale a Bible."

"Who was Enoch?"

"His closest brother."

"Who was Nathan Hale's hero?"

"Sam Adams."

He grinned at that. "Sam," he said. "How familiar." An eyebrow slanted up. The corner of his mouth tilted. "Who was Alice?" he asked then, as if that were the most important question.

"His *girl*."

"Are you busy Saturday?" Nathan Hale had lit a torch to send them both up like straw, and from that day on, Rosalind was Ben Roth's girl. And, damn it all, wasn't she still? She opened her eyes and saw the arch of the trees overhead, the man next to her.

"Will," she said, "we'd better be getting back. I like to be there when Kit's bus comes." They got up, scattering pine needles. What was Will Eddy thinking about, she wondered, when we were quiet? His girls? "Where does she teach kindergarten?" she asked him.

He grinned. "None of your business."

"I bare my soul to you, and you won't even tell me that. Fine thing." Rosalind made a mental note to get a look at the kindergarten teacher at Kit's school.

Down the rocky hill and through the barley field they went, running, laughing, bodies impinging occasionally. Once they heard a gunshot. "Hunters," Will said. "You and Kit be careful. Don't go into the woods without me."

"Oho!" she chortled.

"Rosalind, do you go out? I mean, could we go to a movie, or something—" He broke off, embarrassed, as she averted her eyes. They crossed the lake road into her back yard.

"Sit down," Rosalind said, indicating the picnic table. He sat on the table. The Bosworth-Toller and the *Exeter Book* were on it too. Rosalind riffled pages nervously. "I can't, Will," she said. "I don't *date*. I don't go out. I'm still married, you see. I'm committed to Ben." He nodded. "I'll sleep with you, if you'd like." His face closed; his temples and jawline tightened, and his gray eyes went hard, unreadable. She laughed self-consciously. "There *is* a logic to that, believe it or not. I would really like to make love with you, by the way." *Am I actually saying this?* she heard her mind cry, then bit her lip against the inevitable *What's the matter with me?*

"A logic," Will Eddy finally said. He shook his head. "No, thanks. It strikes me as . . . dishonorable."

He's turned me down, she thought, stung. Her face went proud and stiff like his. "Dishonorable," she said. "That's a harsh word."

"It was a harsh offer," he said. She looked at his face, at his hair that flamed in the sun, his shoulders and his arms in the tweed hacking-jacket. She'd like to measure his wrist, touch his hair, feel the force of that long lean jaw in a kiss. She had an instinct, almost chemical, that making love with him would be good, very good.

He stood up. "If you need any help," he said, "ever, I want you to get in touch with me. I wish you had a phone, but the barracks isn't far. . . ."

"Ah," she said flippantly, "I'll just send up a smoke signal from Calypso." She fluttered her hand upward, pantomiming smoke. "So long," she said. "Lord Peter." They looked at each other, their private senses of insult and hurt almost palpable between them. He turned and headed for his Thunderbird. Rosalind watched the long line of his flanks as he walked, imagined their thrust—ah, never mind.

She opened the *Exeter Book* to "The Husband's Message." "*Nu ic onsundran,*" she muttered. "Now I'm [sic] alone."

· *Super Bowl Sunday*

January 15, 1978

2:45 P.M.

"Why'd you invite the Damians?" Rosalind asked Will from the bed. She couldn't see him; she had put the teabags over her eyes. Her insides were warm, her lips scorched and puckery from one of Barney's devastatingly potent Bloody Marys—so heavy on the Tabasco one sip caused sweat to break under the eyes. The cold wet teabags felt wonderful. She could hear Will gathering Ben's cards into the manila envelope.

"I'm going to put this stuff someplace safe," his voice said. She heard a zipper open and close. Idly she imagined pants with a long, long fly, then realized it must be one of his portfolio briefcases. "My God, Roz!" Will let go a startled laugh. "You look like a corpse with pennies on your eyes."

"They feel marvelous," Rosalind said. "Pope sniffed coffee for headaches. Do you suppose caffeine has medicinal properties?" She felt him tuck the quilt around her.

"Why'd you invite the Damians? I mean, I know you're friendly with Paul, though I can't think why—"

"I'm his lawyer, Roz."

"But why'd you invite them *here,* to the house? Will, are you up to something?"

She heard an exasperated sigh that sounded, to her

trained Shakespearean ear, just a mite exaggerated. "Up to *what?*" Will's voice asked.

"You know, a gathering of the suspects, trapping them all in one room, like the last act of *Hamlet. . . .*" She shivered; the no-exit quality of the last act of *Hamlet* never failed to unnerve her.

"You read too many murder mysteries."

"*Hamlet* isn't a murder mystery. Well, maybe it is. . . ." She heard Will start to laugh.

"I had lunch with Paul the other day," he resignedly recited, "and Paul mentioned that Sarah had been clamoring—'clamoring,' that's what he called it—to see the house. Our house. Well—"

"The *house?*"

"She loves it; she drives by it; she wants one like it. What can I tell you? I hardly know Sarah Damian. From what I've ever seen, she's just a cute, dumb little blonde—"

"Cute? Dumb?" Rosalind sat bolt upright, and the clammy teabags tumbled down her chest. "That . . . *maenad!*" She directed a menacing frown at Will. "I hope she turns on *you* sometime." Will laughed. Muttering, Rosalind retrieved her teabags and gingerly replaced them on her eyelids as she lay down again. "Well, so Sarah was 'clamoring' . . ." she prodded.

Obligingly, Will resumed where he had left off. "Well, what could I do? Say my wife won't let your wife into her house? This was over brandy, Roz, brandy at *lunch,* and Paul was already pretty smashed, so I said, 'Paul, I'll tell you what, we're having some people up to watch the Super Bowl, so why don't you bring Sarah along then?' I figured it'd be less awkward with a lot of people here, and"—he paused—"this is the great thing: it turns out that Paul is really serious about building; he's going to retire here, he says—"

"God, retire," Rosalind interrupted. "Retire! Like an old man!"

"Yeah, well, think, honey. He wants to build a house to retire into. Think of all Andy Grimshaw has done for us—this house is worth three times what he charged us. Let's try to throw a little action Andy's way, that's how I figure it. With Flo pregnant, he can use the money."

Rosalind got laughing and had to realign her teabags. Innocent *again*, Will Eddy. A little help for our friends. "A little action," she murmured. "You talk like a cop, Will Eddy."

She snuggled down into the quilt and thought about Andy and Flo Grimshaw, young, dear friends. One hot summer day while the house was still under construction, Rosalind had been at the site, watching Andy forge a circular stairway out of what looked like seventeen wooden airplane wings and a pile of steel Tinkertoys. As you looked down from above, where Rosalind was, the airplane wings gradually assumed the shape of petals on a flower. On a tall stepladder, in between the screams of his acetylene torch, Andy Grimshaw had kept up a running lecture to Rosalind above and the curious workmen below, who walked desultorily in and out of her line of vision. "These are plumbing fixtures," he explained the steel objects. "Floor flanges and pipe nipples—"

"Nipples?" Rosalind had giggled. She was sitting on a sawhorse, wearing cutoff jeans and sneakers; she let her feet dangle over the stair opening. "Nipples," she chortled.

Under his goggles, she could see Andy's blush, but he said matter-of-factly, "Freudian imagery everyplace, Roz." He turned on the torch again, and deftly he bolted and spot-welded the central post through the mounting wooden petals. Over the awful whine of the blowtorch, Rosalind slowly discerned that an automobile horn was stuck someplace near, droning a baritone to the squealing soprano torch. Abruptly Andy turned it off. Sparks faded like lightning bugs.

"Do you hear something, Roz?" he asked. He knocked on his hard hat.

Rosalind rested one bare leg on her sawhorse, like a ballet dancer. "Halloweeners, probably," she said absently. The horn blared on.

"Roz, it's August."

Below, bare-chested, Rosalind's favorite carpenter appeared, a born-again Christian who surreptitiously penciled crosses on all his own beams and rafters. "Andy," he called up, "it works! The truck phone works! Praise the Lord!"

"Oh, my God!" Andy dropped his torch and leaped from the ladder as from a cliff. Still in hard hat and goggles, he ran off. It was the first time the truck phone had "rung," the devout workman explained upward to a mystified Rosalind. Beatifically, he smiled at her as the horn ceased.

Andy came back, grinning from ear to ear. "Flo's pregnant!" he shouted and threw his hard hat in the air. "Praise the Lord" had mingled with "stud" and "sure shot," as Andy's crew of workmen had clapped him on the back. Rosalind, aloft, had sat back on her sawhorse, stunned. You're too young, she'd wanted to holler down. You're my student. . . .

Sarah can help Andy and Flo, Rosalind hazily thought now, burrowed into her quilt. Aloud, she tried, "I just hope Sarah can keep her hands off the books," and she opened her eyes to see if Will was still there, but everything was soft, murky brown. . . .

"Lazy Daisy," she heard Will's voice as if from a great distance. "Don't wake your mother up." Along her right side, she felt a small, warm body encroach on hers under the quilt,

smelled Daisy, baby shampoo, sweet and dewy. Rosalind
pulled her daughter close. Daisy fit like a pillow.

"Daddy says I can take my nap with you." Rosalind felt
Daisy's elbows dent her stomach. Oof, she thought. "What's
wrong with your *eyes*? You look like a raccoon!"

"Daddy did not say," Rosalind heard Will. "Barney said.
Lie down, Daisy. Do you want to go back to your room?"

Rosalind hung on to Daisy. "I was crying," she told her,
"but now I've stopped, and the tea bags help my eyes."

"Help them *what*?"

"Go to sleep. . . ." Rosalind drifted off.

· *Lucky Charms*

December 1970

I

"Rozzy, I like it here!" His bulky Burberry askew on his enormous shoulders, Barney Chase prowled the living room of the Mud Lake cottage. I feel as if a bear had come to call, Rosalind grinned to herself. Her dad had finally let his hair grow out of the crew cut he'd affected for twenty years, and it curled wildly, all mottled gray and brown, a shaggy, extravagant frieze for his marvelous face. I wonder if he has a girl, Rosalind suddenly speculated: that would explain the hair. She hoped both so and not, then put it out of her mind. Barney raised his big hands upward, expansively appreciating the massive fieldstone fireplace. "Kit, you almost ready?" he bellowed up at the catwalk. "It's nearly noon." His voice filled the cottage. "I've got a limousine outside, and the plane won't wait, not even for the great Barney Chase!"

Barney turned and winked at Rosalind. "The *late* great Barney Chase. Rozzy, I'm fifty-seven years old!" His gravelly lament rose to the rafters. He prowled some more. "This is a terrific place. There's room to breathe. You know what, babe. After spring training I'm going to visit you for a whole week. I'll bet the fishing is great." He gave the quilting frame a thwack, like a pat on the back. "Even this monstrosity fits in. I always felt like I had too many elbows in that little

house of Cynnie's." He sat on the back of the couch, his battered face wistful for a fleeting moment. "You're sure you're
not going to rattle around here while we're gone?" He
looked at Rosalind hard. "It's a grand gesture to give your
lonely old man Kit for the holidays, but why don't you come
along too? Come on," he wheedled. "I'll even pay an extra
luggage charge for your typewriter. I'll buy it a *seat.* Come
on." Barney beckoned her with his eyes and a sly little smile
at the corner of his mouth. "Think of the Florida sunshine.
Come on." Enticingly he squinted one eye and wagged his
head towards the door.

Rosalind laughed at his winsome, tempting face. "Ah, Barney, you old charmer, I can't. I just can't. I've got a thirty-
page paper to type; I've got another paper to *write*; and I've
got to concoct two exams. Exam week is right after New
Year's. I'm going to need every minute of this vacation."
Vaguely she gestured towards the cluttered parson's table
against the windows, and as if he wanted to check her story,
Barney strode over and picked up a stray page from next to
the typewriter.

"What the hell language is *this*?"

Rosalind laughed. "Old English, you clod. And don't think
that's not going to be the devil to type up." Actually, she was
looking forward to polishing the paper, making it perfect:
"*Þæt Wundres Dæl:* The Riddle in 'The Husband's Message.' " At the last class before vacation, she'd read the draft
aloud in the Old English Poetry seminar, and the Chairman
had been visibly delighted with her interpretation of the
fragmented, cryptic elegy. "With a little strategic research,
that'll be publishable," he'd said then, raising a finger in her
direction. "See me after class." To the rest of the seminar,
he'd exulted, "It's moments like these that make the seminar
experience so exciting. She may have cracked 'The Hus-

band's Message'! Remember, you heard it first here. A splendid piece of original criticism, Miss Chase." Rosalind smiled to herself, remembering.

"It's weird to be packing bathing suits." Kit came out on the catwalk. "Mom, can I throw this down?" One-handed, he hoisted a small canvas suitcase, aimed, and tossed it over the railing. It landed in the exact center of the couch.

"What an eye!" Barney came to stand with Rosalind. Kit came frontward down the ship's ladder, as if its rungs were steps. "He's a great kid, Rozzy," Barney said to her. "You're doing a good job. Um, Rozzy, any word?"

She shook her head.

"Ah, that fool!"

"Where's the limousine, Barney? I never rode in a limousine."

"You deprived child!" Rosalind hugged Kit to her. "Did you put in everything I laid out? Both the toothbrushes? Your big suitcase is in the kitchen." She stood on tiptoe to kiss Barney, and his cheek scraped hers; it felt good. Kit hugged her waist while Barney hugged her shoulders. One hand up, one down, she rumpled both heads of hair, her father's, her son's, and she wanted to drop everything and go with them, lotus-eat in Florida for a fortnight. She couldn't; she absolutely couldn't.

"You guys have a wonderful time," she said. "Don't wrestle any alligators," she added, having a jagged memory of struggling with one of the snarling scaly beasts herself when she was Kit's age and in Tampa with Barney. Annabelle, spellbound with horror at Rosalind's recital of the adventure, had called Barney long-distance to chew him out: "You brute, Barney Chase, you unspeakable brute!"

"Rozzy, I learned my lesson," Barney said. "It was a very young alligator, however, and you *creamed* him. Your mother

was the scrappiest kid, Kit; you should have seen her cream
this alligator—"

She laughed and waved her hands at them, flipping them
away. "Go on," she said, "get out of here; don't miss your
plane." Pressing suitcases on them, she bustled them out the
door and stood watching them, Barney in his Burberry, Kit
in his fringed suede jacket, head for the airport limousine. It
was starting to snow. White Christmas, she thought. Ah,
forget Christmas, she amended. The driver, somehow ca-
joled by Barney into driving all the way from the airport to
Mud Lake, hopped out to take Kit's bags. Barney turned.
The wind caught his trench coat, and the plaid lining bil-
lowed.

"Rozzy!" he bellowed. "We'll be in Philadelphia by the day
before New Year's. The Bellevue Stratford—just give a call,
babe, it's only two hours away. Hockey, Roz, you always
loved hockey, you bloodthirsty kid—"

"If I'm finished," she called back. "Ah, go on, Barney, get
out of here!" She waved till the limousine was out of sight.

Within an hour after they'd left, Rosalind was almost
climbing the Mud Lake cottage walls. Her fingers went
clumsy, fumbled on the typewriter keys. All those þ's and ð's
that had to be put in by hand! The typewriter implacably
hummed. "Þæt Wundres Dæl" was virtually finished, the critical fun over, for after class, in a white-hot thunderbolt of enthusiasm, she'd immediately done the research the
Chairman so temptingly recommended. The typing she
could do any time in the next two weeks, while she watched
TV even, and she was hanged if she'd be reduced to daytime
TV, that being her vague notion of the ultimate depravity.
Sighing, she glanced sidelong at the waiting papers on her
parson's table desk.

Pinned to a window screen, a notice from the Registrar reproached her like a white feather for cowardice:

Unless this Office hears otherwise from
PROF. PAUL DAMIAN, your Inc. in ENG. 333
18th CEN. STYLISTICS will turn to an F on
January 8, 1971 at 5:00 P.M.

Rosalind bit her lip in rage at this impending blot on her straight-A escutcheon. She rummaged to find her ancient (well, year-old) notes on the zeugma. Oh, hell, they were scantier than she remembered and almost illegible, having been scribbled in soft lead.

Decisively Rosalind turned off the typewriter. During Christmas vacation the college library was open on Mondays and Wednesdays until five. It was Monday; it was only one o'clock; she'd go to the library and confront the zeugma head on. A drive would do her good. She pulled on boots, grabbed her sheepskin coat and her briefcase, and strode through the lightly falling snow to the Firebird, buoyed up by a sense of purpose and a not unpleasant sense of revenge; revenge on Paul Damian. She'd show him; oh, yes, she would: at exactly four o'clock on January 8, she'd throw the (excellent) paper in his startled, florid face. And maybe a volume of Pope for good measure.

In the Firebird, on the winding road to town, Rosalind frowned over the steering wheel and the zeugma, clicked her teeth, racked her brain. What was a zeugma? A skewed parallel, a yoking of disparate objects, rather like marriage. Syllepsis or zeugma: taking together or yoking. "A single word seems to be in the same relationship to two others but

in fact is not." Examples: "She felt the fabric and alone."
Fowler's "Miss Bolo went home in a flood of tears and a
sedan chair." Poor Miss Bolo. "He killed a quart of whiskey
and himself." A skewed parallel.

Passing Cynnie's little round-porched house on the
Square, Rosalind, braking, remembered Cynnie's Riemann
Sphere, where parallel lines do not exist. Aha! "They appear
parallel, Roz, but they're not," Cynnie had tried to explain.
"The idea of parallelism is a device, Roz; it's pragmatic. Rie-
mann gives you much more freedom for calculation than
Euclid." "Maybe Riemann gives *you* more freedom, Cynnie;
don't get *me* into it." "Roz, leave my syntax alone!"

Veering the car through the vaulted brick front-gates of
the campus, Rosalind worked out an opening paragraph:
"In the eighteenth century, the passion for parallelism was
in its flamboyant rococo heyday, and the restless poets,
taught that nothing was new under the sun, began to jazz up
[sic] their parallel structures. The zeugma stands to parallel
structure as Riemannian [?] geometry stands to Euclidian;
like Riemann, a zeugma is a renegade, an iconoclast." Oho,
that should make Damian's big head spin on its sixteen-inch
axis! For the rest she'd need a few strategic zeugmas to ana-
lyze. She searched her mind and gleefully recited the
famous passage from *The Rape of the Lock*:

> Whether the Nymph shall break Diana's law,
> Or some frail China jar receive a Flaw,
> Or stain her Honour, or her new Brocade,
> Forget her Pray'rs, or miss a Masquerade,
> Or lose her Heart, or Necklace, at a Ball . . .

She was able to park right in front of the library—it's
Christmas vacation, she reminded herself. She noticed she
was humming, "She blew my *nose* and then she blew my

mind," a not especially helpful zeugma, being twentieth century and hardly respectable. Skipping up the library steps, she located another passage rollicking in her brain:

> Some take a lover, some take drams or prayers,
>   Some mind their households, others dissipation,
> Some run away and but exchange their cares,
>   Losing the advantage of a virtuous station . . .

Like *Ben,* Rosalind's mind censoriously footnoted. She wandered into the library, delighted to find it practically deserted, just a few random "townies" about. She climbed the wrought-iron spiral staircase that led to the Poetry Mezzanine and selected a choice carrel near a window. "Some take a lover"; that's Byron; that's nineteenth century; that's no good, not much better than the Rolling Stones. Wait a minute!

"Do a paper on the zeugma," Damian had challenged her at the seminar table. Not "the eighteenth-century zeugma." She had it in his handwriting: "R. Chase—Zeugma." Why not do a bit of pop criticism? "The Zeugma from the Eighteenth—no, the Seventeenth, do it right—to the Twentieth Century: John Donne to Mick Jagger." Gorgeous! There had to be zeugmas in Donne, she airily conjectured; Donne was metaphysical, all strained metaphors, yoking of opposites. She'd tackle some Donne.

Two hours later, reading "The Sun Rising," Rosalind hadn't found a zeugma, but she'd sure found something else:

> Thy beams, so reverend and strong
> Why shouldst thou think?
> I could eclipse and cloud them with a wink,

> But that I would not lose her sight so long;
>   If her eyes have not blinded thine,
>   Look and tomorrow late tell me,
> Whether both th'Indias of spice and mine
> Be where thou leftst them, or lie here with me.
> Ask for those kings whom thou saw'st yesterday,
> And thou shalt hear, All here in one bed lay.

>   She is all states, and all princes, I,
>   Nothing else is. . . .

> This bed thy center is, these walls, thy sphere.

Rosalind caught her breath. *Whew, I'm panting,* she thought. John Donne, the most erotic nonpractitioner of the zeugma ever to— She shifted about on her chair and became uncomfortably conscious of the inside of her body; she could feel (and it was almost all she could feel for a moment) the shape of her vagina, a straight diagonal to the lower center of her. With awe she noted how similar this feeling must be to an erection—an erection in reverse, but not in any sense negative: on the contrary, a powerful, aggressive thing. She felt close to a visceral discovery of essential sexuality. Ah, celibacy can teach us something, she sighed, shifting her weight carefully on the hard chair.

This was awful. Mortifying! What did monks do? Cold showers? She had an unpleasant memory of reading about a priest who'd whacked himself with a belt; well, there was a difference, thank heaven. This won't do, she said firmly to herself. As Francis Jeffrey said about Wordsworth's "Excursion," *This will never do.* Should she call Paul? It was his fault, she illogically figured, for it was his paper she was working on. She could hear him; "Glad to be of service," he'd say, the bastard. "Oh, Lady Rosalind, let me service you," as if she were the Alfa Romeo. She clattered down the spiral stairs to the telephone in the lobby. Seeing the campus directory, on impulse, she looked up Luke DiLorenzo—safe, he'd have gone home, where'd he live? Somewhere out of state, she recollected. Shrugging, she dialed his number in Lacedaemon Hall.

"Matt?" Luke's voice demanded right away.

"Luke?"

"Chase!"

"Yes," Rosalind said, stalling, with an angry flush recalling her brazen (and surpassingly inept) attempt to seduce Will Eddy. "Um, Luke, how come you're still here?"

"I'm waiting for my brother," he said, exasperated. "He was supposed to pick me up on his way from Washington Saturday, and I've been waiting for three days. Now he's put me off until tomorrow. I'm telling you, Chase, I'm starving, and I'm broke. The damned dining halls are closed."

"I could make you supper," she said. Oho.

"Hey, that'd be great."

"How would you feel about, um, a night in the country?"

"You mean with you and Kit?" His voice was guarded.

"Kit's away. He's in Florida with my father."

"Oh."

"Well, make up your mind."

He hedged. "What, ah, did you have in mind?"

"What do you think?"

He laughed. "Chase, I'll be outside Lacedaemon Hall in five seconds flat."

"You need cereal?" Luke DiLorenzo tossed a big box of Lucky Charms into the grocery cart. Rosalind, pushing the cart, looked down at the bounty therein. "Do you need beer?" he'd asked an aisle back, nonchalantly stashing two cartons of Heineken, $4.25 each, in the cart. Nonplussed,

Rosalind now regarded five half-gallons of milk, three thick sirloins, two dozen extra-large eggs, a pound of mushrooms, and five beefsteak tomatoes. A bag of potato chips stood open on top of the milk cartons. Lustily Luke crunched them.

"Just how long," Rosalind demurely asked him, "are you planning on staying?"

He laughed joyously, dark head thrown back. Even his teeth are perfect, Rosalind thought, entranced. He'd shaved off his beard, and his skin was flawless, his jawline strong. Luke wore a down-filled yellow jacket and blue jeans, moved in the supermarket aisles as if he were dancing. "Ah, Chase," he said. "I'm sorry. Ever since the hunger strike, I can't stop eating." He put his hands with hers on the push-bar of the cart, as if to keep them away from the food shelves. "Also," he added, "I just talked to my mother on the phone. 'But Lukey, I made *lasagna,*' " he mimicked, making his voice falsetto. "If Matt and I aren't home by dinnertime tomorrow, she's going to disown us."

"Where's home?" Rosalind asked him, enjoying, to an unconscionable degree, walking next to him. Luke was devastatingly handsome, had the face of an arrogant *cinquecento* prince, the long-muscled body of a swimmer, and she'd wager he was a marvelous dancer—oh, without question the brightest and best of the sons of the morning! She giggled. I'm acting like a love-struck coed, she thought. "Buffalo," he said.

"Buffalo?" She laughed. Such an unlikely creature to come out of Buffalo, New York; she'd been there once, as a child, when Barney was broadcasting Triple A baseball, and Barney quoted her as having chirped Shirley Temple-style: 'Barney, this is the awfullest city. Wherever do they keep the buffaloes?' "Buffalo!" Rosalind laughingly threw at Luke Di-Lorenzo.

"What's wrong with Buffalo?"

"I never knew anybody from Buffalo before."

"Well, now you do," he said equably and maneuvered the cart for her into the checkout. While Rosalind watched the cash register tote up nearly forty dollars, Luke took a Milky Way from the candy rack and ate it, then neatly placed the torn wrapper with the groceries, grinning all the while at the checkout girl. The dazzled girl smiled back, dropping change all over the counter.

At the cottage, Luke carried wood and built a fire, helped Rosalind in the kitchen, sliced mushrooms and onions, made a splendid salad. It was like having a larger Kit around, Rosalind amusedly realized. He is so *helpful*. Ben, she thought with scorn, had never washed a single dish; but then Ben had been awfully good about diapers, she had to amend, feeling repentant. She was also feeling unfaithful. Ah, my prim Victorian Rosalind, Ben would say, do you know how many women I've slept with these past two years? Hundreds!

Luke gave her beautiful quilt only a passing glance, but "Color TV!" he shouted. While they ate, he watched Philadelphia hockey. When the game was over and the dishes finally done, he folded the dish towel neatly on the counter and, at long last, put tentative hands on her shoulders. "You know what?" he asked. "I've been wanting to try that ship's ladder. Why don't you show me around?" He doesn't know how he should go about this, Rosalind realized; he is not yet sure what I 'have in mind.' She laughed, went up on tiptoe and kissed him lightly, took him by the hand and led him to the ship's ladder.

"Up you go," she said.

In her big low bed next to the chimney, Luke helped her undress, his eyes warm, his hands warm on her body. He wanted the light on. His touch was light as air. Young men are getting gentler, Rosalind hazily thought, wondering what Kit's generation would be like. With her hand, a bit impatiently, she guided him inside her, and it was slow and lovely, went on and on. After a bit, Rosalind was poised and tight and ready to dissolve, but Luke kept the pace measured and easy, polite. . . . Well, this is nice, she thought, a change after that battering ram, Paul Damian; still, can't we go a little faster . . . ?

"What are we doing?" Luke asked in her ear. He raised his head. The peace symbol on the chain around his neck bumped her face. "What are we doing?" he asked again— why did they always want one to say it?—but she wouldn't, said primly instead, "*We* is the erotic pronoun," and felt his startled laugh inside her. "English teacher," he said.

Adroitly then, she manipulated her legs up on his shoulders, heard him groan at the sudden change in angle, felt one marvelous deep stab; but then maddeningly, like a perfect gentleman, Luke adjusted himself to the shortened coupling, hesitant, afraid to hurt. "Don't be so careful," she murmured. "Don't be so polite. Let go. I won't break." Tentatively he thrust, then more boldly, then faster as she coiled and whirled round him, and when she contracted, their tense juncture quaked like the earth, then slid back, sand shifting under a wave, oh, perfectly gorgeous.

Luke fell over against the pillows, panting, regarding her with comic awe. "I won't screw for a month!" he said.

"Or at least an hour," Rosalind said, sitting up cross-legged and gleefully tossing her head. I taught him something, she gloated. Ah, the older woman. She laughed, feeling free and wicked. Thank you, John Donne. I am all states, and all princes, he. Luke, all princes, was all curly-haired and sweaty and grinning, lounged against the daisysprigged pillows and the shadowy fieldstones of the chimney. Are there any more at home like you? Rosalind wondered the coy old question. "Does your brother look like you?" she asked him.

He looked startled. "Yes," he admitted. "But he's older. Has some gray in his hair."

"Oh, gray and bent," she teased. "How old?"

"Twenty-nine," he said.

"Oh, that's old," she said. "Maybe I ought to meet your brother." She pulled a pillow on her lap and covered her breasts with it, hugging it to her. She missed her long hair. "What does he do, your brother?"

Luke turned to punch the pillow behind him. "He's an accountant," he said.

"It's nothing to be ashamed of." Rosalind laughed at his expression. "A dull but honorable profession. Does he work in Buffalo?"

"No, Washington." Luke looked away.

"With the government?"

"You know, Chase, I'm starved. Come on." Gracefully he got up and held out his hand to her. "Let's get something to eat." Rosalind followed him thinking, I never went naked down the ship's ladder before. I think I'll go first. . . .

In the morning, as they walked to the Firebird, Luke caught sight of the basketball hoop on the oak tree. "Hey!" he said. He pantomimed a jump shot, then a lay-up.

"I'll bet you're good," Rosalind said, eyeing him up and down as Barney might. She hugged her sheepskin coat around her. God, she felt marvelous, despite having been subjected to television at breakfast, not to mention milk and sickening-sweet, pastel-colored Lucky Charms.

"Go get your basketball, and I'll show you."

"I haven't got a basketball."

"You haven't got a basketball?" He laughed out joyously. "What kind of house is this?"

Rosalind parked the Firebird in front of white-pillared Lacedaemon Hall. Luke looked over at her lazily, his head angled back on the camel-colored seat. "It's been great, Chase." He reached to squeeze her knee.

"I've got a little time," she said, draping her arms on the steering wheel. "When's your brother coming? Why don't you introduce me to your brother?" She was teasing, but Luke looked uncomfortable, stared out the window.

"My brother's with the FBI," he said so fast, it sounded almost involuntary.

Rosalind's body clenched, then went limp. She held her breath a minute, then slowly let it out. She fixed her eyes on a battered old pickup truck, stolid and homely, parked to the side of elegant Lacedaemon Hall. "Indeed," she finally said.

"Oh, Chase, it seemed like a game at first. Matt asked me to keep an eye on you." Luke's body sagged in the bucket seat. "On Ben Roth's wife."

"And did you?" Rosalind stared at the pickup truck. Her eyes ached. She felt like she'd been hit. She remembered how Luke had hung out at her tiny cubicle of an office last semester—so had other students, but he could usually outwait them, and besides she'd rather fancied him; ah, admit it. One day she'd said, "I'm late, I have to pick up my son," and Luke had said, "I'll come with you," and when Kit came out of school, "Hey, do you think he'd like me to take him over to the gym and shoot some baskets?" "I think he'd love it," she'd said, grateful. Then, months later, in her car. . . . Oh, the bastard, the unspeakable bastard.

"I felt like a shit," Luke said. "An absolute shit." Objectively, clinically, Rosalind noted relief in his voice: the magic
of self-castigation. Was he Catholic? she wondered. "I liked
Kit," he went on. "I liked *you*. I didn't find anything out. Kit
never mentioned his father, and I couldn't bring myself to
pump a little kid. When school started again after Easter,
and Matt came by to give me my new instructions, I told him
I just wasn't cut out for spying. Matt had always been my
hero, my idol, and he couldn't believe I wouldn't help him,"
Luke said. "He'd been taking a lot of flak from the Bureau
because he couldn't make contact with Roth in the flesh.
Matt said he'd talk to him on the phone and he'd sound real,
but every time he got close to meeting him, Ben Roth
seemed to vanish like someone on the road to Emmaus. You
and Kit were the bait, Matt said, the only fixed point on Ben
Roth's map, and he needed me to, well, keep an eye on you.
I said, no way, no more, and that was that." Luke paused.
"The whole rotten thing turned me around politically," he
said. "I'm with you now. The hunger strike was on the
level."

"Get out," Rosalind said. "Get out of my car." Luke
grabbed for her hand. She pulled it away and faced him.
"He told you to make love to me, too, didn't he? Get out of
my car."

"Whatever he told me," Luke said, "that time in your car
in September, that was on the level too. I don't make love to
order, Chase." Rosalind put her head back against the seat
and closed her eyes. She felt used and bruised and suddenly
awfully, awfully weary. Then she turned her head and saw
Luke's handsome, earnest face.

"I didn't have to tell you, you know," he said.

"No," she said. "No, you didn't." Then her mind flashed a
picture of her plundered refrigerator, her rumpled bed.

"Well, boy," she said, starting the engine, "shuffle off home
to Buffalo. My best to your big brother," she added, nodding grimly at the steering wheel. Luke put a hand on her
knee. "It's all right," she said. "Just *go*."

II

"Barney Chase's room, please." Disencumbered of the
change she'd been clutching in her hand, Rosalind settled
herself comfortably on the leather-padded seat of the
roomy, old-fashioned phone booth in the corner of the Mud
Lake Tavern. It was only two o'clock in the afternoon of
New Year's Eve, but already the regulars were gathering,
festivity pendent in the air like a gleeful teaser, a noisemaker
jumping the gun. The Mud Lake Tavern was a rowdy old
place, the smells of beer and sweat ground into its floor and
the heads of slaughtered deer fixed to its walls, but the
kitchen served an ambrosial shrimp boiled in beer. Listening
to the phone click through various channels of the Bellevue
Stratford Hotel in Philadelphia, Rosalind began to crave,
then positively covet, some beer-boiled shrimp.

"Barney Chase's suite," an unfamiliar masculine voice said
with great aplomb.

"May I speak to Barney, please?"

"Barney is *out*. May I take a message, lovely lady?" Who
the hell?

"When do you expect him?"

"She-et, I don't know. Tomorrow, probably."

"Mmm, listen, this is Rosalind Chase—Barney's daughter.
Is my son Kit there?"

The voice blared: "Kit, it's your *mama*!" Rosalind held the
receiver away from her ear and frowned at it quizzically.
Kit's voice came on the line.

"Hi, Mom."

"Kit, who was that?"

"Oh, that was Walter. He's an Eagle. He hurt his knee. He's baby-sitting me."

"Where's Barney?"

"She-et," Kit said, "I don't know."

"Kit . . ."

"What?"

"Nothing. Listen, babe, I just wanted to hear your voice and say happy New Year."

"Are you coming to the hockey game tomorrow? Did you finish your papers?"

"Just finished," Rosalind said with great satisfaction. "Just an hour ago. But listen, lovey-dove, I don't think I'll come all that way. New Year's Eve drivers, you know. You'll be back Sunday. That's—well, tomorrow, it'll be day after tomorrow."

"Okay," Kit said. "I don't think they'd let you in the booth anyway. They won't let Walter. *I'm* going to be there," he added proudly.

"Great. Listen, what are you and Walter doing?"

"We're playing Scrabble," Kit said. "I'm *creaming* him," he confided in a loud whisper. Rich raucous background laughter floated over the line.

Rosalind laughed too. "Great," she said. "Hey, are you brown as a berry from Florida?"

"*What?*"

"Are you *tanned?*"

"Yes. I'm almost as dark as *Walter.*"

Rosalind choked. "Well, angel," she said, laughing, "happy New Year—I miss you. I'll see you Sunday. Give Barney my love."

"Okay, Mom. I love you."

"I love you too. Bye, Kit."

"Bye."

Rosalind hung up the phone. Inexplicably, like a cheap act
of grace, a dime came back. She fingered it thoughtfully.
Through the glass door of the booth, a man in a plaid shirt
waved a pitcher of beer at her invitingly. She smiled and
shook her head. She put the dime in the slot and dialed Cynnie's number. No answer. She let it ring on, a yellow phone
between two yellow rockers ringing on and on in Cynnie's
empty house. The dime came back.

She dialed Luke DiLorenzo's room in Lacedaemon Hall.
Her fury at his betrayal had rocketed her through her two
papers, and she'd decided to forgive him. Luke now struck
her as just another hapless victim of the FBI's stupid games,
their Hitler Youth tactics. Besides, he'd inadvertently
spurred her splendid papers. As Luke's phone, too, rang on
and on, Rosalind pictured the papers—neatly typed on
heavyweight bond and ensconced in khaki-colored folders—
on the corner of her parson's table desk. *"Þæt Wundres
Dæl,"* a sound and brilliant critical essay. "The Zeugma from
Chaucer to Jagger," a witty bit of razzle-dazzle in a flighty
New Yorker style. Maybe she'd even send it there; it had a
wacky Barthelme air and could probably pass as a short
story, so nutty was fiction nowadays. Rosalind hung up the
phone, and the dime came back. She consulted the leather-
bound directory—such a posh phone booth—found the
number of the state police barracks, was politely informed
that Trooper Will Eddy was off-duty till Saturday. Oho: the
nurse or the kindergarten teacher?

Pleased finally to be rid of her ill-gotten dime, Rosalind
perched on the phone booth seat and bet on the kindergarten teacher. Last month, at Kit's school, through the kindergarten door, she'd surreptitiously—for quite a long
time—watched a vivacious little dark-haired beauty teach her

small charges to skip; the young teacher had skipped exuberantly to demonstrate, her round breasts bouncing. She'll
be a tub in ten years, Will Eddy, Rosalind warned him, as
she left the booth. The tavern was filling up. The juke-
box whined Tammy Wynette and "Stand By Your Man."
Rosalind waved to the postmistress on her regular stool at
the end of the bar, stepped up, and asked the bartender for
five orders of shrimp to go.

"You having a party?" the jovial bartender asked her.

"No," she said, grinning at him. "Frankly, I am just plain
starved."

"Eat hearty," he advised. "There's a cold snap coming.
The mercury's dropped twenty degrees since noon."

"Make that six orders," Rosalind extravagantly said, putting her foot on the brass rail like the man next to her.

· III

Teeth rattling uncontrollably from the sudden, breathtaking
cold outside, Rosalind burst through the back door of the
Mud Lake cottage into the kitchen, dumped the shrimp in a
big red pottery bowl, and stashed the bowl in the refrigerator. From the interior, green bottles of Heineken glittered
at her, more of Luke DiLorenzo's leavings: your eyes bigger
than your stomach, boy? Heineken and beer-boiled shrimp,
a perfect New Year's Eve dinner for a solitary—if she could
wait. She was delightfully hungry.

Humming, Rosalind went into the living room, hung her
sheepskin coat neatly in the closet, and, with great, energetic
relish, tidied her desk. She patted her two papers fondly.
From the floor she picked up crumpled carbon paper, balled
it, wound up, and pitched it into the fireplace. She laid a fire

to light later. She got the vacuum cleaner from the closet, turned on the television, and, to the accompaniment of *The Edge of Night,* vacuumed the entire room, feeling deliciously depraved to be watching, albeit in sidelong uncomprehending snatches, a soap opera.

The living room immaculate, Rosalind climbed the ship's ladder to her room. She changed the sheets on her bed from daisies to rainbow stripes—my God, had she been on the same sheets since Luke DiLorenzo's abuse of her hospitality? In the bathroom she put out a lavish quantity of fresh towels and installed a new roll of toilet paper. Why, she wondered, is housework so utterly delightful when one has just finished two brilliant papers? and a shower such incomparable bliss. . . ?

Blissfully she took a long hot shower, wandered about naked, pottering, dusting, tidying Kit's room, the guest room; then, wearing just underpants, inspected the closet under the eaves in her bedroom. After much pleasant musing, she pulled out the long kilt Annabelle had sent from Edinburgh. It was new and soft and luscious, yellow and red and green. With sudden inspiration, Rosalind dug around in her bureau and finally located a yellow cashmere sweater she'd had—oh, glory—since Cornell. She clasped the buckles of the kilt and pulled on the sweater. The wavy mirror over the bureau told her she looked beautiful. She always looked beautiful when her papers were done, all misty-eyed from typing. Rummaging deep in her sock drawer, she found the yellow knee socks she'd worn long ago with the sweater, pulled them on, and admired how dainty her feet looked peeping out from under the long kilt. She swung rakishly down the ship's ladder. It was nearly five. She would eat, she decided, at six, when it would be completely dark, then curl up by the fire, an elegant lady of country leisure, and read the new Joan Didion novel she'd (in advance) purchased to reward herself for finishing her papers.

She was arranging beeswax candles on the red parson's table, when a knock came at the back door. She ran, flung the door recklessly wide, and there was Ben. Simply, there was Ben. She heard her own full-throated, triumphant laugh. Of course, there was Ben. How had she known? All day she'd had an unvoiced conviction, an unthought mystical surety that Ben was near. Without a word, roughly, Ben pulled her to him and held her. He was cold; his face was cold, his jacket. His body shivered in her arms.

"You cut your hair," he mumbled into it. "Let me look at you, Roz." He pushed her away, hands on her shoulders. His asymmetrical face was bearded in patches, his hair matted and very long; he wore a truly dreadful fatigue jacket. A very fatigued fatigue jacket, Rosalind punned inanely to herself, trying to stave off her rising alarm at Ben's drained, ashen face. Behind Ben a girl materialized in the doorway. Behind the girl, across the yard, Rosalind could just make out a Land-Rover parked next to the Firebird. The darkness was gathering fast.

"Hi," the girl said. She slammed the door and tossed a rucksack on the counter. The strap on the rucksack was gone and had been replaced by a frayed length of dirty string. The girl wore a fatigue jacket like Ben's, was small and wire-thin, had a horrid cold-sore, crusted red and yellow on her upper lip. Rosalind averted her eyes from the cold sore; she slanted a silent question at Ben.

"Rosalind, this is Muffy," Ben said, waving a hand from one of them to the other. "Muffy, Rosalind."

"Hello," Rosalind murmured. *God, was he sleeping with her?*

"Fuck you," Muffy said affably, as if "Hiya." She opened the refrigerator door. "Holy Christ," she said. "Shrimp!" She seized a bottle of Heineken, unsnapped her jacket, and, with a Swiss army knife that hung from a belt loop, flipped the cap off the bottle. The cap arched through the air and landed in the sink with a ping. "Cheers," Muffy said, raising the green bottle. Rosalind and Ben looked at each other and suddenly, together, laughed. Humming, Muffy browsed in the refrigerator.

"However did you find me?" Rosalind asked Ben, hearing her voice come out brightly animated, the British ingenue again. Ben was staring at her as if at a mirage.

"It wasn't easy," he said. "We got lost. There's a road up a ways," he said, waving his hand back, "and there were these fantastic *ruins*—"

"Ben's like a fucking *tourist*," Muffy observed from the refrigerator, her mouth full of shrimp. "He wanted to stop and *look* at them—" She broke off. "Listen, you two, don't mind me. I'll amuse myself here."

With both hands, Rosalind took Ben's arm and led him into the living room. "Wow," he said. His sleepy-lidded eyes went wide. He tipped his head back, and she saw that old bold profile as if he were in class next to her at Cornell. Then she saw that his eyes were bloodshot, granulated in the corners—dear God, he looked awful. His cheekbones jutted over his patchy, matted beard, and his skin was gray; his hair looked like it hadn't been washed in a month.

"Take off your coat," Rosalind gently urged. She helped him. With the coat came a smell—Rosalind pulled back involuntarily—a musky, feral smell, like a hunted animal might smell, she thought. Ben was awfully dirty, she somberly noted; his jeans were a greasy gray, and his wrinkly blue Oxford-cloth shirt had coffee stains dribbled down the frayed placket. His clothes positively hung on him.

"Ben, have you been sick?"

"Oh, just flu," he said absently. He looked at her, and his

face went teasingly alert, like the old Ben's, the lifted eyebrow, the lopsided, rakish corner of the mouth. "Roz, you
look beautiful. Oh, baby, you look so clean." He wiped his
hand across his mouth. "So fucking clean." He ran his eyes
around the room. "Where's Kit? I have to see Kit."

"Ben, I'm sorry. Kit's not here. If I'd known—well, how
the blue hell was I supposed to know?" Mingled pity and
fury choked her words.

Ben's face sagged back into weary vacancy. "Where is he?"
he asked without interest, his voice dead.

"He's in Philadelphia with Barney. They went to Florida—"

"Good old Barney," Ben vaguely said. He put his hands in
his back pockets and wandered into the room. "Nice place,"
he said. "Hey, what's this?" He stood over her quilt, mitered
on its frame behind the couch. "Roz, did you make this? Oh,
my God, I love it. Nathan Hale," he said. Rosalind went to
stand next to him, pressing her shoulder against his arm.
"Nathan Hale," he said again. They smiled at each other, a
slow, sad smile like a bridge over the years, girders missing,
cables broken and dangling, still a bridge. After a minute,
Ben looked away, back at the quilt.

"Fair Rosalind," he said. With a finger, hesitantly, he
touched the purple velvet she'd used for the doublet and
hose of Shakespeare's Rosalind. There was dirt under Ben's
ragged fingernails. He pulled his hand back. "You could
play Rosalind now," he said, smiling at her. "With the short
hair. Ah, Roz, you look like a beautiful boy." He slid his arm
around her and touched a tentative hand to her breast,
cupped it, gave a little squeeze, and turned back to the quilt.
He gave the spouting Moby Dick a passing glance, then,
"What's this?" he asked, indicating the blank area where
she'd picked out Leda and the Swan.

"Oh," she said, "I botched the first attempt. It's to be Leda

and the Swan, and I'm going to do it again—just like the
Yeats sonnet this time. 'A sudden blow: the great wings beat-
ing still/Above the staggering girl . . .' Right here"—she
pointed—"I'll put Troy's burning tower."

"Troy's burning tower." Ben bent to look closely. He ran
his fingers over the perforations in the fabric. "Did you un-
ravel?" he asked her.

"No, I just cut out the stitches—"

"Penelope," he said.

Rosalind's hand went to her mouth. "Oh, my God," she
said. Shakily she laughed, put out a hand to steady herself
on the quilting frame. "Ben, I even taught the *Odyssey* this
semester. It never occurred to me. Ah, Ben, you God
damned wanderer, you!" She let go one wild laugh, and
then she was crying.

He shot her a look of such smug irony that her tears
abruptly stopped. He was about to make her very angry, she
could sense it, like a raised red flag. "Roz, even your uncon-
scious, it's still *fiction*; it's still shit." His voice was strong and
baiting. Then his eyes faltered. "Real life," he mumbled.
"When're you going to try real life?"

"Real life," she bitterly retorted, "wherever that is. I suppose it's with you, with the 'Revolution.' Look at you, Ben:
you're filthy; you're skin and bones; you smell like a goat.
You look awful, just awful—" She broke off. His face
seemed to welcome her abuse. "Come on," she said. "Sit
down. Let me light the fire."

Settling him on the couch, she felt with alarm the limp do-
cility of his body and hastened to the kitchen. Muffy was sitting on the kitchen counter, legs dangling, shelling shrimp
with rapacious fingers. There were shells all over the
counter and the floor. Quickly opening a can, Rosalind
dumped chicken noodle soup in a saucepan, added water,
turned the gas up high. She took a carton of milk from the

refrigerator and awkwardly poured, spilling some, into a red glass. "That soup's for Ben," she said to Muffy. Muffy grinned.

"Okay," she said.

Rosalind took the milk to Ben, went to the fireplace, lighted the kindling and watched it and the carbon paper catch. A good fire. Kit would be impressed, she thought, poking it. Sparks flew. "The fire feels great," Ben said. He was looking a little better, lounged back on the couch, his feet stuck out towards the fire. He'd put his milk glass on the floor. She picked it up. "Roz, I'm not sick. Quit coming on like a Jewish mother."

"Soup's boiling," Muffy called.

Rosalind ran back to the kitchen. The soup was boiling over. Muffy was frowning at it vaguely. "Is he sick?" Rosalind asked her, as she rescued the soup.

"Who, Ben? Nah," Muffy said. "Just tired. Shit, we're all tired." She drummed her heels against the cabinet as Rosalind poured soup into a bowl. "Mind if I finish that?"

Rosalind carried the bowl of soup to Ben and knelt before him to offer it. He drank, slurping noisily. She unlaced his boots—old army boots, cracked and down at the heels. "Come on," Ben said. "Sit *down*." She sat next to him on the couch. He stamped his feet, wedged toe against heel, and kicked his boots off. The emergent smell made Rosalind's nose quiver, her gorge rise. Ah, but it's Ben, she reminded herself like a charm, it's Ben, flesh of my flesh, Ben. She moved so her kilt flowed over his jeans, took his limp hand between both of her own.

Muffy came in. "Hey, I've got to crash," she said apologetically. "We've been on the road for days. I'm bushed." She yawned wide to illustrate. "Are the bedrooms up there?" She flicked a thumb up at the catwalk.

Rosalind nodded her head. "The guest room's the one on

the far end. There're fresh towels in the bathroom," she ran
on like an eager hostess, "and there's plenty of hot water—"

"Quit nattering, woman," Muffy amiably said. Rosalind
laughed suddenly. Muffy grinned at her. God, that cold sore
must hurt like hell. "Ben," Muffy said, "don't forget, four
o'clock, the Apostle. I'll set my trusty alarm." Muffy started
up the ship's ladder.

"Oh, Rosalind, by the way," she swung round to say, "Ben
can't get it up any more. Nighty-night." Muffy climbed the
rest of the ladder and went whistling along the catwalk. The
door at the end slammed.

Muffy's parting shot, if shot it was, hung in the air like a
psychedelic poster. Rosalind groped for conversation, something civilized, and heard her voice come out as sprightly as
a sophomore's on a first date: "Tell me, Ben," she said, "tell
me about your work," and, still: Was it true? She couldn't
help wondering. Can't get it up? Ben? In college, before
they were married, he'd pulled her into bathrooms in the
apartments of friends for "just a quickie, Roz," and although
no one ever came into the bathrooms (a golden American
rule), sometimes it was a little awkward getting out, Ben
grinning behind her, toilet paper stuffed into her underpants to staunch that magical stuff that could make you pregnant. Can't get it up? *Ben?* "I mean, Ben," Rosalind went
doggedly on, "what do you do now? You can't be organizing
factory workers now that you're underground. What's your
job, your assignment?" She leaned her elbow on the back of
the couch and rested her head on her hand, looking at him.

Ben, in profile (his best angle), appeared flattered to be
asked, clasped both hands around his knee and pulled the
knee back like an urbane young executive in a Barcelona
chair, about to tell a new and charming date about his work.

"Mostly I travel around the country," he said, letting his lazy deep voice roll, "helping the collectives to get it together. You know, how to plan strategy, organize riots, and demos, who cleans the kitchen, how to load and oil the rifles, that kind of stuff. Then," he went on, "there's this technique called Criticism-Self-Criticism: have you heard of it?" Rosalind shook her head. "Well, it's a Third World concept. It comes from Fanon, I think—" He paused, lowered and shook his head. "I can't remember exactly where it comes from. Maybe Mao. Anyhow, it basically consists—this technique consists in—basically, in breaking a person down, for the purposes of rebuilding the person, making him stronger. Cleaner. It's a sort of psychic purge. The group turns on one person—anyone—and 'criticizes' him. Or her. It goes on for hours, ah, sometimes days, until inevitably and violently the person is criticizing himself. Or herself," he added, with a frown. "You'd be amazed, Roz, how well it works. The recipient becomes actually grateful. Afterwards, he's ready to kiss your God damned ass."

Ben shut his eyes and let go a little sound, almost a groan. "The problem," he said, "the flaw in the method, is that it makes those who criticize sadistic. You get to enjoy doing it, especially if it's been done to you. *And it always has been done to you.* That," he said, nodding sagely, jiggling his foot, "got to me. One part of my mind started splitting off. My voice would be spewing constructive abuse like everyone else, but my head would be saying, 'You like this, Ben Roth; you're a fucking sadist, Ben Roth. . . .' "

He paused and glanced at Rosalind, as if to let her comment. The instability of his tone, the lack of conformity between his gestures and his words, had her totally disoriented. "Yes," she finally agreed, "I can see where that would happen."

"Then," Ben went on, leaning his head back against the couch and looking up at the catwalk, "there was the fucking." He looked for all the world as if he were reminiscing about college. "At first, it was fun—lots of randy girls, you know." He cocked a winsome, boyish grin at her. Rosalind nervously whirled a hand as if to say, yes, do go on. "Well, the fucking became—*as everything inevitably does*—political. In all the collectives there'd be one or two what we call 'monogamous couples,' too fucking devoted to each other. Counterproductive to the aims of the collective. Well, we—from the Bureau, the leadership—devised this method whereby we'd kill two birds with one stone, so to speak. When we visited the collectives, we'd spend the days on strategy and criticism; then at night, we'd fuck the women of the 'monogamous couples.' " Frowning, Ben shook his head at her. "The women were tough. You could usually reason with the men, but the women held out." Ben rubbed his hand over his eyes.

"You mean," Rosalind asked, "you'd visit these collectives and rape the women?" She wanted to scream, but her voice came out noncommittal, merely interested. She felt like the straight man in an absurdist play.

"Not rape!" Ben turned on her. "Not rape. It wasn't rape." He covered his face with his hands. "Oh, Roz, sometimes they'd cry, they'd beg. I got so I couldn't do it. Even if they didn't cry, even if they wanted it, and, God, they could want it, I just couldn't. I couldn't. That's what Muffy was talking about. She's been trying to help." Ben clenched a fist and raised it towards the catwalk. "You see, they didn't keep it quiet. Oh, shit, no, the collectives have no secrets. We're all in this together. They'd talk about it. 'Ben still loves his wife,' they'd say. 'Ben is basically monogamous.' It would start off all sweet and understanding, then these girls'd be standing over me: 'What's the matter, Ben? Aren't we pretty enough for you, Ben? Do we smell bad? Why don't the pump work, Ben? Why can't you fuck us, Ben? You're an elitist, Ben; you're a shit, a wimp—' " He broke off, flung his head backward and moaned, "Ah, Roz, I've been in hell." A wordless cry started to rise to the timbered ceiling, then plummeted.

Horrified, dumbfounded, thunderstruck, Rosalind put her arms around Ben's shaking shoulders. He was sobbing— dry, rasping sobs that made his chest heave. He turned his head and burrowed it against her breasts, pushing, as if to say, Not enough tits, where are the tits? He pulled her down on the couch and pressed his body against hers, his hands scrabbling at her breasts, his head rolling and grinding at her face, her neck. Lower down, she couldn't feel him, then she could a little, and he raised his head and said, "Roz!"

He got up on his hands and knees. He shoved her sweater up, exposing her breasts. She saw them from above, their nipples pink and startled. He pulled the fringed juncture of the kilt apart. Rosalind saw her yellow knee socks, her bare thighs. "Take off your fucking pants." Rosalind raised her buttocks and squirmed out of her underpants. Ben shucked his jeans—he wore no underwear, she noted peripherally. Muzzily she watched Ben as if she were elsewhere, a god looking down on his frenzied, purposeful motions.

He grabbed a scarlet sofa-pillow and wedged it under her flanks like the first time, she remembered hazily, in his room at Cornell, and she'd wondered what on earth that was for, the pillow. Leverage, he'd said. Now, he looked at her consideringly. With both hands, savagely, he shoved her knees apart, knelt between them, veeed his hands together like a child pantomiming a diving airplane, veeed them around his penis, and tried to push himself inside her. She could feel his fingernails snag at her softest parts; oh, God, she tried to wriggle away, but, "Hold still," he commanded.

He pushed his body on her, with his elbows, angling her

knees apart so she could feel her thighbones grate on the joints of her hipbones, oh, it was awful, but after a minute, the fingernails retracted, and Ben said, "Come on, Roz; move, Roz; fuck, Roz," so she tightened her muscles and pulled, relaxed just a second, tightened, and felt him grow till he filled the space, his space after all, the space he'd hollowed out, the first after all, and she closed her eyes and tried to relax, but her splayed legs were cramping, he was thudding against her uterus, then he bit a nipple hard, and when she arched her body in pain, he came, groaning, whimpering, in a prolonged spastic wiggle that she felt inside her, such an agonizing climax to all that, poor Ben who used to laugh when he came, and then he collapsed hard on her, a dead weight.

Rosalind opened her eyes and saw her yellow knee socks rakishly tangled across Ben's spare, bare flanks. In the knee socks, her legs looked limp as a dropped puppet's. She raised her eyes to the timbered ceiling. Then, on the catwalk, she saw Muffy. Her eyes confronted Muffy's. Muffy's expression was impossible to read—was Muffy jealous of Rosalind? Was Muffy happy for Ben? Oh, dear God. The cold sore dominated Muffy's face like a clown's makeup.

This is too much, Rosalind thought. This will not do. Like Wordsworth, *this will never do,* and so she closed her eyes, and when she dared open them again, Muffy was gone. Ben was breathing heavily on her, his mouth against her breast. There was dark blood on her right nipple and at the corner of his mouth. Idly she contemplated the top of his head, his greasy, matted hair on the soft yellow cashmere of her sweater. He had quite a lot of gray in his hair, she noticed. Quite a lot of gray, and he wouldn't be thirty until June. She pulled the soft sweater down over her mangled breast. She pushed the scarlet pillow out from under her. She manipulated herself around Ben, to the outside of the couch, so that she could hold him with her arms, her body. She would keep him with her this time, she vowed, and when it got warm again, she'd take him and Kit to the ruins of Calypso, she planned, falling suddenly asleep.

Rosalind woke with a start when she felt Ben struggle over her. "Go back to sleep, my fairest Roz," he said. He kissed her cheek. "I'm just going to take a shower." Roguishly he grinned down at her. "I'll be back."

"Don't leave," she said. She saw it was still dark outside the windows.

"I won't," he said. "Not for long." Then she could hear the shower upstairs off the catwalk, could hear Ben singing the wordless, operatic song he always sang in the shower. . . .

It was daylight when Rosalind woke again. She sat bolt upright, her body alert but her mind unfocused. Someone had put a blanket over her. Near her hand, she saw a scarlet pillow clotted with a white substance in the vague shape of a sunburst. Gingerly she touched it. It was still sticky, a mess. She'd have to throw the pillow away. Fortunately Maisie Ritter had a lot of them. Scarlet pillows. Through the front windows, she could see Mud Lake, all swirled, thick ice, immobile, like the lowest circle of Dante's Inferno—

"Where?" she cried aloud. "Where've they gone?" She fell sideways off the couch. Frantically, her knees like water, she climbed up the ship's ladder, ran into all the rooms off the catwalk, but they were empty. The bed in the guest room was rumpled. The towels in the bathroom were damp. Rosalind careened back down the ship's ladder, almost falling, and ran to the back door. She opened it. The freezing cold day loomed like a transparent sheet of ice before her. The

Land-Rover was gone. The air took her breath. She closed
the door, leaning back against it, breathing hard.

On the counter near the sink, amid fragmented shrimp
shells, she saw two white bowls, two silver spoons. In the
milk that remained in the bottom of one bowl, yellow marsh-
mallow moons floated, one pink heart, two green shamrocks,
and little fantastic brown shapes: Lucky Charms. Rosalind
raised the bowl and peered into it, as if to consult an augury
therein. Then she flung the bowl at the back door and
watched it shatter, spilling its coy contents all over the galley
kitchen, her body racked with a great and shuddering sense
of release.

One white bowl and one scarlet pillow, she grimly toted up
the damage after a minute. Not bad, for New Year's Eve.

Part Two

"Barney Chase!" Sarah Damian effused, clapping her hands. "I just can't believe it. My big brother had pictures of you all over his room, when we were children, back in Illinois. Paul, why didn't you *tell* me?" Barney preened, thoroughly delighted. Rosalind, watching the show, lounged against the front door and grinned slyly at him. To her right, near the Ficus benjamina, Paul Damian was practically kissing Annabelle's ringed hand.

"I saw your magnificent Cleopatra at Stratford in 1970," he murmured in the silken voice he affected sometimes, usually in class, never in *bed*, Rosalind unexpectedly thought. She shook her head to clear it. Annabelle, she recollected then with amusement, had been a truly dreadful Cleopatra, just too staunch a blonde to carry it off. Annabelle now, with a little perplexed wince, asked Paul incredulously:

"You *liked* my Cleopatra?"

"Rosalind!" Sarah turned round to her from Barney but seemed to avoid her eyes a little, focusing slightly to the left. "I adore the house." Blushing, she turned again, this time to grab Paul's arm. "Paul, don't you adore it?" Sarah wore a white shirt, a velvet waistcoat, tartan trousers, and still sported her neat Dutch bob; the blond of her hair had faded slightly, but no gray was visible. She looks like she could be Paul's daughter, Rosalind thought, recollecting that Sarah was only five years older than herself—Sarah must be thirty-nine, she computed. Sarah was younger than I am now, Rosalind realized with a start, when she threw the books at me. Sarah looked the same: a face that fury could not jade, the rounded cheeks still rosy and smooth. Her blue eyes sparkled, their whites clear as a baby's. Random pillow-confidences began to filter back like snowflakes into Rosalind's oddly waiting brain, confidences from Paul's irrepressible babble before, during, and after lovemaking. Sarah was his second wife, had been plucked by him, a randy assistant professor, from the ranks of sophomore English at Southern Illinois, thirteen years his junior. "She looked so clean, Rosalinda, so wholesome. She was a cheerleader. My first wife was a bitch, such an intractable, difficult, frowning, *intelligent* woman. I thought Sarah was just the ticket. A ticket to hell! God, what a jealous woman. A hell of a cook, though. Come on, wench," he'd said then. "Let's cut the chatter," and he'd wrestled her over, moved on her again. . . .

Rosalind blinked, caught Paul Damian regarding her as if he knew what she'd been thinking, a lascivious, heavy-lidded, knowing look. Oh, damn, he'd probably willed it into her head, for she didn't, honestly didn't, find him at all attractive any more. He was too heavy; his face was jowly; his years of heavy drinking had woven a crimson web across his nose and cheeks. God, Paul was fifty-two years old now! Uncomfortable, Rosalind looked back at Sarah who had discovered and was now rapturously appreciating the Ficus benjamina which had grown fast as a weed, fast as Kit, in the new house. A perfect mesomorph, Sarah still moved in a bouncy cheerleader style as she circled the Ficus, touched random leaves lightly, a harmless, worshipping bacchante.

Annabelle, regal in a Valentino caftan of dusky violet wool, regarded Sarah with indulgent amusement as she herself took firm hold of Barney's arm. Watching Sarah's capers about the Ficus, Rosalind felt suddenly rather hollow-cheeked, too slender, too stylish, like a paper mannequin on the pages of *Vogue.* She'd dressed with an eye to Cynnie as the competition, had donned for the first time a fawn-colored dirndl Annabelle had "picked up" for her in New York; with it, she wore rust-colored suede boots and a soft fawn cashmere sweater Will had most extravagantly given her for Christmas; and under the cowl neck of the sweater, she'd hung one of Andy Grimshaw's masterpieces: a large pendant of suede on leather rimmed with pewter, the suede like abstract patchwork in rust and umber and brown.

"What a splendidly *healthy* Ficus!" Sarah was crowing. "What do you do to it? What kind of plant food?"

"It's the light," Rosalind modestly said. She raised a hand towards the skylight overhead, feeling a bit limp of wrist and emaciated—God, Sarah did look wholesome. There was snow on the skylight. The skylight sent Sarah into ecstasy. "Rosalind, may I see the house? I am just dying to see the house!"

"Kit!" Rosalind called, hearing her voice come out a trifle strangled. "Kit!" Kit came bounding down the spiral stair-case. He wore jeans and a turtleneck, looked quite suddenly teen-aged and old to Rosalind. She averted her eyes from the tight crotch of his jeans (she'd been finding stiff towels in the laundry lately) and reached up to rumple his hair, having to reach up rather far. "Kit, would you show Mrs. Damian around?" To Sarah she said, "Kit's the perfect tour guide. I'm beginning to sound rehearsed. Why don't you show her the upstairs first, Kit? I hope you made your bed," she added, glad she'd remembered to put her quilt away from Sarah's eager, prying, artsy-craftsy eyes. Kit said, yes, his bed was made, and, smiling engagingly, led Sarah off, up the hand-sculpted wooden spiral staircase.

"Call me Sarah," Rosalind heard her say to him. "Are you called Kit for Christopher Marlowe? How enchanting!"

In the kitchen with Will, both of them deftly mixing drinks—martinis for Paul and Barney, both on the rocks, one with an olive, one with a twist, one with two, one with three splashes of vermouth, a Dubonnet on the rocks for Annabelle, bourbon and soda for Sarah—Rosalind grinned up at Will and said, "You're right. Sarah's a *mark*. We got a little action to throw Andy's way."

Will looked at her and laughed. "You sound like a moll," he said. "I could call him," he suggested. "Call Andy."

"Why don't you?" Rosalind assented. "Yes, call him. There'll be loads of food—I mean, look at the size of that casserole." She flicked a hand at the huge, hand-thrown, earthenware pot in which Sarah had deprecatingly presented her aromatic *bœuf bourguignon*. "I'd better put that in the oven. Call Andy, Will," she urged. While, in a proprietary way as if she'd made it, she stashed Sarah's marvelous pot in the oven, Rosalind could hear Will with Andy on the phone.

"Yeah," Will was saying, grinning at Rosalind, "Roz says she's a *mark*. That means a pushover. You know how Roz talks, Andy; she talks like a guttersnipe." Rosalind got laughing. "No, Andy, don't bring anything, just Flo. Get your ass over here. Roz says get your ass over here."

"I never said that word in that context in my life," Rosalind reproached him after he'd hung up. Will still wore his ancient jeans, but he'd put on a white shirt and a tan suede vest, looked as elegant as Lord Peter *en déshabillé*. She nuz-

zled her body against him, with her arms around his waist
pulling him close. He fondled the soft cashmere of her
sweater, ran his hands down to her buttocks, then reluctantly put his hands in his pockets.

"Later, love," he said. "A tour's going through."

"There's always the bathroom."

"Uh-uh. Remember when he brought the sightseers in
when we were in *bed*?" They both laughed; then, in resigned
unison, picked up drinks to carry to the living room.

"Roz, what's he doing here?" At the door, Cynnie Talleyrand Pettinger held out a pot, kissed Rosalind's cheek,
and glowered at Paul Damian, visible in the living room,
talking to Annabelle by the brick fireplace that soared all the
way to the lofty cedar ceiling. Drinks in hand, they looked
witty and urbane: the after-theater crowd. "Where's Barney?
Walter's parking the car. It's really snowing hard. Roz,
where did you get that skirt?" In outrage Cynnie stared at
Rosalind's skirt. Dramatically she dropped her lynx coat to
the floor exposing an identical fawn-colored skirt. "I went all
the way to Philadelphia for this skirt, Roz!"

Rosalind, left holding the pot, laughed gleefully. "Annabelle brought it. You know, 'Just a little Anne Klein I
picked off the rack at Bergdorf's for you, dear.' "

"Damn Annabelle!" Cynnie laughed her lovely, tinkling
laugh. "What size, Roz? Oh, hell, Roz, you're too thin. I hate
you." With her skirt (an eight to Rosalind's six), Cynnie wore
a ruffled blouson in pale blue; their outfits actually didn't
look anything alike. An amazingly adaptable skirt. Over her
shoulders, Cynnie floated a soft and webby shawl the color
of barley in the sunshine. Cynnie looked, as always, a creature from some far-off, ethereal realm.

"Cynnie!" Barney came round from the living room into

the hall and swept Cynnie into his arms. Cynnie seemed to dissolve like smoke against his big easy body, his rumpled tweeds. She lifted one foot off the floor, like in an old movie, and kissed him resoundingly on the mouth. They let go of each other, and both winked, in unison, at Rosalind.

"Roz." The mellow, shaded baritone of Walter Pettinger came from the door behind her, a voice that by a process of synesthesia seemed to echo the colors of his lustrous skin. Walter squeezed her shoulders and kissed her cheek. "Let me carry the pot for you, lovely lady." Walter held the pot easily in one big hand, a rakish prop for his dashing Harris tweed suit.

"Did Cynnie drag you to Philadelphia for that?" Rosalind asked him. "Walter, you look like The Juice turned fashion model. You look like Robert Lovelace on a seducing spree." She grinned at him; she loved his face, handsome and arrogant, head held high and back, but there was something about his eyes—the way the eyebrows rimmed the eye-sockets—that gave him the look of a shy forest creature, a spectacled bear, or a kinkajou.

"I made the stew," Walter proudly drawled. "I made it out of beer and flour and bacon drippings, and it is ambrosial, just like my mama made it down on the old plantation."

"The old plantation down on One Hundred and Thirty-first Street," Barney said laughing. Walter laughed, too, a wonderful rich laugh.

"Walter's a super cook," Cynnie lazily said, putting one hand on Barney's shoulder, the other on Walter's, draping herself between them. "You should try his African vegetables." What are African vegetables? Rosalind started to ask, but Daisy and Joe came bumping and sliding down the spiral stairs.

"Cynnie!" they cried. "Walter!" Cynnie released the men and knelt on the floor to hug Daisy and Joe.

"You beautiful, beautiful babies."

"Babies!" Both Daisy and Joe pulled away, indignant.

"That was *hyperbole*," Rosalind said to them, like a school-teacher. "What's hyperbole, Joe?"

"Ex-ag-ger-a-tion," Joe said slowly. Rosalind fondly chuckled.

"You're doing it again," Walter said. "Joey's going to grow up just as smart-ass as Kit."

"What did John Donne write, Daisy?" Rosalind went on, afraid she was showing them off but wanting to avert Daisy's tempestuous red-headed reaction if she wasn't called on to perform when Joe was.

"John Donne wrote metaphysical poetry," recited Daisy in a little singsong voice.

Cynnie got up from the floor. "*I* taught Kit Riemann's Zeta Function," she proudly said, "when he was only seven. Where is he? Where's Kit? I haven't seen him since this morning in the drugstore. Where's the man in my life? Kit!" she called.

At 5:45 the doorbell rang again. Rosalind stopped flirting by the fire with Walter Pettinger and ran to answer it, to let in the Grimshaws. "You darlings!" she exclaimed, flinging wide the door. Their eyes beamed at her through the falling snow outside.

"Hi, Roz," they said together. "Sorry we took so long." Rosalind hugged them both. She loved them, thought of them as a younger brother and sister, stood fondly back to look at their eager, bright-eyed faces. Flo, a feisty little Jewish girl from The Bronx, had softened with her pregnancy (seven months now), and even her hair, once severe bangs and crisp flipped-up ends, seemed wispy and feminine. She wore a soft olive-colored smock with billowing sleeves that Rosalind had passed along to her, declaring that Daisy was her last, absolutely her last baby. "I had to hem it up six inches," Flo confided now, making a wry face. "Roz, why didn't I grow tall like you?"

"Because then you'd have been too tall for Andy," Rosalind told her. She kissed Andy Grimshaw's pink, soft cheek. It got pinker. Not quite as tall as Rosalind, Andy was sandy-haired and chunky, still as baby-faced as he'd been when he'd walked her from classes long ago. She saw him glance with surreptitious pride at the suede pendant around her neck. "D'you like it?" she asked him, as if he were a little boy. ("I know Andy and Flo are married," Rosalind had once exclaimed to Will, "and I know they're grown up, but I still think of them as students. I can't help it." "Wait'll Kit brings home a girl, Roz," Will had said. "You are going to *faint.*")

Now, as if they were children, Rosalind took Flo and Andy each by a hand and ushered them into the august and (by now) rather rollicking company in the living room. Carefully she introduced them to Annabelle and Barney, then to Sarah and Paul. "Are you the man who built this marvelous house?" Sarah Damian eagerly asked Andy. "Oh, come over here with me; I want to talk to you," and Sarah took Andy by the wrist and settled him with her on the couch. "Do you think it could be done in redwood?" Rosalind heard her begin. *Man,* Rosalind was thinking; Sarah called Andy a man.

"Barney!" Kit's voice boomed into the room from the kitchen, where the television was. My God, what a deep voice, Rosalind thought in a thorough daze. "Barney! It's time! It's time for the Super Bowl. Red Grange is tossing the coin!"

Barney's battered face ran a regular gamut of emotions. He grabbed Annabelle by the hand. "Come on, everybody, it's time for Super Bowl Twelve!"

· I

"Kit, get that, would you?" Someone was knocking on the back door of the Mud Lake cottage. "It's almost time for the kickoff. Who could be knocking?" The television was on, and both Rosalind and Kit were poised on the couch before it, heads leaned forward, elbows on knees, watching intently the Colts and the Cowboys run onto the sun-dappled emerald-green Poly-Turf of the Orange Bowl. "Can you believe it's seventy degrees in Miami and zero here?" Rosalind brooded sidelong. The knock came again. "Kit, for God's sake, will you get that?"

Kit heaved an exaggerated sigh, reluctantly got up from his place on the couch next to her, and went towards the kitchen and the now pounding door. Like Rosalind, in honor of the day, he wore a Barney Chase football jersey as a tunic over his jeans and turtleneck. Barney was supposed to "drop in" at the NBC broadcast booth sometime during the first quarter, and they were both very excited. "Here's 'The Chase,'" Curt Gowdy would say. Kit and Rosalind would whistle through their teeth and cheer. . . .

Johnny Unitas did not look good, Rosalind observed critically; he looked older than Barney and did not move anywhere near as well; and then she frowned at Craig Mor-

ton, who should not, she firmly believed, have been suffered
to push Roger Staubach out of the Dallas starting lineup.
Staubach's going to be *great,* she silently fumed, one of the
brightest and best: whatever are you thinking of, Tom Lan-
dry?

"Luke!" She heard Kit's excited voice from the kitchen.
"Luke!" *Oh, brother.* "Mom, look who's here! It's Luke.
You're just in time for the Super Bowl, Luke." Rosalind
turned her head ironically to regard the rather hangdog
approach of the unexpected, uninvited guest. Luke Di-
Lorenzo, looking damnably, impossibly handsome, grinned
ingratiatingly at her. He wore his sunny-yellow down-filled
jacket and held, on one hip, a box frivolously wrapped in
shiny red paper with a big yellow pom-pom tied rakishly on
the top. He looked cold; his cheeks were ruddy, the collar of
his jacket turned up. Kit was beaming with pleasure. Kit
loves Luke, Rosalind thought repentantly, then angrily.

"How'd you get here?" Rosalind asked Luke.

"I hitched," he said.

"With that box?" Rosalind began to smile, then giggled, finally laughed. "Ah, sit down. Take his coat, Kit. But you
have to be *quiet,*" she warned Luke severely. "Kit and I are
very serious about this game."

"So am I," Luke mildly returned. Rosalind felt him sit
down on the couch next to her. Sideways she was conscious
of his thigh on a parallel with hers. Kit sat down on her
other side.

"How was your vacation?" she asked Luke, without looking at him. His long thighbone shifted.

"Great," he said. "My brother Matt fell in love and got
married all in one week. She turned out to be the richest girl
in Buffalo." Rosalind laughed shortly. Leave it to big
brother, she thought. "He's quitting the Bureau," Luke

leaned to tell her quietly. "You don't have to worry about him anymore. He's going to work for Teresa's father."

"Teresa," Rosalind said. "Is she pretty?" She turned her head for a second towards Luke.

He shrugged. "Not bad. And, oh, Chase, is she ever rich!" They both laughed, then looked quickly away from each other.

"Luke," Kit said tentatively over Rosalind, "what's in the box?" Rosalind saw that Luke had put his frivolous burden on the other side of him, on the couch. The red wrapping glowed against the umber of the couch like a new sofa-pillow. Rosalind averted her eyes but not in time to miss the vision that floated like a sunspot: the sperm-clotted red pillow she'd had to throw in the garbage more than a fortnight ago, along with a shattered white cereal bowl.

"A peace offering?" she asked Luke.

"Yeah," he said. He grinned impudently at her. "But not for you. It's for Kit." Rosalind felt Kit's excitement jiggle the couch next to her.

"Why don't you give it to him?" she asked Luke. "You unconscionable *tease. . . .*" His eyebrows lifted.

"Sorry, Kit," he said. He passed the box along. Kit tore at the wrappings. Rosalind took the yellow pom-pom and held it in her hands, like a flower.

"Mom, it's a basketball!" Kit gleefully exclaimed. "Luke, it's exactly what we needed. We have a basketball hoop outside."

"I thought you might be able to use it," Luke said casually. He leaned back on the couch and crossed one knee over the other, leaning his body a little towards Rosalind. She crossed her leg away from him. He put his arm along the back of the couch. Kit nudged Rosalind with the basketball.

"Mom, isn't it terrific? It's a Rawlings."

Rosalind nodded coolly. Then she started to laugh. "Oh, you!" she said suddenly to Luke. She grabbed the basketball from the startled Kit and bashed Luke in the chest with it.

His handsome head back, he grinned insolently at her, holding his hands on the basketball, keeping her off. "Be a lady," he said. They both laughed, eyes embarrassed at first, then easy on each other's faces.

"Thanks," Rosalind said. "Thanks for the basketball." She tied the yellow pom-pom around her wrist, like a bracelet. Then she tensed. "They're kicking off," she said. "I didn't even see the coin-toss." An intense, concentrated silence filled the timbered living room of the Mud Lake cottage. . . .

"Oh, God, they are all so tight!" Luke DiLorenzo groaned halfway through the first quarter. "It hurts to watch them. Look at Unitas's hands. You'd think it was cold there."

A pounding came at the back door. "Shit!" Rosalind said. Both Kit and Luke looked at her in surprise.

"Mom," Kit reproached in a murmur. Luke laughed. I must use obscenities more often, Rosalind thought, feeling rather proud of herself. The pounding at the door continued. Neither Kit nor Luke moved. Finally Rosalind got up and, keeping her head turned towards the TV, made a wandering progress to the back door.

"Keep your shirt on," she muttered, opening it. A jowly man with a mouth like a prissy rosebud scowled at her. He wore a big black overcoat. Behind him was Will Eddy, dapper in the Confederate gray of the Pennsylvania State Police and an absurd fur hat with a chin strap. His gray eyes warned her, warned her about . . . something. . . .

"Will, I like your hat!" she said too brightly, trying to dissipate the particles of her gathering alarm. She heard her voice catch.

"Rosalind Chase?" the man in the black overcoat asked her, coming into the kitchen. He flashed a badge in her face; her stomach plummeted. "Or should I say Roth?" Will Eddy came in, too, closing the door. "Where," the FBI man demanded suddenly, "is Mark Rudd?"

My God, they really do say that, Rosalind dizzily thought, trying to gather her wits. The man kept his eyes on her face, waiting for an answer.

"I don't even know Mark Rudd," she said, trying to sound reasonable, but it came out defiant. "I saw him just once, from a distance. . . ." Her voice trailed off. In confusion she looked at Will Eddy, whose face shocked her. It looked like hers felt, strained and full of dread.

"He's not here to help you," the FBI man said. "He's here to help me." Rosalind lowered her eyes. She saw the yellow pom-pom on her wrist, the number 33 emblazoned across her chest. It had to happen sometime, she told herself like a charm, I knew it would happen sometime, it's better to get it over with. "Where'd you see Mark Rudd?" the man demanded.

"Um," she said, "it was at Columbia in the fall of sixty-eight, November, I think—near the sundial. He was making a speech. He was saying—"

"Ah!" the man said, disgusted, waving his hand at her to make her stop. "Where's Bernardine Dohrn?"

"I don't know. I've never met Bernardine Dohrn."

He gave her a crafty, speculative glance. "Where's Ben Roth?"

"I don't know."

"You do know him?"

She nodded.

"He's your husband, right? Will you come along with us, please?" Panicked, Rosalind looked at Will Eddy. He shrugged, but his face was terribly, terribly concerned.

"All right," Rosalind said. "Just a minute." She turned, and the FBI man grabbed her arm as if to stop her escaping. "Just a fucking minute," she snarled at him, then thought, My God, I have never said that word aloud in my life before. What's the matter with me? "I have to get a coat, don't I?" She went as far as the red parson's table and called, trying to make her voice steady: "Luke?" His head turned, and so did Kit's: curly black and curly blond, two heads over the back of the couch and the quilting frame. She smiled. "I have to go out for a little while. Will you stay with Kit till I get back?"

"Sure," Luke said.

"Mom, you're going to miss Barney!" Kit's face was incredulous. As if she were going to a ball Rosalind put on her sheepskin coat. She bent to zip up her boots, damn it, getting her jeans caught, tearing them, wresting them out of the zipper.

"Lovey-dove," she said to Kit, standing up straight and smiling at him, "you watch very carefully so you can tell me all about it. I shouldn't be long."

"Okay." The two heads, black and blond, turned back to the television screen.

"All right," Rosalind said brightly to the two men in the kitchen, "bring on the rubber hoses." Under his crazy fur hat, she saw Will Eddy's aristocratic face lurch into visible pity and fear.

Through the stunning cold that gathered outside the back door, Rosalind walked between the two men, her coat heedlessly open. So zero was she at the bone that she was aware of the actual cold only as a mild and distant annoyance. A gray Plymouth was parked next to the Firebird. Will Eddy opened the front door for her, and she got in. He started to get in next to her, but the FBI man said, "You get in back,

Eddy. This isn't a cozy country outing." As the door shut, Rosalind moved as close to it as she could get. She could feel Will Eddy get in behind her. His door slammed. The FBI man started the car. They drove along the lake road towards the main road, but just before the main road, the FBI man turned the car abruptly off, onto a dirt road.

"This isn't the way to the barracks," Will Eddy said. Rosalind turned in her seat so she could see him a little.

The FBI man ignored him. He whistled a little tune. "This is the way," he said after a moment, with satisfaction. He pulled the car up to the edge of the woods. Through the evergreens, like a mirage, Rosalind could see the ruins of Calypso. She felt stunned; she hadn't come this way before; Will Eddy had brought her across the barley field and up the rocky hill. For a moment she thought that Calypso had suddenly materialized in another place, like Brigadoon. This must be where Ben and Muffy got lost, she remembered then, as from another life.

"Get out," the FBI man said. Will Eddy helped Rosalind out of the car as if they were going to a ball. She liked his fur hat. They followed the FBI man toward the crumbling wall of white marble and through an open space. There was something in the center of the circle on the snow-flecked pine-needle floor. Litter, Rosalind idly thought, garbage.

But it wasn't litter. It wasn't garbage. It was Ben. His body was frozen; his arms folded over his stomach, shredded and frozen there, frozen with blood, the middle of him scarlet, frozen scarlet, frozen blood, frozen. His hair and his beard glittered with hoarfrost; his eyes stared, glazed, wide-open, opaque, frozen. Do eyes freeze? she wondered wildly. Out, vile jelly. The frozen expression on his face, she recognized it—the moment after pain, one eyebrow raised, the tensed mouth: Why, I'm hurt, he always seemed to be saying, like a

child. His mouth was shiny and blue-red. Rosalind let her
eyes rest on Ben's mouth. Had he kissed her? Kissed her
good-bye? "Go back to sleep, my fairest Roz," she heard him.
He'd kissed her. He'd taken a shower. She'd thrown the sofa
pillow away, thrown it in the garbage like litter, like trash,
flesh of my flesh. . .

Without warning, her insides contracted. She felt hot liquid scald her throat. "Pig!" she screamed at the FBI man.
"Motherfucker!" Her cry rose to the arch of the trees, then
seemed slowly to fall and bounce off the surrounding, waiting marble walls of fallen Calypso. Rosalind felt vomit
stream down the front of her, spatter the big 33 on her jersey, and she tried to turn her body away from her mouth.
The vomit spewed into the sheepskin collar of her coat.
"Motherfucker," she tried to say again, but more hot vomit
choked her.

"See," the FBI man said complacently to Will Eddy.
"Didn't I tell you she was one of them?" Rosalind felt warm
hands on her shoulders from behind, hands that moved to
her head as she retched, and she felt gratitude that such
people existed, one in a thousand who could hold one's head
while one helplessly vomited. She wasn't one, couldn't even
hold Kit's head, but Ben could, Ben, and Will Eddy could
hold hers despite what she'd just shrieked to the heavens,
and she turned, gasping, to him.

"I didn't mean you, Will," she said, vomiting all over the
Confederate gray of his uniform.

"I know, I know," he murmured, stroking her hair.

Despite the FBI man's disapproving moue, Will Eddy kept
his arm firmly around Rosalind's shoulders as, in grim and
swirling silence, the three of them walked back to the gray
Plymouth. Three more cars had pulled up next to the
woods; people were hopping out, many, many with cameras.

Rosalind ducked her head when the first flashbulb assaulted
her eyes; but then, proudly, she lifted her chin to confront
them, thinking of Annabelle . . . young Annabelle playing
Rosalind in *As You Like It,* tilting her chin defiantly at Duke
Frederick when he called Rosalind her father's daughter:
"So was I," Annabelle retorted, "when your Highness ban-
ish'd him./Treason is not inherited, my lord." Annabelle spat
out "my lord" like a curse. Rosalind had been seven, Kit's
age, when she first saw Annabelle play Rosalind at the
Winter Garden; now, she let herself go back into the
darkened theater, let Will Eddy hold her up, lead her
through the Forest of Arden. . . .

Back at the cottage all three of them trooped in as if they
lived there: Rosalind, Will Eddy, the FBI man. Will Eddy
dropped his fur hat on the kitchen counter. As if in a
dream, Rosalind admired his ruffled, flaming hair. It looked
warm as fire. The FBI man ushered them into the living
room. The curly black head and the curly blond head still
faced the television screen. Luke's voice called out, "It's thirteen to six. Two lousy field goals and one blocked extra
point. What a bungled game. . . ."

Kit turned around on the couch and went up on his knees
to look at Rosalind. His face was alight. Rosalind stood holding onto the quilting frame. The yellow pom-pom was still
on her wrist. "Barney said 'Hi, Kit' right on the air, Mom.
Didn't he, Luke? Mom?" Luke DiLorenzo turned around
too. Rosalind saw his startled brown eyes range from her to
(presumably) the FBI man and Will Eddy, whom she could
feel behind her.

"You." She heard the FBI man's voice. She turned. He
was staring at Luke, his rosebud mouth puckered with consternation. "You can go," he said to Luke in a dismissing
way.

"Go?"

"Yes, go! Get out of here."

Luke looked at Rosalind. "I don't have a car," he said.

"Shit!" the FBI man ejaculated. "Well, keep your mouth shut. I'll give you a ride when I leave."

Kit came around the couch. "Hi, Will," he said. "What's going on?" Rosalind saw panic raddle Kit's usual poise, that seven-year-old urbanity she so extravagantly admired. His expression broke her heart. She made a motion to grab him to her, but Will Eddy stopped her.

"Everything's all right," Will said to Kit. With his body and a warm smile, he guided Kit back around the couch to the television screen. "This man wants to ask your mother a few questions, that's all."

"Is he a professor?" Rosalind heard Kit ask. She watched the tall figure and the small figure as if they were in a play. Kit must have built a fire, she noticed idly. Or Luke. Shadows flickered from the flames and the gaudy color TV all over the room, shimmering.

"Who's winning thirteen to six?" she asked Luke.

"Dallas," he said, uneasily. The FBI man was scrutinizing him from the side. Suddenly Luke's body moved, jarring the soothing firelit shapes on her periphery. He caught the basketball that Will Eddy passed to him over the couch.

"Why don't you and Kit go out and shoot some baskets?" Will suggested, as if, wouldn't that be fun, shooting baskets in the zero cold; a lot more wholesome than being cooped up watching the Super Bowl.

"Sure," Luke said. "Come on, Kit!" Luke dribbled the ball to the closet. Kit ran over. "Think fast!" Luke passed the ball to Kit. Kit caught it and threw it to Rosalind. Her hands wouldn't move. Luke retrieved the ball from under the quilting frame. He and Kit put their coats on and went out through the kitchen door.

All through the long, jangled afternoon, Rosalind could see the Super Bowl flicker on the television screen and hear the basketball bang against the backboard on the oak tree. Policemen riffled through books and rummaged through drawers, scrutinized the crockery in the kitchen cabinets, sniffed the herbs and spices on the rack over the stove. Rosalind answered rude and impertinent questions, feeling that someone's rhythms, perhaps her own, were off, out of sync. No, she hadn't been jealous of Muffy. It hadn't even occurred to her to be. She'd rather liked Muffy. She loved Ben; she loved him; why, she'd made love with him, right here, here on the couch, in front of the fire.

"Why are they dusting for fingerprints?" she asked abruptly. She looked behind her at all the bustling activity. One man kept taking pictures. "Why are they dusting? It's been seventeen days. Do you think I'm a slattern?"

"We're not here to pass judgment on your morals," the FBI man priggishly said.

Rosalind saw Will Eddy hide his one smile of the day. She looked at Will and she looked at the flickering television and she heard the reassuring, battering basketball; and then she looked back at Will Eddy and said to him as if it were a profound and original discovery, a prayer from deep in her heart: "Thank God for sports."

"I beg your pardon?" the FBI man asked her, startled into politeness.

· II

When Rosalind woke up the next morning, Kit was asleep in her bed next to her, and Cynnie had replaced Will Eddy on the living room couch. Will Eddy had tucked her and Kit in

bed together and told them he'd stay till the morning. Hazy-
eyed, Rosalind stood on the catwalk and looked down at
Cynnie, gracefully asleep on the couch, her soft ash-brown
hair against a scarlet pillow, her legs decorous and parallel in
embroidered jeans. It's a good thing this happened during
the midsemester break, Rosalind thought, then thought,
What a stupid thing to think. She didn't feel too awfully bad,
she was surprised objectively to note, as she tried walking
along the catwalk to the ship's ladder. The widow's walk. She
was wearing a high-necked Victorian nightgown with flow-
ing sleeves and dangling ribbons, she saw, looking down at
herself, and she wondered if Will Eddy had helped her into
it. She couldn't remember; oh, God, she'd been tired to the
bone. She could remember him helping Kit into his pajamas.
. . . Should she send Kit to school today? How much had he
absorbed?

Last night she'd told him, and after the first violent tears—
a child's tears, thank God; she'd been afraid he might be
stoic, or else adult, whatever that was—Kit had asked in a
burst, "Did it hurt?" Oh, she'd put her hands on his
shoulders and pulled him close, rubbed their faces together,
his cheeks slick with tears, chapped and ruddy from the zero
cold of the outdoors. Barney's jerseys mingled together, silky
and undulating in the firelight, the mingling like a kinship
ritual. Blood.

It was as if Kit could feel Ben's blood, Rosalind mused
now. Kinship. *"Did it hurt?"* The identification! She stood at
the top of the ladder and ran both hands around her waist
where the organs were so politely enclosed, the rib cage intact, the blood channeled and contained. Flesh of my flesh.
Did it hurt?

"Roz!" Cynnie sat up, as always immediately wide awake.
Her sad, down-tilted gray-blue eyes regarded Rosalind with

infinite softness. "Ben's dead?" she asked then, rhetorically, and for a fleeting second, her face focused, as if she were at a horror movie and not altogether hating it. "That man from the FBI was horrid."

"Ben's dead." Rosalind sat down on the couch next to Cynnie as gingerly as if she'd just given birth. Ben's dead, her mind repeated soberly. If he hadn't come here, he'd be alive. "Cynnie, do you think I should send Kit to school?"

"Well, he wasn't in any of the pictures," Cynnie said. She waved a vague hand toward the red parson's table. Rosalind looked, saw newspapers. "You were," Cynnie said. "You look gorgeous. So does that dreamy cop. Who *is* he?" Cynnie wanted to know, sitting up straight, crossing her legs Indian fashion. "He let me in. He decided it'd be better if you woke up and saw *my* beautiful face." Cynnie preened a little. Then her face went serious. "Roz, are you all right? I mean, you're not in shock or anything, are you?" She looked closely at Rosalind's face. "You *look* all right," she said.

"I think maybe I *am* all right," Rosalind said. They both laughed a little. Rosalind let the jittery laugh impel a sentence from her, a sentence that felt fully formed and waiting: "Oh, God, Cynnie, I wouldn't say this to anyone but you, but it is almost a relief—" She stopped. Heartless. It sounded heartless, but Cynnie was nodding.

"Well, of course," she said.

(A millstone, he was a millstone. I loved him, loved him. Well, of *course*.) Frightened by the jumble of her thoughts, Rosalind tried to baste some words together to cover the wadded rags and tatters below. "I feel released," she began painstakingly for Cynnie. "I don't feel that terror that drives to the bone anymore." In fact I don't feel anything anymore. (Close and warm, the two of them in the iron bed in the whitewashed villa near Granada. Ben's Fulbright year. A crucifix over the bed. "Lorca was killed near here, Roz.")

"Who do you think did it, Roz?" Cynnie asked.

"I don't know." Rosalind felt her body start to tip, and carefully she slid back to rest her shoulder against the couch. Who did it? Nobody did it. I did it. A god from a machine did it.

"You can ride out the publicity, Roz," Cynnie assured her. She posed, slipped her thumb under her chin. "You've got straight A's."

Straight A's? Had she missed something, some vital conversational link? Rosalind gazed, unseeing, at Cynnie. ("Your father was killed here, Kit." "Lorca was killed here, Roz." A different Ben. Ben loved the cathedrals in Madrid; he never tired of tracing the myriad Stations of the Cross. Miles they'd walked around churches, Kit perched on Ben's shoulders. "Look at Veronica's Napkin here, Roz." Federico García Lorca, shot without a trial. Ernesto "Ché" Guevara. Nathan Hale, bareheaded on the scaffold.) Rosalind let her voice become audible again: "The tragic rhythm," she said slowly, as if it were very important. "Ben became tragic." When had she said that before? Rosalind looked down at her lap where her hands were demurely folded. How funny. Usually she moved them when she talked, especially to say things like "the tragic rhythm." She saw Cynnie's finger touch her folded hands.

"There's Kit," Cynnie said, looking up at the catwalk. "Kit," she called. "Surprise! I'm going to run you to school this morning."

"I like the bus," Kit said, coming down the ship's ladder like a monkey. Rosalind reached out to hug him, and so did Cynnie; they started fighting over him, laughing and tickling. "Hey, cut that out," Kit said, indignant.

"You're sure you want to go to school, lovey-dove?" Rosalind felt connected to her body again. Roughhoused into it.

"I'm sure," Kit said.

"People might say something."

"She-et," Kit said, "I know."

"Don't say that word!"

"You said it yesterday."

"I did not. I said *shit*," Rosalind enunciated carefully.

"You said *shit*, Roz?" Cynnie asked, interested. "I never heard you say shit."

"Well, I did. What Kit says is 'she-et.' He picked it up from that Philadelphia Eagle who's a friend of Barney's."

"Eagle?" Cynnie made a delicate, puzzled, little face. "Is that a football player?"

"Yes!" Kit said, exasperated.

While Rosalind showered and dressed, Cynnie scrambled eggs, made bacon, coffee, toast. She'd brought a whole larder of food in an old-fashioned wicker picnic basket. Together, they saw Kit off at his bus, both of them waving while he averted his eyes.

"We're embarrassing him," Cynnie finally said. "Let's go in. He'll be okay, Roz. How many second-graders read the newspapers?"

They tidied the cottage. The police had been careful, but there was still powder they'd used to lift fingerprints, and all of the crockery had been disarranged. Cynnie went through everything, sniffed the herbs on the rack over the stove to see if anything had been planted. Cynnie vacuumed. She even vacuumed Rosalind's quilt. Then she turned on the television and flopped down to watch a soap opera. Rosalind copied Cynnie. "Don't you love midsemester break?" Cynnie asked her. "Just think, if we were married, it'd be like midsemester break all the time."

"Cynnie, you wouldn't stop teaching."

"No, I guess not. I guess I wouldn't. Still, I'm twenty-eight years old. I wouldn't mind being married."

At noon came a frantic pounding on the back door. Cynnie crawled off the couch to answer it. Rosalind was propped at the other end, doggedly making the television push back the circles on the edge of her mind where Ben hung out—scarlet pillows and Veronica's Napkin. "Barney!" she heard Cynnie's excited cry.

"Where's Rozzy?" Barney's gravelly voice demanded. "Is she all right?" He came blustering into the living room, a big shaggy bear, his overcoat all crooked. Rosalind turned on the couch to look at him. Then she got up and ran around the couch to him. He held her, picked her up in his arms, cradled her, kissed her hair as if she were a little girl. "Baby, baby," he crooned. He put her down. "Are you all right?" he asked. "You *look* all right."

"I'm all right. Or I'm going to be. Are you all right? For God's sake, Barney, you're wearing a pajama top."

He looked down at himself and covered his face with his hands. He got laughing. "I was in bed in Miami," he said, "when I heard it on the eleven o'clock news. I raced like a madman to the airport, called Walter, and Walter picked me up in Philadelphia this morning. Christ, Rozzy," he groaned, "I walked around two airports and sat on a jet, in my pajamas!" They both got laughing. This is all right, Rosalind thought, as if slowly working out a problem in logic. It's all right to laugh.

"What's so funny?" Cynnie came into the living room. Following along behind her were Rosalind's student, Andy Grimshaw, and a gorgeous black man in a black leather jacket. A Black Panther? Rosalind wondered. What the hell?

"Andy," she said, dealing with him first, "how did you get here?"

"I hitched," he said. His blue eyes were wide, like a scared child's. "Walter here and your father picked me up on the road. Is there anything I can do? I thought you might need a baby-sitter, but your father said—" His baby face was full of confusion.

"Andy, you sweetheart. Kit went to school, but maybe later." Rosalind kissed his pink cheek. He blushed. She was terribly, terribly touched. "Cynnie, aren't students nice sometimes?"

"I told him I thought you'd send Kit to school," Barney explained. "It's what I would have done."

"Kit wanted to go," Rosalind had to admit. "I don't think I would have made him."

"Rozzy," Barney said earnestly, looking uncomfortable about the other people, but ignoring them, "the worst thing you can do right now, for either of you, is cling to Kit. He's seven; he barely *remembers*—"

"If Roz hadn't sent him, *I* would have," Cynnie interposed, cutting short the subject just as Rosalind was about to sink into what Kit didn't remember. "Roz," she said brightly, "have you met Walter?" She indicated the beautiful black man who now stood behind Andy, more than a head taller. Cynnie cupped her hand and pretended to whisper, "I think he might be the one who taught Kit that word."

"I'm forgetting my manners," Barney said. Then he forced a laugh and said, "Well, what can you expect from a man who's still in his pajamas, for God's sake? Walter Pettinger, this is my daughter, Rosalind. I gather you've already introduced yourself to Cynnie." Barney gave Cynnie a slightly disapproving glance. Cynnie had taken hold of Walter's arm, as if to say, I want *this* one.

"We spoke on the phone," Walter said, shaking Rosalind's hand. He had a rich, lazy voice. "And I'm a friend of Kit's—that's one fine little boy you have. I'm sorry for your trouble." His dark eyes were warm.

"Thank you," Rosalind said, feeling something start to enclose her—frozen images, Lucifer in the lowest circle of Dante's Inferno, hoarfrost and blue-red lips. She shuddered violently. Barney put his arm around her, and she leaned to his warmth.

"Rozzy," he said gently, "I've spoken to Annabelle, and she's on her way. 'Hang Gertrude,' she said on the phone, 'I'm sick to death of the woman. I'll give my understudy her big break.' " His warm laugh made Rosalind laugh a little.

"That sounds like good old Annabelle," Cynnie lazily said. "Hey, Roz, are you going to be able to put everybody up here? Let's see, Kit's bed is single, there's a double bed in the guest room, I wouldn't recommend the couch—no, Roz, you can't. You can have Barney and Annabelle," she said generously. "You and Annabelle do still sleep together, don't you, Barney?" Rosalind stared at Cynnie, who was really being outrageous, even for Cynnie.

Barney looked hangdog, then defiant. "Yeah," he said. "Annabelle and I sleep together. What's it to you, minx?"

"Well," said Cynnie, lowering her eyes modestly, "I just thought I might take Walter home with me tonight when I go." Both Barney and Walter looked at Cynnie in amazement. "If Walter needs a place to stay, that is," Cynnie concluded with an airy whirl of her hand.

"May I hitch a ride, Miss Talleyrand?" Andy Grimshaw asked politely from the red parson's table. Everyone turned. Rosalind had forgotten he was there. He wanted to help; he'd come all that way. She went over to him.

"Andy, would you like to help me, oh"—she cast round for a plausible activity—"make some lunch for this rowdy bunch?" They *were* rather rowdy, she could hear now that she was away from them; their voices commingled soprano, baritone, bass; their laughter was infectious. Andy must have felt left out. "It was awfully nice of you to come," Rosalind told him, then went on teasingly, "especially since you already got your A."

"Miss Chase, are you all right?" Andy asked her, alarm and concern warring for control of his baby face.

"Oh, call me Roz," said Rosalind. She stopped as she realized how flippant she sounded, and thoughtfully she studied Andy's face. Ah, I show more mirth than I am mistress of, her mind quoted reproachfully, but it wouldn't do to say it aloud. Andy doesn't approve, she gleaned; he's shocked to find levity in this presumed house of mourning. He's glimpsed the hard core of comedy that lurks like a . . . what? A minotaur in jester's motley, at the dead center of tragedy: *laughter,* the guilty secret kept by the huddled survivors, the laughter of the forlorn but undefeated hope. Of course, really, to be fair, Andy is viewing an unusually . . . bizarre demonstration of this truth, Rosalind musingly decided as she continued to ponder his face. Oh, this is an appalling heritage I've cut my teeth on, this muddle of sportsmanship and the-show-must-go-on. But of course the show *must.* Even Kit knows that.

"I *will* be all right," Rosalind lifted her chin and told Andy, "if everyone just keeps on talking. And laughing. Fortunately that's what my particular people happen to be good at. Wait'll you meet my mother. Oh, brother. Come on." She took Andy by the hand, squeezed his hand because it was shaking, or hers was, and called to the rest of them, "Come on, everybody. Let's see if we've got enough food for lunch. Come on, Cynnie." Cynnie and Walter were dawdling by the quilting frame. " 'Thrift, thrift, Horatio,' " Rosalind muttered to herself.

Super Bowl Sunday

January 15, 1978

Halftime, 7:30 P.M.

"Roz, how can you pander to men like that?" Cynnie demanded in a petulant voice. "Nobody ever let *us* play football. Of course," she amended as, swirling identical fawn-colored skirts, she and Rosalind turned the corner from the kitchen into the lofty dining room that, through an openwork brick wall, overlooked the sunken living room, "who'd want to? It's like the army. Football's stupid; only men are that stupid."

"This isn't a good game, Cynnie," said Rosalind, who, having yelled and gesticulated every bit as obstreperously as Barney or Kit or Walter all through the really lousy first half, felt obliged to defend football. "Super Bowls are almost always bad football. The players are too tight. They've been idle for two weeks. Even Roger's tight today."

"Roger," Cynnie murmured sidelong. "How familiar, Roz."

"Oh hell." At a loss, Rosalind gazed at the dining room table which, in its present round, contracted condition, would seat only six. She started counting heads in her mind. Beyond the wall of bookshelves that separated the dining room from the kitchen, Annabelle, Flo Grimshaw, and Sarah

Damian were collaborating in whispers on garlic bread and a Caesar salad—in whispers because on the other side of the kitchen counter where the television was, Barney, Andy, Paul, and Walter were engrossed in the halftime montage of old Super Bowls. Will and Kit (the latter under duress) were upstairs putting the overexcited, boisterous Joe and Daisy to bed. Eleven people. "Cynnie, we'd better wait for Will to come down. He'll have to put the leaves in the table."

Cynnie ducked down and looked under the table. "They're right under here, Roz. Gee, this table works just like my great-aunt's. Where'd you get it?"

"Will's dowry," Rosalind said absently. "We never had room for it before." Would the Caesar salad be enough? Should she make some kind of vegetable to go with the meal? Cynnie had crawled under the table. Rosalind bent to see what she was doing. Flushed of face, smiling, Cynnie emerged.

"Cynnie," Rosalind asked her speculatively, "what are African vegetables?"

"Ah, no, Roz," Cynnie laughed. "I'm not telling. Walter wouldn't tell *me*; I had to eat them and guess."

"Cynnie, I don't believe there are any specifically African vegetables."

"Roz, there are lots of things specifically African," Cynnie said and laughed a slightly lascivious laugh. "Come on. Help me pull the table apart." Clumsily following Cynnie's exasperated instructions, Rosalind eventually managed to do her part with one end. Then Cynnie manipulated the underlying leaves until the table turned into a long oblong, nearly filling the room.

"I never had both the leaves in before," Rosalind said, feeling rather awed. The table quite usurped the room. Rosalind felt the day begin to overwhelm her.

"I can tell," said Cynnie. "They don't match. Where do
you keep your tablecloths?"

"In the cabinet under the windows. But I'm sure I don't
have one big enough for this table. I should have had you
bring one, Cynnie. Oh, I didn't think! I'm always so rattled
on Super Bowl Sunday; I don't know what's the matter with
me; it's been seven years. . . ." Her voice trailed off. She felt
perilously close to tears.

"Take it easy, Roz." Cynnie was going through Rosalind's
stash of Dansk tablecloths, a regular rainbow of them, but
none of them big enough. "We can put two tablecloths
together. Hey, what's this?" Cynnie pulled out a fancy scarlet
tablecloth wildly embroidered in silky white thread. She
flung it around her shoulders like a cape. "This is beautiful,
Roz. It isn't big enough, but it's beautiful. Where'd you get
it?"

Rosalind's stomach felt queasy. I haven't had anything to
eat, she excused it. Just a Bloody Mary. "Annabelle sent that
a couple of years ago, from the Middle East. Israel, I think."
Inexplicably Rosalind shuddered as Cynnie spread the cloth
out on the end of the table near the windows. The silken
white embroidery made a flamboyant, coruscating sunburst
in the center of the scarlet square. "I hate it, Cynnie. I've
never used it."

"You hate it?" Cynnie was amused. "What's wrong with
it?"

"It's . . . hideous. The pattern."

"Roz, it's lovely. Look." Cynnie spread a bone-colored
linen tablecloth on the lower end of the table. "It'll be perfect for the two different meals." Cynnie moved to the
center of the oblong table, jiggled the crack open, slid the
hems of both tablecloths through, closed the crack, and the
two cloths came together in a knife-edge straight line. "This

end'll be for the aristocracy and Sarah's *bœuf bourguignon*—
did you smell it? Gorgeous! The plain end will be for the
proletariat and Walter's stew." Chortling with delight, Cynnie took salt and pepper shakers from the sideboard and
strung them along the line where the tablecloths joined.
"You know, below the salt."

Rosalind, her gorge rising—Can I be pregnant? she wondered. No, I can't possibly be, she decided, picturing a neat
row of pills in a rectangular compact—turned away from the
table and took two bottles of Côte de Beaune from the
wine rack tucked into the bookcases. Gingerly, because Will
was careful with his wines, she put one bottle at either end of
the table. "No, Roz," Cynnie said patiently, removing the
bottle from the plain cloth and placing it with the other bottle, square in the center of the ugly, embroidered sunburst.
"With Walter's stew you have to serve beer. Below the salt,"
she decreed, "the proletariat will have to be content with
beer. The stew's made with beer."

"Beer?" Rosalind wrinkled her nose. "Cynnie, it doesn't
seem fair."

"Since when has society been fair? The stew needs beer,"
Cynnie said. "I hope you have some beer."

"I think there's some Heineken." Rosalind let her mind's
eye rummage through the refrigerator.

"Perfect. That's a classy beer. Walter uses Löwenbräu in
the stew."

Cynnie was certainly generous with Walter's stew recipe,
Rosalind thought, and pounced: "Are yams an African vegetable?"

Cynnie jumped. "Roz, I'm not telling!" The two of them
looked at each other and laughed, Cynnie sheepishly, and
then she went back to contemplating the table. "Roz, I'm
going to put Barney here, at the head." She touched the chair

nearest the windows. "With the aristocracy. Barney hates beer anyhow. And, at the foot, we'll appropriately put Kit. Kit can have some beer, can't he? We'll serve it in wine-glasses."

"Cynnie, no—"

"Oh, bullshit, Roz. Walter gives Kit beer when he comes over. Oh, Walter's teaching Kit a lot, Roz." Cynnie's laugh pealed delicately.

"Walter gives Kit beer?" Rosalind frowned. She was count-ing out napkins. "Cynnie, do you remember that student of yours who taught Kit how to roll joints? I think you're a bad influence, Cynnie."

"Billy," Cynnie reflectively said. "Billy just got his doctor-ate from Stanford."

"He *did*?" Rosalind stared. She remembered Billy as an in-genuous, peach-fuzzy boy.

"It happens, Roz. Students grow up. Even children grow up. It'll happen to Kit," Cynnie said airily. Then she glared at the table as if it were an impossible mathematical equa-tion. She counted on her fingers. "Roz, we don't have an even number of people. D'you think it's too late to invite someone else?"

"For God's sake, Cynnie!"

"All right, all right. Roz, where're your place cards?"

"Place cards?"

"Roz, do you have *any* cards? Blank ones, I mean."

Rosalind heaved an exasperated sigh. "I might have some *index* cards."

"They'll do. Bring me some. Eleven. And a felt-tipped pen. I'll take care of the seating, Roz, and I'll even set the table. Come on, Roz," she prodded. "Move, Roz." Rosalind, suddenly dizzy, held on to the table. "Get me the cards and the pen. Are Barney and Annabelle back together, Roz?

Never mind. I can tell. Annabelle's too old for the stage, isn't she? Yes, she is," Cynnie answered herself. Exultantly she circled the table, tapping her fingertips together. "I see just how to arrange the seating." Cynnie stamped her foot suddenly at Rosalind. "Move your ass, woman!"

· *Heroic Couplets*

February 1971

· I

"You're Annabelle Chase's daughter," a feisty voice accused.

Expecting "You're Paul Damian's mistress," or "You seduced a student," Rosalind, just through the paneled door of the Library-Library (as the room was actually called, even in bronze on the door), girded to brazen out a day-before-the-new-semester sherry party, her first appearance on campus since Ben's murder broke in the media, stared nonplussed at the short stiff fellow who stood before her like a thumb. The Shakespeare man, her mind identified him, while her body, instinctively guarding her glass, checked out her periphery: all English Department chitchat had not ceased at her entrance, sherry glasses had not spilt their amber contents on the fine old Oriental rug, nobody was pulling volumes of Henry James's New York Edition to throw. A distinct anticlimax, this stubby and truculent Shakespeare man, who wore his hair in a balding page boy suspiciously like Shakespeare's. Going on sabbatical he was, leaving Rosalind his Shakespeare course—if they hadn't taken it away from her. Thoughts nettlesome and persistent had plagued her throughout the skewed and brittle mourn-

ing of the midsemester break: what if the department, im-
pelled by some gentlemen's agreement she didn't know
about, expected her to fade quietly out of the third act, like
the Fool in *Lear*? What then? Where go then?

Rosalind tried to fob the Shakespeare man off with a
vague smile, but he just stood there, as if they were having a
dialogue. Around them swirled the offhand, antiquated gos-
sip that passed, at sherry parties, for literary conversation;
and Rosalind, used to quiet after two weeks ensconced at the
cottage with just Kit and Barney and Annabelle, felt the
banter batter her ears from all sides. "Donne wasn't a *believer*. Whatever gave you that idea? The poor man just
needed a job." "John Keats was a tough little cockney, and I
never read 'im without dropping all the *h*'s." "Hiding her
poems in the attic—that's classic anality. And all those dashes!"
"You're Annabelle Chase's daughter."

The Shakespeare man was trying again, in the same belli-
cose tone. Dear God, Rosalind ranted internally, last week
someone printed WHORE in orange lipstick across my windshield; do you think you can scare me by calling me "Annabelle Chase's daughter"? Sticks and stones, my good man.

"Yes," she finally said, however. "Yes, I am." She waited.
He probably hadn't liked Annabelle's Cleopatra last summer
at Stratford. Well, neither had she. The sins of the mothers . . .

"Ah!" he said. "Ah!" He tipped his pageboy to one side
and contemplated the ceiling, while a rapturous little smile
flirted with the corner of his mouth. The prolonged gesture
exposed the underside of his chin, and Rosalind noted that
he was trying to grow a pointed little beard. "The divine Annabelle!" he breathed. He rocked on his heels. Then he
frowned at Rosalind. "I hope you're not going to make a
circus out of my Shakespeare course."

"I hope not too," Rosalind replied with spirit. Oho. She still had his Shakespeare course.

"Acting isn't everything," he pronounced sternly; and while Rosalind was doing a double take on that in her mind, suddenly he leaned at her and barked, "How do you think the Plague affected the Elizabethan theater?"

"Oh, a lot!" Rosalind said, drawing back.

"Exactly!" said the Shakespeare man. He beamed on her. "I'm off to England," he confided. "Right now. The Plague, you know. Research. Good luck!"

Be careful you don't catch it, Rosalind wanted to call after him as, even walking like a thumb, his Shakespearean bob inflexible as a wig, he seemed to glide around her and out of the door. She found herself edging toward the wall, where it was quiet. The Plague! She remembered a burly, bearded student showing her an exam this Shakespeare man had made up, the student professing to have thrown up en route to her office, the sissy. "How, exactly, is drawing and quartering accomplished?" "How many Londoners died of the Plague in 1599?" "Describe a bear-baiting." "Name three places severed heads were displayed on pikes, marking them on the attached map of Elizabethan London."

"Miss Chase," the student had complained, "do you think that gory stuff is relevant? I'm a pacifist." Ah, the greatest theater in the language had drawn its blood, its energy, its *life* from those heads on the pikes and the stacked bodies of the Plague victims, Rosalind had tried to tell him, for Elizabethan London was as real to her as her own life, as real as Cornell or Grant Park in Chicago or Low Library at Columbia, as real as a baseball diamond, a football field, or the quilt she was happily embroidering. Tragedy blossomed, and not just tragedy, comedy as well. From the same blooded roots, the same hogshead of ale. "They joked about the Plague on the stage," Rosalind had told the student. "Joked?" "What else were they going to do?" Rosalind had eloquently asked.

What else? she asked herself wryly now, limp and weak-kneed in the Library-Library. Could she go through the crush in the room to the sherry table on the other side? No, she could not, not right now. Her legs were unaccountably shaking, fluttery waves that started at the thighs and worked down. She leaned her shoulders against the honey-colored wainscoting and tried to assume a lounging posture from which to count the house. ("Counting the house is the only cure for stage fright"—a flower of maternal wisdom.) For reassurance Rosalind looked down at herself and Annabelle's notion of consolation, a new outfit she'd somehow contrived to acquire for Rosalind on her lavish way to Mud Lake (she'd come all the way in a chauffeured limousine): "Driver, stop just a jot while I pop into Bendel's; Fifty-seventh Street is difficult at the rush hour, my good man, not impossible," she'd chided, tapping his shoulder. Rosalind gave her eyes a downward moment to appreciate the intricately fringed dark-gold suede jerkin and skirt, the hunter-green silk shirt against the golden wall, and then she raised her head.

The Library-Library wasn't large, but the ceiling was high, the lighting mellow and shadowed, faces dim. Students were there, she saw. That's why it was so crowded. English majors must have been invited. She saw Susan Jasper, who smiled at her, waved, but then lowered her head. Susan wouldn't know what to say, Rosalind knew. *She* wouldn't know what to say. Perhaps the Shakespeare man's approach had been the best possible; its sheer contentious irrelevance had put her on her mettle.

Catty-corner halfway across the room she saw the handsome, white-haired Chairman with two of the senior English faculty and a bright-eyed, tubby little man she didn't know.

The Chairman caught her eye, but she looked hastily away, startled by her own cowardice, humiliated even; and then a single face arrogated her eyes, usurped her attention: Luke. In profile, near the sherry table, talking to two girls, one of whom was very pretty and wore a skirt that barely made it over her buttocks. What was Luke doing here? Was he an English major? she stupidly wondered, as if, in the encounter that probably impended, his major would be the salient feature. She fixed her eyes on Luke's elegant profile, admiring dispassionately the casual grace of the set of his head, and then she watched as uneasily he moved it, his head, flinched almost, tried to deflect her gaze, but he couldn't. He turned and looked at her. He hadn't been at the inquest. Nor had his brother.

Lucky Charms in the stomach, marijuana in the bloodstream: breakfast. "Certain portions" of the body had been gnawed by animals, the medical examiner had apologetically reported. Rosalind could feel again Barney and Annabelle on either side of her at the inquest: Barney's huge shoulder, Annabelle's small, slender shoulder: equal strength. A rock and a wire. Like lovers they'd been, the fortnight they'd spent with her and Kit. A yoke "like gold to airy thinness beat" seemed to hold them together, however far, however long they were apart. Rosalind's mind drifted. John Donne, Dean of St. Paul's, not a believer? Was that possible? Dreamily, she watched Luke detach himself from the girls—oh, he was smooth. ("Excuse me, I just have to say hello to Nemesis over there by the door.") He paused at the sherry table and then wove, a basketball player in slow motion, through the crowd to her. From the flossy literary patter about her, Rosalind caught one raised and exasperated masculine voice: "It wasn't *Emily* who was the lesbian in the family; it was Charlotte. Have you never seriously scrutinized the imagery in *Villette*? Well, if you must do an honors thesis on lesbianism in nineteenth-century lit, you had better." And Rosalind smiled, and Luke, arriving, appropriated the smile as his own.

She looked up at him, and her hands recollected the texture of his hair, the softest hair imaginable, like putting one's fingers into a dark cloud, she remembered thinking that night on the daisy sheets, and her body remembered his body; but it was all past tense. Bereaved, she thought with wonder. I am bereaved. Would there be sex again, any sex? She realized she doubted it. Her body doubted it. Her body felt memory, but not desire. The center of her had turned to ice along with the bloody center of Ben. The first and the last. Ben.

"Hi," Luke said. He handed her a sherry. He stood next to her, leaning down protectively, the impeccable gesture, the perfect arrangement of her space. *Galantuomo,* Rosalind thought, and she stood away from the wall, feeling poised, feeling safe.

"Thanks," she said. "Thanks for the sherry. And thanks for the basketball. My father and Kit played a lot." She sipped it, the sherry, horrible sherry. "Are you an English major?" she asked.

"Yeah," he said. "Business minor." She watched him range his eyes around the room. Watchful, he was. Guarded. He had the gaunt look he'd had during the hunger strike. "How's Kit?" he asked, keeping his eyes alert to the room. "I wanted to come up; I wanted to call, but they told me not to." He laughed shortly. "They!"

"Kit's okay," said Rosalind. "I dropped him at Cynnie's to come here." (Break a leg! Kit had called to her when she set off on foot for the party, the angel.) "I also locked my car in her garage. People have taken to writing things on it." She laughed too. She felt a welcome camaraderie. "They!"

"What a hell of a thing for Kit," Luke said. He leaned his

shoulders back against the wall. Rosalind leaned against it too. They weren't looking at each other, she realized; they were looking at the room, nerve endings as attentive to the shiftings of groups as two anthropologists doing a study. "A hell of a thing for you." Luke inclined his head a little and asked, "What do they write on your car?"

"Whore," said Rosalind. "Not murderer. Not yet." Then she asked, keeping her eyes front, "How's your brother?" Sidelong she saw him lift his chin and rub his head on the wainscoting.

"I'm not supposed to talk about it," he said.

Rosalind pinched thumb and forefinger hard on the stem of her sherry glass, but it held. "When I was ten," she said with feigned evenness, looking straight ahead, "I was at camp, and one rainy day we were sitting in the bunk talking about sex, and one little girl wouldn't join in, and somebody said, 'What's the matter, Connie? Don't you know about it?' and Connie said, 'I know about it, but I'm not supposed to talk about it.' We were *ten*," she said, snapping her teeth together. "What do you mean, *you're not supposed to talk about it?*"

They eyed each other sideways for a minute, and then Luke's troubled face lightened. "Well, hell, Chase," he mildly came back, "I don't mind talking about *sex*."

"Damn your eyes, Luke," Rosalind said, and then bitterly she laughed. "Look at us, will you look at us? our backs against the wall, me afraid to cross the room, scared to look at the Chairman—"

"The Chairman thinks you're terrific," Luke said, and Rosalind was just about to say, Whatever do you mean? when Paul Damian came through the paneled door, turned right, and stopped like a garish piece of pop sculpture in front of them. He wore a bright plaid jacket, cut, as were all his jackets, rather like a zoot suit. Sarah, who'd had classes in Advanced Tailoring, made them for him, to Rosalind's erstwhile amusement. Sarah sewed the huge shoulder-pads in by hand, using an elaborate hemstitch that Rosalind had once scrutinized with interest in a motel room—ah! Paul looked from her to Luke, Luke to her; and his face went cherry-red and stayed that way, his feet seemed fixed in cement, the muscles of his jaw locked on the vertical.

"I—I—I—" he stuttered.

"Hi, Paul," Rosalind brightly tried, nodding her head in dismissal.

"Ah—ah—ah—" he stuttered. Rosalind and Luke looked at each other in consternation. Was he all right? Would he have a heart attack? A stroke? But he looked all right, just absolutely at a loss. Razzle-dazzle Damian, Rosalind thought, with a sad, internal grin.

"Paul," she assured him, "you don't have to talk to me. Paul, for God's sake." He really did look miserable, poor man, turned to stone. "I don't want to talk to you either," Rosalind reasoned with him. "There's no need to be chivalrous."

"Uh," he tried. "Uh." He tipped his head a little, as if he couldn't believe the sounds that were coming out of his mouth.

"Paul!" Rosalind said, exasperated. Still, she thought, the FBI and Sarah must have made a formidable team. He's brainwashed. More gently she urged, "Go and get some sherry. Just nod your head and move along to get some sherry. Go on." He didn't move. Rosalind found herself laughing a little, helplessly. Luke reached out his hand in front of her, and, like a stiff-armed puppet, Damian shook it.

"Um, Professor Damian," Luke deferentially began, "I'm

really into heroic couplets, and I was wondering—" Just then, from across the room near the sherry table, came a flash. Rosalind's eyes blacked, but the tableau was fixed, a lurid miniature on her eyelids. Eidetic imagery, she identified it. What a strange sensation! She saw a photograph of herself flanked by Paul and Luke, their arms stretched in front of her as if she were their captive in a children's game, their hands clasped on a level with—

"I'll kill the son of a bitch!"

The flash had loosed Paul Damian's tongue, but Luke would not release his hand. Hands down, they drew close, like Indian wrestlers. "Easy, sir," said Luke, his tone polite, unflappable.

"Why, you, you—" Damian broke off, tipping his chin at Luke like a defiant, street-smart, aging kid: Jimmy Cagney in *Angels with Dirty Faces*. "Punk!" He found the word. Do we all ape the movie heroes of our generation? Rosalind wondered, diverting herself from the unfortunate fact that the three of them were now the target of all eyes. Look at Luke. Cool Hand Luke. Really into heroic couplets! How'd he come up with that one? And now there was action around the sherry table.

"Look at the Chairman!" Luke said, his eyes lifted and alight. He let go of Damian's hand. The cynosure shifted. At the sherry table, deliberatively stroking his bristly mustache, the white-haired Chairman cast cold downward eyes on a pudgy young man who clutched a camera to his chest as if it were a threatened black kitten. Fast, the two of them started walking towards the door, and as they drew near her own spellbound trio Rosalind heard the photographer whine, "There's still such a thing as freedom of the press," and the Chairman retort, "Beat it, buddy"; and the cowed photographer, taking strides almost longer than his legs, achieved

the paneled door, and took off like a pusillanimous bat out
of hell down the hallway.

An instinct to disband, scatter, disperse—how had they
been so unlucky as to be caught together?—seemed to strike
Rosalind, Paul, and Luke all at once; Rosalind could sense
their quivered knees, their darting, quickened eyes; but then
the Chairman, a broad grin on his usually austere face,
joined them and recomposed the scene: a professor, a graduate assistant, a student, after all. "Rosalind." He smiled
warmly over at her. "Paul," he said easily, throwing an arm
over Damian's plaid shoulders, "good to see you! Hello,
Luke. How's the heroic couplet project coming on? Isn't it
refreshing," he asked Paul, "to encounter an undergraduate
with a knack for *style*?"

"Uh, yes!" Damian said, clearing his throat. His voice came
out too loud, but the Chairman squeezed his shoulders ap-
provingly. "Heroic couplets," Paul got out then.

"Now, what I really came over for," the Chairman went
on, "was to ask you two if I might borrow Rosalind for a bit.
There's someone who's most eager to meet her, and I prom-
ised I'd see what I could do," and all in one peremptory,
sweeping gesture, he released Paul's by now rather squashed
shoulders, took gentle hold of Rosalind's elbow, and, leaving
Luke and Paul to sort themselves out like mortal suitors
rejected for a god, steered her through the now aggressively
attentive assemblage as if they were quite alone. Rosalind felt
people draw back from their path, recede to nervous fingers
scribbling in a margin.

"I was most damnably sorry to hear about your misfor-
tune," the Chairman inclined his head to tell her. "If there's
anything I or my wife can do. . . ."

"Thank you," Rosalind said. Looking up at him, she felt
her smile tremble. The warmth of his and the pressure of

his hand on her elbow steadied it. He stopped their walking and looked down at her straight.

"I can't tell you how gratified, how proud, really, I am to see you here today. It's . . . heroic." His eyebrows mocked his hyperbole a little, but in the next breath he said, "I've been fighting like *hell* to keep you, and I'm relieved to know I can count on you for grace under pressure. *Sustained* grace under pressure. I can, can't I? You'll teach your classes, take your classes. For a toehold that's hard to dislodge, you'll get a start on your dissertation. Can you do that, after what you've been through?"

"I think so," said Rosalind, feeling her eyes widen at his cagey program for her survival. "I do want to stay."

"Good!" He started them walking again. "There's an old friend of mine I want you to meet," and as they approached the bright-eyed, tubby little man she had noticed before, the Chairman suddenly asked her, "Would you believe I was once a great fan of your father's? He was my impossible ideal—the man of action." The Chairman laughed a little, reminiscently. "Do you know what I'm thinking right now, Rosalind? I'm thinking I should have smashed that importunate little beast's camera." He shook his head ruefully. "My wife is always telling me I lack follow-through. Oh, I should have smashed the camera. What a moment that would have been!" He lifted his splendid head and laughed a fine and hearty laugh.

·   II

"Why didn't you smash the camera?" had been the tubby little man's first words. "I'd've smashed the camera!" "Oh, Malcolm, don't," the Chairman had painfully winced. "What

was the point of ejecting him, if you weren't going to smash
his camera? Oh," he had gone on, rubbing his hands
together longingly, "I have always wanted to smash a camera!" She'd been rather the belle of the ball, Rosalind decided now as, from the almost empty cloakroom, she
collected her coat, a new duffel coat, dark green and warm
and unobtrusive. Annabelle had thrown her sheepskin coat
in the trash. There had been vomit all over it, crusted, reek-
ing.

A scarlet pillow. A cereal bowl. A sheepskin coat.

Batting down images that surfaced, unbidden, like bones
from a flooded graveyard, Rosalind paused next to a pillar
on the portico to realign her thinking. Something nice, she'd
been thinking. "I say, hello, Rosalind!" Ah, yes, the belle of
the ball. Various senior faculty members, wistfully deferen-
tial, had wandered up and wandered away, but she'd been in
the constant company of the Chairman and his old friend,
an Englishman from Cambridge, who, it had gradually
emerged, was one of the top medievalists in the world. He'd
read her paper, *"Pæt Wundres Dæl,"* "with an attention positively lustful." He was excited about it.

Wafted a bit by his praise (and wasn't scholarship a
gorgeous refuge from the world?), Rosalind went lightly
down the lighted library steps and had reached the end of
the walk before she noticed it was dark. A kind of iron-gray
darkness, raw and chill. Well, after six and February, of
course it was dark, she told herself. Which way should she
take to Cynnie's? She paused where two roads met at a right
angle in front of the library. Her body felt her quandary;
her body also felt unnecessarily alert. She hadn't been out
alone on foot for some time, and she didn't like it much, not
in the dark. She could call Cynnie to come get her . . . oh,
no! Scare Kit, scare Cynnie, and anyhow she'd have to wait.

Rosalind looked down one road to the front gates. The horizontal, clawed branches of the oaks that lined its edges loomed blackly in the murky light; and then there'd be that long stretch of sidewalk along the brick wall of the campus where there were no buildings. The other road stopped at the back of the Administration Building, but from there she could cut across the baseball diamond and go through the parking lot of Lacedaemon Hall, which fronted on Cynnie's street where there were houses; cozy, lighted houses with smoke wisping out of chimneys on a night like this. Briskly clicking her restless heels, Rosalind started in the direction of the baseball diamond, which had really tipped her hand when it came down to it: sports a solace, like scholarship. The ivory tower and the broadcast booth. Her heart stupidly hammering, she guided her untidy thoughts back to "Malcolm" and his bright-eyed advice on "The Husband's Message." Could she properly handle the Christian allegory he had shown her, hidden in the poem, even hidden in her paper? She knew nothing of hermeneutics and Biblical exegesis, and yet slowly Malcolm had drawn the precious clue out of her. " 'The Husband's Message' is inscribed on a little piece of wood," he'd hinted. "A little piece of wood. Now, Rosalind, tell me, what else wooden, that is to say, made out of wood, might matter to this Anglo-Saxon girl who receives the message?" "Ships," Rosalind had said. The girl was to board a ship and sail to her bridegroom. "Um, sticks and crossbows. Tools. Huts." "What else?" Malcolm had prodded, giving it to her, generous, a true teacher. Rosalind had caught her breath—why was she reluctant to say it? "The rood," she finally said. "The cross."

He'd twinkled at her. "See," he said to the Chairman, "I thought she could say it." Like a schoolboy, he punched the Chairman's arm. "You Americans. You think you'll say any-

thing, face up to anything, but religion embarrasses the *hell*
out of you. Rosalind, don't let him turn you into an obdurate
realist like himself." "Obdurate realist!" the Chairman had
chuckled, as Malcolm went on to Rosalind, earnestly now:
"You have that little piece of wood so eloquent it seems to
speak; you have the bridegroom calling his bride to join him
in the native land across the rough sea waves, and you're
right into the Song of Songs and Christ calling to his
Church. You can't shirk it; it's there." He'd warmed to his
subject. "Allegory isn't old hat. We make up allegories all the
time; we allude; we perpetuate old stories. Look at people's
names. Look at your own name, Rosalind. A whole other
story flickers behind you. You came into the world not only
with your own beauty, but with Shakespeare's," and the
three of them had smiled shyly round at each other, and
then Malcolm had practically and persuasively wound up,
"At any rate, don't limit the scope of that immensely suggestive paper; promise me you'll follow it through."

Rosalind smiled into the darkness behind the Administration Building. Malcolm had a journal in mind for her re-
vised paper. He was ambitious for her. Mightn't she consider
doing a book on all the three Old English elegies? Nothing
definitive had been done yet, not even much good. She'd
asked, tentatively, about a dissertation, and the Chairman
had winked his approval. Why not? he and Malcolm had
concurred, nodding to each other, smiling. Your dissertation's already a third done. Weaving through the circular,
icebound commemorative gardens behind the Administration Building, Rosalind suddenly laughed out loud. A medi-
evalist? Her?

She visualized a life quiet and monastic, slow-measured
and stately as a tapestry. The ivory tower. Yeah, yeah. From
the stand of poplars that bordered the gardens, she ap-

proached the baseball diamond. It was deserted. (Well, of course it's deserted, it's February.) She went around the backstop, touched home plate for luck, then marched straight over the pitcher's mound. (Luke pitched, she remembered. Also woo. Oh, zeugmas were the devil to shake! That one was terrible.) Rosalind touched second base and veered into right field, which was separated from the parking lot of Lacedaemon Hall by a high hedge. Good thing it wasn't left field, she thought idly, or there might be a lot of broken car windows in the spring. Only that elite minority, left-handed hitters, to fear. Ben was left-handed. Ah! She stamped her feet. She put up the hood on her duffel coat to cover her head from the sky. Annabelle had thrown away her sheepskin coat. Annabelle had taken her own makeup kit and expeditiously, as if WHORE on a windshield in orange lipstick were a minor theatrical accident, expunged it.

"No, Roz," Will Eddy had told her with a tired little smile, "calling in women who wear orange lipstick will not speed the investigation." "It happened at the supermarket, Will. Who'd be following me to the supermarket?" "A crank, Roz." "Isn't it *poison pen*?" Then they'd both laughed, weary, giddy laughter. Will was having trouble with his superiors, Rosalind knew. Trouble over her. "Your boyfriend the cop," the FBI man called him. "Your boyfriend the professor." That was Paul Damian. Glad he'd graded my paper, Rosalind thought now, cold-bloodedly, before the FBI got to him. She imagined "The Zeugma from Chaucer to Jagger" in its khaki folder with the scrawled red grade:

Unwillingly Rosalind giggled. He'd given her an A+. Ah, poor brainwashed, stuttering Paul!

The high, prickly hedge that delineated right field and protected the adjacent world from baseballs confronted her. Rosalind eyed it uneasily. She felt a longing for the Village of Caliban's aged and mottled sidewalks just beyond Lacedaemon Hall, sidewalks with staid, nineteenth-century dates cut every few squares. She didn't want to go through the hedge. If she'd gone the other way, she'd already be on the sidewalk of Cynnie's street. It's not the briar-hedged Sleeping Beauty's castle, she reasoned with herself. It's Lacedaemon Hall. Luke lives there. Andy Grimshaw lives there. Fast, she slipped through a brambled opening and emerged in the parking lot. There were lights in the windows. She felt, suddenly, overlooked. Someone watching. Well, of course someone's watching, she argued with herself. People look out of windows. It's a *dorm*. People wait for people.

She hurried. She found a gleaming Porsche next to a battered old pickup truck, thought the word *zeugma,* and moved quickly between them, letting her coat brush the shiny Porsche rather than the rusty pickup. She found she was walking very fast, then running. Adrenaline was pumping; her heart and temples were pounding. In an extravagantly wide arc, she ran through the parking lot to the gate that led to the street. Without at all wanting to, she ran fast along the sidewalk towards Cynnie's house, ran as fast as she could, as if her body were a car with a jammed accelerator. Isn't it fun to run? an inane piece of her mind sang, while her jangled intellect thought, This is *fright*. Fright is something animal, a sense. What is an emotion, William James? Which comes first? Fright, the physical sensation, or fright, the emotion? The physical sensation; you were right.

Right about fright./Isn't it fun/to run? The silly song kept singing as Rosalind ran along the brick wall of the campus and grappled for whatever it was that had scared her so. She didn't know/what had scared her so. I feel *hunted,* her intellect intruded, hunted as Ben felt hunted, and now I can't bear the thought of how afraid he was; it's almost worse than him being dead.

Did it hurt? Kit asked. I ask, Were you scared? Oh, Ben, I am scared, and what I want now is . . . Kit.

The brick wall of the campus ended, and on her other side—so many sides! before, behind, between, above, below—she became conscious of the Square across the street where the Civil War cannon made a jagged silhouette against the lights of the town, and she started dodging around the immense old trees that jutted into the sidewalk, and she yearned for the pools of light the lampposts made, and when she got to the pools of light, she missed the darkness between them, and isn't it fun/to run?

The turn into Cynnie's house stopped her song and broke her rhythm. Rosalind stumbled on the stairs, bashing her knee, hurtled headlong across the round front porch, banged her shoulder against the recalcitrant door, and catapulted through, straight into Walter Pettinger, who had his hand on the doorknob. "Roz!" he said. He put his arms around her and with one hand cradled her head, while he patted her back with the other as if she were a baby. Her breathing seemed to rasp the quiet air of Cynnie's house. Rosalind rubbed her face against Walter's sweater, and her eyes took refuge in the misty, nubby texture of the yellow Shetland wool. After a minute, Walter moved his hands to her shoulders and pushed her back to look at her.

"Lady," he said, "you look like you just made an eighty-yard run. Let's get this coat off you and sit you down by the fire."

Sit you down, Father/rest you, her mind resumed its antics on a higher plane, as Walter, patiently, doing all the work,

unbuttoned her duffel coat and removed it, arm by painstaking arm. "Hey, that's nice," he said, flicking the fringe on
her suede jerkin. As air began to circulate around her over-
heated body, Rosalind shivered. "Kit," she said. "Where's
Kit?"

"Kit's fine," Walter said. Surreptitiously, he was glancing
out the front door and windows, eyes hooded, un-
fathomable. "Kit's washing greens in the kitchen with Cynnie. That's a tough and tender little guy, Roz. Let us not
alarm him." Walter was locking the door, bolting it, putting
the chain lock on. That chain lock is new, Rosalind abruptly
thought. Cynnie never had a chain lock. Cynnie never even
locked the door. I've made this village into Morningside
Heights. "Kit took over the greens for *me*," Walter went on.
"That's good looking out. My hands were turning green."
He waved his big, long-fingered hands in the air, a wide-
receiver's hands held with the visible memory of the shape
of a football. Rosalind admired the shaded colors, the lighter
palms limned in the crevices so that even from a distance she
could see he had an enviable lifeline: a survivor. Walter
prowled about a moment, and then he turned and asked, all
business now, "What happened, Roz?"

"Oh, Walter, I feel such a fool. Nothing happened. Just all
of a sudden I had this sense of being, well, menaced. . . ."
Oh, she didn't like the melodrama of the word *menaced*! And
she didn't like how taut and military Walter's body had gone.
"It was totally irrational," she asserted then, flopping her
hands sideways in a flamboyant shrug. She sat down on the
crewelwork love seat near the fireplace and busied herself
removing her boots. She frowned at her right knee, which
had a swollen, livid look.

"Menaced," Walter repeated. "Watched, followed, threatened, hunted." He seemed to pull each word down from the

ceiling. "That right?" Reluctantly Rosalind nodded and looked at her lap. Her fingers fiddled with the embroidery on the arm of the love seat. She kicked her boots away. "Roz, I grew up on the streets," Walter said. He pulled his breath in through his teeth and lifted his chin. "That is a feeling I know, and I also know that when you feel it, there is highly likely something to it."

"Ah, not these streets, Walter," Rosalind demurred, and her hand waved the subject away, like a Frisbee. Who did it? Who killed Ben? Certainly nobody *here*. "Hey, Walter," she said then, with a smile that started as a diversionary tactic and turned to a smile of pleasure as she realized what was wrong with this picture. Walter lived in Philadelphia. "You came back. I didn't know you were coming back."

Walter abandoned his wary stance and put his hands in the back pockets of his trousers, let go one light laugh, shook his head, and treated her to a baffled, quirky grin. "I never left," he said. "That crazy little white chick in the kitchen has been working some kind of witchcraft on me." And he laughed with delight.

Rosalind laughed out too. "You're kidding!" she said. She sat eagerly forward.

Walter laughed softly, just the edge of the sound catching the air, an echo of laughter. "I wish I was," he said. "Never thought this would happen to me. Never got caught once. I'm thirty-two years old, and I'm head over heels like a kid over a flat-ass white girl who's even got blue eyes. Blue eyes!"

Lightly he moved around, laughing to himself, and Rosalind laughed with him, light, throaty laughter. The pleasure on his face was wide open and irrepressible—oh, he was in love, all right! How like Cynnie to pull off such an unexpected, dramatic shotgun of a play—what a quarterback she'd have made! Cynnie, who disdained football. . . .

Jolting as the juxtaposition had struck her at first (white/black/Riemann Sphere/Gridiron), the more Rosalind turned it around, Grecian-urn style, the more she liked it. Cynnie Talleyrand and Walter Pettinger. It even scanned. It was as neat and startling and complete as a heroic couplet, yes, pun intended, Rosalind thought emphatically to herself—oh, there'd be problems! Heroic problems. But watching Walter's wonderful grin as he moved, his litheness that somehow scaled him to Cynnie's living room, his yellow sweater that harmonized with the spindly rockers, Rosalind could only think: perfect. This juxtaposition, this connection, was somehow as perfect, in its own offbeat way, as Barney's and Annabelle's similarly incongruent (but uncannily durable) connection was perfect. . . .

"I never realized before," Rosalind started to tell Walter, "that Cynnie is exactly like my mother—"

"Roz!" Like a flashbulb, the lights came on in the dining room, and Cynnie stood dramatically backlit in the doorway. She wore a soft mauve dress with little puffed sleeves and a low, square neckline; her hands were fists on her hips; her gray-blue eyes were scandalized and blazing. "Exactly like *Annabelle?*" As Cynnie headed like an arrow for Rosalind on the love seat, Walter, laughing, backed off, got out of her way, and sat down hard on one of the yellow-painted rockers. Like a flamenco dancer, Cynnie whirled round and pointed an imperious finger at him.

"What do you mean, flat-ass?" she demanded.

From behind, fascinated, Rosalind watched Cynnie pat her derriere complacently; and then Cynnie laughed a wicked laugh, and under the gathered mauve skirt her flanks shifted hard as she did a wildly suggestive bump and grind for Walter. Delighted, Walter laughed too. He rocked his chair. All of a sudden, Rosalind wanted to cry. She

wrapped her arms around her body and huddled close to
the soft arm of the love seat and tried to compose her face as
Cynnie sashayed over to her. "Hey, Roz, I like that," Cynnie
said. With covetous fingers she felt the suede of Rosalind's
jerkin. "Yum, luscious. Now, take it back," she went on,
fingers pinched on the suede.

"Take what back?" Diverted from tears, Rosalind pre-
pared to defend her jerkin.

"I'm not like Annabelle. Say it. Roz, I know she's your
mother, but I thoroughly *loathe* Annabelle." Cynnie rolled
her eyes ceilingward, comically affronted.

"All right, you're not like Annabelle," Rosalind agreed.
"You're a mathematician."

"Right!" Cynnie said, mollified. She unclamped her
fingers. Rosalind sat back, wondering why that had been eas-
ier than she'd expected. Cynnie was usually more tenacious;
but now Cynnie was looking at Walter. "D'you know what
Walter's knee looks like, Roz?" Cynnie asked in eloquent non
sequitur. "I mean, the one he's had seven operations on. It
looks like a piecrust. I love it; I love his bad knee." Her voice
was delicate as frost.

"A piecrust?" Walter gave her a quizzical look. Cynnie ignored him.

"I love him. I'm in love, Roz. I'm going to tell all my
students. I'm going to write it on the blackboard tomorrow
with DON'T ERASE at the top—" Rosalind started to laugh,
and then Cynnie laughed, the sound like a vibraphone, and
Walter reached out fast and pulled her into his lap in the
rocking chair.

"You crazy, crazy white lady." Softly Walter rubbed a fist
down Cynnie's cheek and neck and, resting his forearm on
her breast, caught his fingers on her collarbone, ran his
thumb round her upper arm, chestnut-brown against the

soft cream of her. His other hand was down, underneath
her, hidden by her skirt. License my roving hands and bid
them go/Before, behind, between, above, below, Rosalind
thought, and sighed. She tucked a foot under her on the
love seat and shamelessly watched them kiss, a slow, hot kiss,
and the chair rocked, and Cynnie moved one searching
hand to Walter's hair, and Walter's shoulder shifted and his
hidden hand seemed to rock the chair, and Rosalind had
never seen Cynnie's body, never seen any woman's body, so
pliant, so yielding. Lingeringly, after what seemed an unconscionable time, they stopped kissing and glanced over at
Rosalind in vague apology, and Cynnie's face was open, vulnerable, soft; she looked . . . melted down. Walter's eyes
were sleepy-warm. "Oh, sugar," he said, tipping his head
back against the yellow-painted rocker.

Perhaps I'll become a voyeur, Rosalind wistfully contemplated, feeling her breath a trifle ragged, feeling also the
quite indecent way she was sitting on her foot, and, yes, all
that . . . quickening was still there; and then she thought of
scrabbling fingernails and WHORE on a windshield and
Muffy's cold sore—oh, God! There's love, she thought
fiercely, and so bloody what? She wrested her errant foot
from underneath her and, having to flounce about a bit, arranged her body in a decorous dancing-school posture. She
decided to join poor Kit in the skullery, washing greens,
whatever greens were.

"Hey, wow," Cynnie just glimmered, reluctantly extricat-
ing herself from Walter's lap and the rocking chair.

"Sugar, not so fast," Walter, groaning a little, reproached
her. He crossed his legs and folded his arms on his knee.
Was that the knee like a piecrust? Rosalind aimlessly wondered. Walter rocked the chair fast.

"Kit must have finished with the spinach," Cynnie said

mistily. "He washes it so carefully, Roz. Oh, wow, there's lots of spinach. I'm weaning Walter from steak, Roz. Did you know they eat it for breakfast in training camp? Isn't that the most barbaric thing you've ever heard?" and just then Kit came in, drying his hands on a towel.

"Hi, Mom," he said, all golden hair and blue denim. "How was the sherry party? I've been washing spinach. We don't have to *eat* here, do we? Cynnie," he said then, plaintively, "will you look at this? My hands are turning the towel *green*."

Super Bowl Sunday

January 15, 1978

8:00 P.M.

Fearing she'd miss the second-half kickoff, Rosalind left Cynnie in the dining room at the "aristocratic" end of the table, meticulously and beautifully Greek-lettering the names of the dinner guests on index cards. Cynnie had taken a year of Greek in college just to learn the calligraphy, Rosalind recollected, amused. "No, Roz, I didn't learn any Greek," Cynnie had patiently explained. "Who wants to know Greek?" Now Cynnie wrote letters to friends in *italiano bastarde*. She was justly famous for the exquisite equations she chalked on the blackboards of her classrooms (and left for others to erase); her personal style at the blackboard was also much admired. Once Rosalind had come to pick her up after class, and a student was standing in the hallway looking through Cynnie's door. "I come fifteen minutes early every Monday, Wednesday, and Friday just to watch her," he dreamily told Rosalind, and together they'd watched Cynnie sway to the rhythms of binomial theorem and the chalk, deliver her undulating, over-the-shoulder lecture with breathy suspense. "She believes in imaginary numbers," the student had remarked confidentially, his eyes on Cynnie. "She's very convincing about them too."

Flo Grimshaw was mashing anchovies in the kitchen. Rosalind took one look at them, pinky-gray and hairy on the cutting board—how could pregnant Flo stand it?—caught sight of the whisked raw egg also destined for the Caesar salad, summarily abandoned all hope of the second-half kickoff, and repaired in haste to her bathroom upstairs. Quickly she genuflected by the toilet, easily she vomited, flushed without looking, and instantly felt better. She even felt hungry. Sarah's *bourguignon* steamed in her imagination, rich and winy. Solid food. What had she vomited? A Bloody Mary? Surely that had been metabolized hours ago. Rosalind drank a glass of water and brushed her teeth. She ran hot water to wash her face. Like assorted imps of the perverse, Ben's Lucky Charms floated to mind, pastel confections kept intact through stomach acid, miraculously spared by the bullet that had shattered the rest of what was important in his body— Lucky Charms. They won't save your life, but they'll sure as hell survive you.

"Mom?"

Rosalind, her face buried in a washcloth, jumped. Kit materialized in the bathroom doorway. Stripling-tall and tentative, he leaned one shoulder against what Andy called the jamb, cocked his head at her, and asked, "You all right?"

"Oh, I'm fine," Rosalind assured him. "What's up?"

He assumed his favorite tough-guy mask. "Y'know my buddy in Arkansas?"

"Yeah, yeah," she said, like a moll. "So, what's up?"

"You have to marry him."

"And why's that, buster?"

"He's pregnant." She got laughing. Kit stood in the doorway watching her, having more to say, but not knowing how to say it; she would have to give him the chance.

"How's the game?" she asked. "I missed the kickoff."

"Worst game I ever saw." Kit came into the bathroom and

rested his backside against the terra-cotta counter. "Wiess is in. They took Morton out, thank God." He picked up a hand mirror from the counter and held it aloft, located the back of his head in the big mirror and looked at it. "Morton was quarterback then, y'know? But for Dallas. Isn't it weird?"

Rosalind resisted an impulse to play dumb and ask, "Then?" She knew when. "Things recur," she said, hanging up her washcloth in a painstaking, exemplary manner. "You think they go away, but they come back in different shapes. Like Andy's wooden 'allegories.'" She leaned back against the counter with Kit, the tile cool through her skirt, and thought about Andy's bosky woodland scene that reversed to menacing shapes, a crumbling temple, a hunter with a bloody gun. Grimly, she conjured up another two-sided jig-saw puzzle: a bright-green football field, Super Bowl XII on the verso of V, Craig Morton here, Craig Morton there, but see how the uniform has changed. The bloodstains, ladies and gentlemen, are superimposed. . . .

"That crazy puzzle!" Kit said. "It is just too *hard*. It's more like a punishment than a Christmas present. Like coal in your stocking," he said with a little laugh. "Daisy and Joe are scared of the bad side." Kit flashed the hand mirror in front of Rosalind's face. "Will can put the puzzle together really fast, have you noticed? I told him I think he practices late at night." Kit put the mirror down. He reached over and gave the trunk of the Dizygotheca elegantissima a shake. It whirred like a baby rattler. Or a baby's rattle, Rosalind's mind played for time. "I'm always surprised that plant is real," Kit said. Then he said, "Mom, for us the bad side of the puzzle came first, didn't it?"

"What do you mean?"

"Oh," he said, "you know. Death, destruction . . ."

"Oh," she said. "Oh, them." We'd better clear out these abstractions, she decided, these Tolkienesque shapes and mushroom-shaped clouds. "You mean your father."

She turned her head sideways to look at him. His head was turned sideways to look at her. He nodded.

"Do you think about him much?"

"I *try* to," said Kit. "He gets away, but it seems it should be important. Who did it, Mom? Doesn't that drive you nuts?"

"It used to," she said, honestly. "I couldn't believe it when the FBI dropped the investigation." Lightly Rosalind touched his knee. One of her fancy, embroidered patches was on it, a butterfly. "Do you remember him, Kit? Can you see him?" You're getting to look like him, she didn't say.

"Not see," Kit said, tipping his head. "Hear. I can hear him laugh. I can sort of feel him, but I feel him as if I'm little, you know? Picking me up. Sitting on his shoulders."

"You were always on his shoulders," Rosalind said. She laughed. She tried to see Ben. All she could come up with was the bearded and laughing photograph the FBI had used on its Wanted poster. The revolutionary outlaw. Foolishly, she'd wanted a poster, but hadn't known how to go about getting one. Oh, he'd looked beautiful—so romantic and so out of reach! "Do you remember Spain?" she asked Kit, trying to find a good memory for him. "That was the last time the three of us were really together."

Kit's eyes ranged around the bathroom, looking for Spain. For olive trees and crucifixes. "No," he said. He pushed himself up to sit on the counter, let his shoulders slump, and examined his hands. He flexed his fingers. "The last time I saw him," he said slowly, "I thought he was a soldier." Kit's voice was deep, but its rhythms had gone childlike. "We were at Cynnie's and he had a beard and I didn't recognize him. I was scared. I came down for breakfast and he was there and

I was scared. 'I have to go to school now,' I said. 'It's time for me to go to school.' "

Rosalind caught her breath. Oh, no, he feels bad about that, she thought, looking at his face. The "flying visit." The "Dearest Ché" letter from the quilt had already brought back that unfortunate . . . family reunion, part of it, and here was Scene Two lurking in the wings. There'd been the blue books and "The Wreck of the Deutschland" and the fitful night, and then Ben had been up at dawn making cryptic long-distance phone calls, and Cynnie had come down dressed for school, had said something about the phone calls, and Ben had called her—Rosalind winced, remembering—"a capitalist cunt." Had Kit been downstairs yet? She wasn't sure.

Oh, Ben had been awful! She'd had an exam in Victorian Poetry. "Let Kit stay here with me," Ben had caviled, already angry she wouldn't cut her exam. "Since when this attachment to bourgeois education, Roz?" Rosalind hadn't wanted to leave Kit with him, wouldn't have put it past him to stash Kit in his Land-Rover and take him away with him. Ben was bearded, dirty, wearing army-surplus, and stridently en route to a "War Council"; his new-militant language had ranged without warning from the messianic to the profane: Jesus routing the motherfuckers out of the temple. God, he'd scared *her*. She looked at Kit now, safe in her bathroom, and she could see the wary, frightened seven-year-old through his dark-lashed, troubled eyes. "I made you go to school," Rosalind told him. "I even took you. We didn't know he was going to leave." When she'd gotten back from her exam three hours later, Ben had gone. She'd been furious—with Ben, with herself, with the Victorian poets. Especially Gerard Manley Hopkins.

"But I wanted to go to school. You knew that," Kit said. "I

didn't want to stay with him." Then he said, "You married Will awfully soon." His tone was noncommittal, but she caught her breath. *Et tu,* Telemachus? His golden head was turned. Ben's profile, she noted involuntarily.

"It depends on how you look at it," Rosalind began, with difficulty controlling her breathing. "Soon after your father died, but not soon after he left . . . me." *Us,* she'd started to say, but it still seemed unfair thus to attack Ben and unsettle Kit. "Will and I almost didn't get together at all, did you know that?" She bit her lip, raised a hand to erase those evasive words from the air, as from a blackboard. Cravenly she was trying to divert Kit from the subject, and she shouldn't. "Kit, why did you say that? About my marrying Will soon? Did somebody say something to you?"

"No," Kit said. "Who would say something? Hey, Mom, come on. We've got company. We'd better get downstairs." He slid off the counter and started for the bathroom door. Rosalind followed. Had she scared him off? Had it gotten too heavy? In the bedroom, near the three shallow stairs that led to the hall, she caught his arm.

"Really?"

"Really, Mom. I guess I'm just realizing for the first time how fast everything moved back then. It makes my head spin. There was us—you and me—and then, in a flash, there was Will and Joe and Daisy, and it was as if the other time, the time before you and me, had never happened." He smiled at her, an angel's smile, a smile like Will's. "You, um, smoothed my transitions for me, Mom."

She smiled back. He had a lovely vocabulary. "Are you sorry?"

"I love Will," Kit said. "He's a great father, but—"

"But he's not *your* father?"

"No, no, that's not it. It's that I feel he really *is,* that Will

really is my father, and I'm not sure I should." Kit's eyes
confronted her straight. "Did he love me?"

"Will loves you very much."

"Not Will!" Exasperated, Kit sat down on the top step. He
put his elbows on his knees, his face in his hands, and looked
at her over his fingers.

"Ben?"

"Yeah, um, Dad. Did I call him Dad?"

"You called him Dad. Maybe Daddy. You were pretty
young."

"I didn't call him Ben? You know, like you call Barney.
Did I, Roz?" he queried with a quick grin.

She grinned back. "No, sonny boy." She reached out both
hands to pull him to his feet. "We didn't want that. Too
show-biz, you know."

"We," Kit extrapolated. "You and him?"

"Well, yes."

"Did he love me, Mom?"

Rosalind took a deep breath. "The last time he came to
the cottage, right before he was killed . . ." Kit was watching
her face carefully; no lying now, and no mistakes. ". . . he
said, 'Where's Kit? I have to see Kit,' and when I told him
you weren't there, he was disappointed, his spirits collapsed,
sort of, and things didn't matter after that." Tears hung in
Kit's eyes. Rosalind put her hands on his shoulders, and for
a second he seemed too big to hug, too like a man, masculine; but then she thought, screw you, Oedipus, and pulled
him close. He snuffled into her hair, and when he stopped,
"Ah, babe," she said, "why haven't we talked about this before?"

Kit pulled back and put his hands on *her* shoulders. His
eyes were pure and lucid as Daisy's after a tantrum. "Honestly, Mom," he said, letting his amazingly resilient grin sur-

face, "I've just started to really think about it." He cocked his
head and listened. "Sorry, split infinitive," he apologized.
Rosalind shook her head in wonder. "You know," Kit went
on, "my friend Caleb's adopted, and a couple of the others
have stepfathers, but nobody has a real mystery like I do.
I'm going to be asking you more. Will you mind?"

"Of course not." Slowly they moved through the bedroom door into the hall.

"You know what I wonder most?" Kit was going on. "Who
did it, that's what I wonder most. If we knew that, we could
put him into perspective, you and me. We could put him—
Ben, Dad, Ben Roth—back together again. Now if we try to
look back, at the past, it won't hold still." He resorted to her
analogy. "It's like a jigsaw puzzle that isn't put together."

"Whee," Rosalind said. "What have you been reading?"

"*Moby Dick*," he said. "Salinger's *Nine Stories*." Then he
frowned quizzically, one arched eyebrow raised. "Why?"

"I was kidding," she said, reaching to brush an errant
golden strand from his forehead. "You're just getting so
smart, that's all." She laughed. "Smart-ass too, Walter says."

Kit gave her backside a little slap. "Flat-ass," he said.
"That's what Walter says all you white girls are." Then he
gave her one of Ben's wicked, lopsided grins. Ah, Ben, she
thought, you'd love him.

"Wise-ass," she said to Kit. They got to the top of the
spiral stairs.

"After you," he said.

"After you," she said. They bowed to each other. Kit went
first. At the first turning he asked her: "Do you remember
the ship's ladder at Mud Lake?"

"Of course I remember the ship's ladder at Mud Lake."

"Did we go on a ship to Spain?"

"Yes, we did." Rosalind smiled. It had been a student ship,
full of bright Fulbright scholars. A wonderful ship.

"I think I might be able to remember Spain," Kit said. "I'll work on it. Thanks, Mom." He ducked around the Ficus benjamina and clambered up the stairs to the kitchen. "What's the score?" she heard him shout.

[Peter Wimsey] renewed his offer of marriage on an average once
in three months, but in such a way as to afford no excuse for any
outbreak of temperament on either side. One First of April, the
question had arrived from Paris in a single Latin sentence, starting
off dispiritedly. *"Num. . . . ?"*—a particle which notoriously "ex-
pects the answer No." Harriet, rummaging the Grammar book for
"polite negatives," replied, still more briefly, *"Benigne."*

Dorothy L. Sayers, *Gaudy Night*

"What do you *mean* they've dropped the investigation? Who
did it?" Rosalind, exasperated, asked Will Eddy. They sat,
the two of them, at the picnic table behind the Mud Lake
cottage, drinking Heineken from frosty green bottles. It was
a freak warm afternoon in late February, and the rich
fungoid odor of thawing earth filled the air, sweet and
pungent. Rosalind had been grading papers—they were
spread out all over the picnic table; she had red ink on her
hands and in her hair. Her class enrollments for the spring
semester were staggering, the rewards and the punishments
of a lurid publicity. One class—her Shakespeare class—had
eighty-five students, and they'd had to move her to a lecture
hall. Hard work, but perhaps worth it. The department just
might keep her on if her usefulness could keep pace with

her notoriety. Thank God for *"Pæt Wundres Dæl,"* Rosalind
often thought, and thank God for Malcolm's enthusiastic en-
dorsement. The Chairman had been marvelous on her be-
half, had gone to the President to keep her. "Who's the
murderer?" Rosalind asked Will Eddy again, looking at him
through the green Heineken bottle.

He shrugged—broad, bony shoulders in a dark-green
loden coat. "They don't know. 'Person or persons unknown.'
It's my impression, from scuttlebutt I've picked up here and
there, that the FBI does not want any more of its secrets
dredged up. It's probably because of the DiLorenzos."

"Maybe they did it," Rosalind said. "Well, not Luke, but
what about his awful big brother? Where was *he,* at the crack
of dawn on New Year's Day?"

"That won't wash, Roz, much as I'd like it to. Matthew
DiLorenzo was on his honeymoon. From Saturday, December twenty-sixth to Thursday, December thirty-first, he
and his bride, Teresa, were at a posh motel overlooking
Niagara Falls; and on January first on a plane to Rome. It's
all documented, bureaucratic black-and-white."

"Niagara Falls?" Rosalind stared, then started to laugh.
"He married the richest girl in Buffalo and he took her to a
motel in Niagara Falls?"

"Five days in Niagara Falls and then two weeks in Rome.
A traditionalist. God, I've grown to hate the FBI." Will
frowned and looked around him. Mud Lake was finally
muddy, Rosalind noticed. Green slime decorated the shore-
line. "When are you going to get out of here?" Will asked. "I
don't like your being here."

"Tsk," she said. "*I* do."

"Why don't you move back in with Cynnie Talleyrand?"

"I was going to," Rosalind said, "but Cynnie's getting married. Hey, did you know? She's marrying Walter Pettinger."

"The Philadelphia Eagle?"

"The former Philadelphia Eagle. He's giving it up. My father's having a fit. He feels responsible." She laughed, thinking of Barney's comic outrage at the impending nuptials. "Walter's black," she added, wondering if she'd get a reaction out of Will Eddy. She didn't.

"I know," is all he said. "I *do* follow football, Roz." He frowned again and looked around. "I still think you ought to get out of here. I feel watched, just sitting here. Don't you?"

"No," she said. "Well," she added, being honest, "sometimes at night— Oh, I can't. It's complicated, and it's stupid, but I almost have to stay here. First there's Maisie Ritter—"

"Maisie Ritter? Marsh's wife?"

"Yes. She's a former student of mine, and she's the one who rented me the cottage. When all the publicity broke, Marshall—that's what Maisie calls him, Marshall—wanted to put me out of here, and Maisie, bless her heart, threatened to leave him if he did. Marshall capitulated. How can I possibly undercut Maisie's first heroic stand? And then there's the Roths. I do not want to appear to them to be running scared." Rosalind swigged some beer.

"The Roths? You mean Ben's parents? I thought they'd disowned him."

"Yeah. Well, now they've surfaced and are asserting belated 'ownership' right and left." She bit her lip. "First they wanted Ben's body, and now they want Kit." Saying it aloud frightened Rosalind. She'd managed to keep a lid on panic by not talking about the threat to Kit, but now her voice came out shaky and scared her.

"Start at the beginning," Will said. He put his hand on hers on the picnic table. "What happened?"

Rosalind took a deep breath. "Soon after the inquest I got a letter from the Roths' lawyer. They'd heard—read—I don't know, that I was going to have Ben's 'remains' cremated." She winced. "It seemed the cleanest, most decent thing to do. I mean, he'd been shot; he'd been gotten at by animals; he'd been cut up by pathologists—well, it's what I'd want someone to do for me. But the Roths said it was 'against their son's religion.' " Rosalind laughed wildly and incredulously. "Ben's religion! And they asked for custody of the body so they could give him a decent burial somewhere way out on Long Island. Long Island!"

"I hope you got a lawyer," Will said.

"No, no, I didn't." Rosalind frowned. "I didn't think of that. I wrote a letter to their lawyer," she went on, "and I said I was sorry, I hadn't realized I was violating any religious code, and that I'd bury him, but I'd bury him here, in Caliban, because that's where I live and Kit lives, and if the Roths want to visit Ben's grave, it's only three hours from New York, and nobody's stopping them. It's not much farther than Long Island."

"Okay, so what happened?" Will had let go of her hand. He was looking worried.

"I got another letter. The lawyer said all right about Ben's body, but that now the Roths were considering suing for custody of Kit, their grandson—"

"They got that idea from *your* letter. Damn it, Roz! On what grounds?"

"He didn't say."

"Roz, you need a lawyer."

"A lawyer? Oh, Will, that seems so drastic. So . . . grown-up. So *serious*."

"Roz, it's custody of your son. That's a serious, grown-up matter."

"You mean you think they could really get him?"

"I have no idea."

"I was worrying—"

"About what? Come on, Roz."

"Oh, grounds—as you call them. Could they, say, allege that I'm . . . promiscuous or something? Did you see that awful tabloid article about Paul Damian and Luke? Oh, he should have smashed the camera, the Chairman. Shake hands and come out 'swinging,' the caption said."

"No, I guess I missed that one." He gave her a wry smile.

"I come out looking like an Iris Murdoch character." She bit her lip. "Could they take Kit away on that kind of grounds? I mean, in addition to the silly little blot on my escutcheon of being a possible murderess." She laughed bitterly. "Could they say that I'm promiscuous?"

"I don't know. How many men have you slept with?" he flippantly asked, lifting his beer bottle.

"In my life?"

"All right—your life." He toasted.

"Three."

"Three?" He choked on his beer.

"Yes. Ben, Paul Damian, and Luke. What is so funny about that?" He was laughing his fool red head off, Will Eddy. He buried his head in his arms and laughed helplessly, spilling beer out of the green bottle. Miffed, Rosalind started gathering up the threatened student papers. Will sat up, gradually controlling his laughter into small, sporadic explosions. Rosalind stood and looked at him haughtily. "I'm going to take these papers inside," she said.

"Bring me the letter, would you?"

"What letter?"

"The letter from the Roths' lawyer about Kit. I'll take it to a lawyer I know."

"Oh, would you? Oh, thanks!"

Rosalind returned with the lawyer's letter and an odd, tickling sensation in her brain. A bee in her bonnet, a hunch that seemed wafted on the earth-smell of the air. She handed Will the letter. He read it through and stashed it in a pocket of his loden coat.

"Will," she said tentatively.

"What?"

"Let's go up there."

"Where?"

"You know."

"Oh, no. Not me."

"*I'm* going. The snow's finally melted. Who knows what we might find?"

"Yeah, who knows?" he glumly echoed.

"I'm going," Rosalind said. She started for the Firebird. His khaki-colored Thunderbird was next to it. She could hear him walking along behind her. She got into the driver's seat of the Firebird. Will got in next to her. She drove along the lake road to where the dirt road veered off. It was muddy but the Firebird made it. Rosalind pulled up next to the ruins of Calypso. They got out and, without speaking, walked into the marble circle.

It was as hushed as an ancient Roman ruin. The magic had survived the winter tragedy. Rosalind looked up at Will's half-averted face, his red-gold, flaming hair against the tall evergreens, and it could have been November again when they were new to each other; and she laughed suddenly, a light, rather tipsy laugh. She put her hand up and touched Will's face with one tentative finger. The tip of her finger felt alive. We've never touched, Rosalind realized; not on purpose. With her finger, slowly, she traced the arch of his cheekbone and the honed hollow beneath. She touched her knuckles to his jawbone as if she'd just punched him, then felt the muscle at the corner of his mouth move as he smiled. He rubbed his jaw against her fingers and lifted his own hand to run his finger lightly across her lips, just touching the wet inside, parting them, then moved his hand round her ear to the back of her head. Rosalind leaned her head back to feel the weight of his hand. She could hear her hair whisper in her ears as he stroked it. "Your hair's getting longer," Will said. "Soft. Beautiful." His voice was husky.

Rosalind looked full into his gray eyes. The greens around and the flecks of sunlight gave them facets, like jewels. His eyes seemed to open her eyes wider; she kept looking; she wanted . . . more. She slid her hand down his neck and maneuvered it under the rough collar of his loden coat and the crisp collar of his shirt to the juncture of neck and shoulder where there was, oh, God, bare skin, incredibly smooth, soft, warm. A pulse beat there. Rosalind caught her breath and saw Will catch his breath. As her roving hand explored the mysterious intricacy of his shoulder, she felt his hand move down the back of her neck, under her hair, under her sweater, his fingers adjusting to her backbone as to a musical instrument. She ran her own fingers lightly along his collarbone back to the declivity where the points met under his throat and sighed at the elegance of the joining. Bones. She was aware of bone under flesh under skin, aware of structure—the structure of him and the structure of her. The desire she felt was bone-deep.

She couldn't wait. The measured, erotic choreography of their questing fingers suddenly maddened her. Her ears drumming, she seized his wrist with both her hands and, as if to wrestle him down with her on the pine-needle floor, moved to the side, her knees tensed and bent. Will stood his ground as she pulled at him. He was laughing. "Don't rush," he said, and from the encircling, encroaching pines, a shot cut the air like a knife, an arrow.

"Oh, God!"

Will's hand was on his shoulder where her hand had been. Blood was on his hand. The wool of his loden coat was burned away in a wide arc. He lifted his hand and Rosalind could see into his shoulder. She had a glimpse of white bone before the blood welled in. How extraordinarily intimate, she thought for one wild moment, and then she started to scream. Not Will, her mind implored; not Will too.

"Don't scream," Will said. "Don't scare . . . whatever." He rocked a little but stayed upright. "The thing. The thing is, we get out of here fast," and the urgency of his dim voice focused her panic, and Rosalind took him by his good arm and wrapped it around her shoulders and felt his lean body close and tried to hold him up as he had held her up—was it just last month?—for the same walk. From the shock and the sudden draining of desire, her own legs were none too steady, but they held, they moved, and she got him to the car. Gingerly she helped him into the bucket seat of the Firebird, arranged his legs for him, as he couldn't get the second one in, and then leaned to look at his tilted face. Blood dark as wine was already staining the shoulder of his loden coat. He looked awfully, awfully pale. "Thanks," he said. "You're beautiful, Roz."

"So are you," she said and touched his cheek and made haste for the driver's seat. Not Will, she thought. Not Will. Spinning wheels on mud, she got the Firebird turned around, and they jolted hesitantly along the shifting, oozing ruts towards the main road. Her snow tires bit the mud; mud stippled the windows. The lake was fleetingly visible, sparkling but opaque. Mud-dark lake, Rosalind's mind chanted; wine-dark lake. Not Will. Not Will.

The windshield wipers smeared and finally cleared the green-brown mud, and with relief Rosalind picked up speed on the winding, bouncing road to town. After a few minutes,

Will said, "You'll get a ticket, sure as shootin', Nancy Drew."
His voice was light and lilting. Startled, she looked over at
him.

"Watch the road," he groaned.

"You're in shock," she said. He laughed.

"I'm in shock from your driving. Slow down!" He laughed
again.

"It's all my fault," Rosalind said. "I'm a jinx. I think I
knew someone was there. I almost smelled it." Will got
laughing, a kind of groaning laugh.

"Will, I am terribly *sorry*—"

"Save your apologies. Save them for the cop who's going
to give you a ticket."

Rosalind glowered at him. He couldn't be very badly hurt
to be talking so flippantly. She concentrated on her driving,
took dangerous tight corners, passed all other vehicles on
principle, kept the speedometer at a steady, hurtling
seventy-five, till finally, at the emergency entrance to Caliban
Hospital, she stopped the Firebird with a great, dramatic
screech. She fumbled with her door, got out, ran round the
car to his door, flung it open, and looked in at the wounded
side of Will. Oh, God. His face was very white, and he was
lounged back against the camel-colored bucket seat, smiling
lazily at her. His gray eyes had an incandescent gleam. She
could see the blood soaking through his loden coat.

"Will," she said, alarmed, "can you walk?" She looked behind her, to the Emergency Room door. The walk was awfully long, and there was a step at the door. "I'll have them
bring a stretcher," she decided, her body tensed to run.

"No stretcher!" Will held up his hand. "Just a minute." He
rolled his head against the seat and laughed at the windshield. "Oh, brother," he said. "I feel drunk."

"Why not a stretcher, Will?" Rosalind desperately asked.

He'd been so vehement! She wanted to call for help. "Stretcher-bearers!" she remembered someone hollering once in a movie. Stretcher-bearers!

Will turned his head back to her. "Pride, Roz," he said, as if that were an explanation. Exasperated, she rolled her eyes and let her breath out loudly. "Listen, Roz," Will went on, waving his hand in lazy circles, "I hope that now you'll get out of there, out of the cottage, out of Calypso."

"Oh, for God's *sake!*" Rosalind exploded. "Come *on.*" She lunged at him, but she didn't know how to get him out. Her hands fluttered with indecision. His bloody shoulder was towards her, and she didn't dare touch it. The blood was . . . congealing. Finally she bent and reached in and grabbed his ankles and put his feet on the pavement. There was mud caked on his beautiful boots. Rosalind wiped her hands on the backs of her jeans. Half-turned around, Will looked at his planted feet in bemused wonder.

"Rosalind, you're out of your mind," he laughed at her.

"Damn your eyes, Will Eddy, if you don't help me, I'll—"

"You'll what?" he challenged.

"I'll have them bring a stretcher, that's what!"

Will lurched to his feet. Blood smeared the camel-colored seat like finger painting. "No stretcher," Will said. Again, Rosalind draped his good arm around her shoulders and, as his body hit hers, felt a surge of deep affection. She saw his face when, stung, he'd turned down her 'dishonorable' proposal. She saw him in Confederate gray hold her though she vomited. She saw him help Kit into his pajamas, kneeling to button them up.

"Come on," she said gently, as if he were Kit. "No stretcher. You don't need a stretcher." Like a wobbly centaur, they started together slowly towards the door. What would happen to him? she wondered. Who would take care of him? She was feeling awfully maudlin, as if she might cry. She looked at the pavement, where blood dropped in dots like bright paint. Will lived all alone. He had no family. We really need each other, she reasoned sentimentally, as she took hold of the hand that hung over her shoulder and tightened her other arm around his waist. "You can stay with us, Will, when you get out. I'll take care of you," she told him, her voice soft and husky. "I'll change your bandages. You can protect us, and in the night, you can hold me and make me forget. . . ." She tipped her head sideways to look up at him. His forehead was damp, the red-gold of his hair darkened into tendrils. He bent his mouth to her ear and flicked his tongue in.

"Screw it out of you?" he asked. He put his head up and laughed a crazy, lazy laugh. Bewildered, Rosalind pulled his dangling hand to keep him walking. She looked at him. Together, they listed up the step. "Rosalind, I'm a man," Will said, "a whole man"—he gave his shoulder an ironic downward glance—"at least I was. I won't stud for you, Roz."

"Stud?" Rosalind asked blankly as, still holding him with both hands, she manipulated the door open, using her hip, then her buttocks, to keep it open. She gave Will a nudge, and he moved through.

"Enchanting as I find you—oh, hell." His head flopped over a little.

"Stud?" Rosalind repeated. The weight of the closing door scraped across her back. "Stud?" Finally, she absorbed what he was saying. Oh, she was furious at being so misinterpreted! Did he think she was making a *pass*? Hadn't he been as moved as she had been, in the woods? What did he want, a proposal of *marriage*? "Why, you prig! You . . . extremist!" she suddenly hissed, startling herself. "You fanatical perfectionist! You all-or-nothing 'whole man'!" People in the bright-orange chairs of the waiting room were looking up as the two of them swayed across the slippery vinyl, and Rosalind had to content herself with one final epithet as they approached the desk: "You bloody impossible *romantic*!" Will gave out a great laugh, like a howl.

"Will Eddy!" The receptionist at the desk leaped to her feet. She wore a clinging electric-blue minidress and loomed like a small psychedelic nightmare. "Gunshot?" she asked tersely, as if this were a beleaguered inner-city hospital, then spared a minute to look Rosalind up and down. "Call Carol on three," she told a skulking orderly, "and tell her Will Eddy's in Emergency! Thank you," she said perfunctorily to Rosalind and muscled her out of the way, taking Will's good arm on her own shoulders. Will's face registered a comic surprise at the change in support. As the electric-blue young woman took him towards a door marked DOCTORS ONLY, Will turned his head and waved his dangling hand at Rosalind.

"Sticks and stones," he said, wagging a finger at her.

"What do you *mean*, you still can't tell me any details? I'm the one who brought him in. This is his blood all over my sweater. I've been here for two hours, and now it's time for my son's bus."

"Well, I suggest you go and meet it, or whatever you do with it." The receptionist cranked a paper into her type-writer. "Try calling information here in an hour or two. They may have a report on Mr. Eddy's condition then." She started typing.

"Well, you see, I haven't a phone—"

"That's hardly my fault," the receptionist said, being really unwarrantedly nasty, Rosalind thought. What the hell . . . ?

"Couldn't I see him just a minute before I go?" Rosalind leaned with her fists on the desk. "You tell me he's alive, but I'd like to see for myself." And apologize. Oh, dear God, the names she had called him!

"Are you a relative?" the receptionist asked, not stopping her typing. As Rosalind opened her mouth to speak again the receptionist suddenly stood up. "You've made enough trouble here for one day," she said. Rosalind, startled, ran the back of her hand over her eyes. Earlier, pacing, she'd knocked over a large round ashtray that had proved unexpectedly full of water, but she didn't think that qualified as making "trouble." The priest who was dampened by the filthy water had agreed with Rosalind that sand was a more usual deterrent to fire in such a receptacle. She was amazed and disoriented by the receptionist's rude treatment, her outright hostility. Did the woman know her? Recognize her? Simply hate her on sight?

"As you should know," the receptionist smugly continued, "a gunshot wound is a police matter, and if you don't leave my waiting room immediately, I will have no recourse but to summon a policeman." Completely taken aback, Rosalind stared, fought angry tears, then whirled around and strode out of the waiting room, trying by her manner to make her retreat a gesture of defiance, but it was hard going. In a white-hot fury she drove back to Mud Lake.

Later, as soon as she dared without alarming him, Rosalind took Kit to the Mud Lake Tavern for dinner so she could use the phone. The hospital informed her that Will Eddy had been discharged "some time ago." The next morning, when she got up, the Thunderbird was gone. She'd spent the night holding on to Kit, as if the Roths might steal him in the darkness, and although she'd barely slept, she hadn't heard the T-bird.

. . .

A week later, she got a letter from an attorney in Caliban, informing her that he'd managed, through their lawyer, to persuade the Roths they had no claim on her son. The letter concluded, "There will be no charge. I'm delighted to be able to do a favor for Will Eddy, who has done so many for me. With all best wishes. . . ."

Will probably fixed tickets for him, Rosalind thought, feeling horrid, burdensome tears of gratitude well in her eyes. There'd been not a word from Will Eddy since she'd so carelessly deposited him, bloody but unbowed, at the receptionist's desk in the Emergency Room of Caliban Hospital. He'd run into his nurse, Rosalind was dolefully convinced. In retrospect she was positive that was the "Carol on three" the fiercely loyal receptionist had summoned.

· Super Bowl Sunday

January 15, 1978

9:30 P.M.

From her allotted place "below the salt," Rosalind glowered at Cynnie, on Barney's left, sharing the head of the table "above the salt." At least Rosalind had been granted Will across the table from her and had Walter on her left, although Walter was above the salt and thus involved in passing the Côte de Beaune and the *bœuf bourguignon* and had his head turned towards Flo Grimshaw, who was in the place of honor between him and Barney. Across the table Andy Grimshaw on Cynnie's left and Sarah Damian on Andy's left made up the remainder of the "aristocracy."

Holding the stem of her wineglass of Heineken, Rosalind tried to catch Cynnie's eye to show her that she was glowering, but Cynnie wouldn't look at her, just kept right on flirting outrageously with Barney. On Rosalind's right Cynnie had—unforgivably—placed Paul Damian, who'd already refused beer and insisted on bringing a large tumbler of Scotch to the table with him. Rosalind wouldn't look at him, although he kept nudging her knee with his knee. Next to Paul, Kit was drinking beer from a wineglass: Rosalind could see him out of the corner of her eye at the foot of the table; and, in between Will and Kit, so was Annabelle drinking

beer, with a lust akin to Kit's. "I adore beer," Rosalind heard
Annabelle confide to Kit. "Don't you?"

Grimly Rosalind ladled out Walter's stew to her fellows
among the proletariat, repeating to herself the Dorothy
Parker line: "You cannot persuade her with gun or lariat/To
come across for the proletariat." And while she grimly ladled
out the stew and thought the Dorothy Parker line, Paul and
Will started up (or perhaps resumed) a rather heated, incomprehensible argument about Hubert Humphrey's memorial service. Rosalind, having missed the television
coverage because she'd been asleep with teabags over her
eyes, couldn't quite discern the bone of contention, although
she began to find her attention sporadically caught. "It's not
that I object to Nixon's being there," Paul leaned forward
belligerantly to say; "I object to the *seat* he got."

"Ah, you're splitting hairs," Will demurred from across
the table. Paul glared at him.

Rosalind, finally diverted from her resentment of the aris-
tocrats, rushed with oil for the troubled waters. "Paul may
split his hairs," she quipped to Will, "but never, never his in-
finitives." Will laughed.

"Ah, the Queen of the Zeugma." Paul Damian raised his
tumbler of Scotch in ironic tribute. Rosalind giggled and
handed him his stew.

"The Queen of the Zeugma. Is that a ship?" Annabelle
asked. Both Rosalind and Paul Damian started to laugh.

"It's about the size of the African Queen," Will told Annabelle, deadpan.

"Or the Queen of the Nile," Rosalind mischievously put
in. "God, you were an awful Cleopatra, Annabelle."

"I was," Annabelle agreed. "I was dreadful." She turned to
Kit. "Where's the Zeugma River, Kit?" she asked him, as if
she were contemplating a cruise.

"It's on the Paris-Chinese border," Kit came back, and cracked up at his own wit.

Rosalind choked on her beer and had to be patted on the back, an awful thump from Paul Damian. "That's a Salinger story," she tried to explain to a mystified, affronted Annabelle, "called 'The Laughing Man,'" but even saying the word *laughing* set her off again. Paul Damian pounded her. "Stop that, Paul!" From her place above the salt, quick as a flash, Sarah Damian turned. So did Walter Pettinger, evidently drawn by the laughter.

"How's my stew, Roz?" he asked her.

"Lovely," she managed before she choked again, and Walter expertly patted her back. A great pair of hands, she thought, feeling nostalgic about the days when he was a wide receiver. Her throat receded. She would live. Actually Walter's stew *was* lovely, and she asked him about it, how he'd kept the carrots crunchy, the onions *al dente,* the peas green, and then she remembered again the mysterious African vegetables, and, "Walter, what are African vegetables?" she asked him. "Cynnie won't tell me."

"Oho, so she won't," Walter said, laughing. "Even Cynnie doesn't know the secret ingredient."

"What is it?" Rosalind asked.

Walter leaned to whisper.

"You're kidding!" she exclaimed, pulling back. "Where on earth do you get a goat?"

"Got yours, didn't I?" Walter said. He started to laugh.

"Oh, for God's sake!" Rosalind sputtered, then got laughing too. This table is quite mad, she thought with pleasure, and waved to Kit, who was grinning at her.

Kit cupped his hands around his mouth. "Did Walter get your goat, Mom?"

"I must sheepishly admit," Rosalind replied—it was irresistible—and Kit's laugh boomed, raucous and hearty.

"Kit's getting big," Walter observed sidelong to Rosalind. He sent his rich drawl traveling down the table in front of her. "Hey, Kit," he called, "did you have a date with a lady friend on New Year's Eve?" The whole table started to listen, as to a comedy routine.

"I *baby-sat* for Daisy and Joe," Kit answered Walter, with a mock glare at Rosalind.

"You were extremely well paid," Rosalind countered. "He *asked* to baby-sit," she told Walter and the listening table at large.

"I baby-sat Kit one New Year's Eve," Walter laughingly reminisced, "and I didn't get paid one red cent. Not a cent. All I got for my trouble was creamed at Scrabble—by a seven-year-old kid."

Laughter criss-crossed the table. Rosalind's vision blurred. Her pulse speeded up. Like a coffin-nightmare, she felt the telephone booth of the Mud Lake Tavern close around her. She could hear Tammy Wynette singing "Stand By Your Man."

"Barney," she called to the head of the table, her voice coming out shaky, "Barney, where were you that New Year's Eve?"

Oh, what kind of time was this to force a reckoning? she was chastising herself, but it was too late. Barney stopped laughing with Cynnie. "What New Year's Eve?"

"The New Year's Eve Walter stayed with Kit. The New Year's Eve you weren't at the Bellevue Stratford in Philadelphia." Oh, dear Lord, oh, dear Lord, no, she was praying. . . . Everyone at the table looked curiously back and forth from Barney to Rosalind, Rosalind to Barney, everyone but Cynnie, who elaborately contemplated her wineglass, holding it up to the light. The ruddy wine sparkled like new blood.

"Barney," Annabelle demanded imperiously, "*where were*

you?" She held her head poised like Lady Macbeth with her dander up.

Barney mumbled, "I was at the Sheraton Hotel in Scranton, Pennsylvania."

"The Sheraton Hotel in Scranton, Pennsylvania?" Rosalind incredulously asked him, feeling relief run through her body like a swift shot of whiskey. "Whatever *for?*"

Cynnie's soft, breathy voice floated into the breech. "He was with me," she said, as if awfully bored with the whole conversation. "Scranton is, you know, halfway between Caliban and Philadelphia," she added lamely as Walter, Rosalind, and Annabelle all leaped to their feet and stared at her. Walter's chair tipped over.

"Tsk," Cynnie said. She looked around at them. "Walter, sit down," she said, flapping her hand at him. "Honestly, you are so insanely jealous. I didn't even know you then." Walter got laughing, got shaking his marvelous dark head, as he retrieved his chair and sat obediently down. Cynnie turned to deal with Annabelle next. Rosalind watched her lean her head nearly to Barney's shoulder in order to see Annabelle, standing erect and full of fury, between the seated Will and Kit.

"Annabelle, you and Barney were separated," Cynnie called. "You had lovers, Annabelle; you even told me about them. Remember that London violinist with the mimosa all over his flat? And good old Barney," Cynnie went lazily on, putting her hand on Barney's broad shoulder, lightly flexing her fingers as if she were playing a violin, "wouldn't give you up. He wouldn't divorce you. Shit, I wanted to *marry* Barney." Barney lowered his head and shook it glumly. "But, no, Barney was just like Roz with Ben—loyal to the end. Like daughter, like father," Cynnie languidly wound up. "Stubborn, stubborn. . . . Sit *down*, Annabelle." Annabelle sat down. She opened her mouth, then abruptly closed it. Cynnie's voice went on. "It's just as well," she dreamily said, touching Barney's cheek with a fond finger. "Walter's more my age." Walter was shaking with suppressed laughter. Rosalind was still standing. Cynnie looked over at her, nonplussed. "Roz," she said, "I thought you knew. Didn't you think she knew?" she asked Barney.

"Yeah," Barney said. "I was sure she knew." They both looked at Rosalind with interest.

"I didn't," Rosalind said. "I didn't know." Feeling absurd, she sat down hard. Well, for God's sake, she thought: Cynnie and Barney. She could see Will laughing at her from across the table. He must have known all along!

"*I* knew," Kit said. Everyone looked at him. Oh, no. Rosalind recognized the reckless look on his face. It could happen in any sort of adult company, that sudden, burgeoning audacity as erratic as puberty. He should be in bed, Rosalind thought. It's a school night; he probably has homework. "Well, I didn't exactly know at the time," Kit went on nonchalantly, looking as impudent as Ben used to, coming with her out of a hastily utilized bathroom. "I was only seven. It's something I figured out later. You know how when you're little, things pass over your head, but they don't disappear. Later, when you grow up, you figure them out. I mean, Mom, I knew about you and—"

"Kit!" both Rosalind and Will gasped. Rosalind felt Paul Damian cringe away from her.

"Luke," Kit finished, looking a little startled.

"So did I!" Cynnie was roguishly delighted to find a partner in crime. "I had my eye on him too," she said mischievously.

"Cynnie, please," Walter rebuked her. "You know how insanely jealous I am." He winked across the table at Sarah Damian, who frowned in a perplexed, suspicious way.

Cynnie ignored Walter. "Luke DiLorenzo was positively

dreamy," she went on. "He looked like a movie star. A young Henry Fonda. Whatever happened to him?"

Hearing, across the table, Will quietly telling Kit to go do his homework, Rosalind speculated aloud to Cynnie, "Luke's very high up in the Mafia in Buffalo, New York."

"You're kidding!" Cynnie leaned forward, fascinated.

"Of course I'm kidding, Cynnie. How would I know that? No, actually, Luke's an extremely successful"—she paused for effect—"gigolo. He'd have been a splendid gigolo." Cynnie giggled. God, I'm getting to be a bigot, Rosalind thought. What next?

"Luke's an accountant," Flo Grimshaw leaned forward to tell Rosalind over Walter.

"You're kidding!"

"No, I'm not," Flo said, looking puzzled. "Roz, who'd kid about being an accountant? He's in Buffalo, he's married, and he has five children."

"A basketball team," Barney said.

"Five!" Rosalind exclaimed. "Good heavens."

"How do you know all this, Flo?" Andy asked her from across the table.

"I read it in the alumni bulletin," she said.

"Maybe he's an accountant for the Mafia," Rosalind said.

Andy laughed abruptly. "Could be," he said.

Flo said, "I had an awful crush on him, Andy," as if to get in on the confessionals too.

"Shit," Andy said. "Who didn't?" He looked down the table. "Night, Kit," he said.

"Good night, everybody." Long-suffering Kit waved, going out through the kitchen. They could hear him clatter down the stairs.

Rosalind and Will caught eyes across the table and escaped to the kitchen to make coffee. From behind, Rosalind grabbed hold of the back pockets of Will's jeans and with her knuckles kneaded the lean flanks beneath. "Will," she asked him, hearing inexplicable excitement vibrate in her own voice, "what are all these true confessions? Have you ever heard anything like it?" She leaned against his back; she fancied she could feel an electricity in his body. He turned his head from counting spoonfuls of coffee.

"Be alert," he said. His gray eyes glinted. "I mean it, Roz."

"You think we're going to find something out?"

"If we watch. If we don't miss it."

Rosalind tugged, then let go of his pockets. "Henry James said, 'Try to be someone on whom nothing is lost.' " She bit her lip.

"That's it," Will said. "Exactly." He plugged in the coffee.

Rosalind began to feel apprehensive. "You want something to happen here? Now?"

"Baby, you still have nightmares. You deserve to know why your life was so disrupted, and so does Kit. Kit's been asking me a lot of questions today. 'Did you know my father?' 'Did my father know Luke?' " Will turned around and leaned against the counter. "You heard him at the table. Why do you think I sent him upstairs?"

"Because he was being outrageous. I mean, he really was."

"Bullshit. No more outrageous than you and Cynnie. Kit was playing Sherlock Holmes. And he's right. There's a chemistry here tonight. Kit felt it. Can't you feel it? You're usually so sensitive." Will slipped his hand around her waist, moved it up, impatient. Oh, he was turned on, alive in every cell; Rosalind could feel it through his hand. Her body quickened at his touch; her mind wondered if she wanted to know whatever it was they were going to find out.

More wine was poured, more beer. Paul Damian asked for more Scotch. Rosalind and Will brought out cheese and fruit, coffee. It was late; the food was all gone; but as if they were all in thrall, no one left the table. Conversation settled into cozy clockwise twosomes: Walter and Flo; Barney and Cynnie; Andy and Sarah; Will and Annabelle. Rosalind, left to the tender mercies of Paul Damian, who was quite tipsily mellow by this time, again started thinking daggers at Cynnie for her seating arrangement. "Rosalind," Paul leaned dangerously close to ask, "do you notice anything funny about this table?"

"No," Rosalind said.

"Sweetheart," he mumbled, "are you and Will up to something? I mean, look around you, all the suspects. This table—it looks like a setup for Percival Dane."

Rosalind laughed. "It does," she agreed. "Maybe he'll come walking in in his embroidered waistcoat."

"He doesn't wear the waistcoat any more," Paul said. "In the last one, I put him in a pinstripe suit, to keep up with his advancing years." Ruefully he patted his own paunch. Ick, Rosalind thought. Paul reproached her: "You mean you haven't read the latest Percival Dane? I *know* I sent you one. The pinstripe suit is crucial to the climax."

"I will. I will. I'd been saving it for the midsemester break. I'll start it tomorrow."

He cocked her a canny look. "*Are* you and Will up to something?" he asked.

"Will says he's not. I'm certainly not. Actually, it would have been nice if Percival Dane had shown up," she giggled to divert him. "Cynnie was annoyed about the lack of symmetry. Percival would have made an even dozen."

"Like the Last Supper," Paul Damian gloomily said.

"There were thirteen at the Last Supper," Rosalind quibbled, "counting Jesus."

"Pedant. Okay, after Judas left."

"Ah, the fun was all over then. 'Take, eat: this is my body,' " Rosalind shuddered suddenly.

"I didn't know you'd gotten religion," Paul said. He looked her up and down, the old rakehell style. Rosalind felt Sarah Damian's eyes dart from across the table. "The faithful wife," Paul went on. "What a waste. . . ." Under the table he put his hand on her knee.

"Paul, damn you, stop that," she hissed *sotto voce.* "No, I haven't gotten religion," she went briskly on for Sarah to hear. She smiled coolly at Paul. "I taught the Gospels last semester, as a novel from four points of view. Along with *The Sound and the Fury.*"

"Pretty jazzy," Paul said. He gave her an avuncular, professorial nod of approval.

"It was terrific," Rosalind said. "The Gospels *are* a novel." Before her mind's eye, she saw Da Vinci's *Last Supper,* soft, misty *sfumato*; and all at once the muted colors went garish, and illuminated, like a reproduction you might pick up in the back of a Catholic church, near the holy water. *Like a card you might find in someone's wallet. The Apostles' Creed.* Rosalind felt a jolt in her brain as if two stray wires had, for the first time, touched. *Ben, don't forget. Four o'clock, the Apostle.* Raising her voice, trying to control its timbre, she asked the table at large, "Who were the Apostles?"

Everyone stopped talking and looked at her. "Matthew, Mark, Luke, and John," said Barney, and shrugged. Golly, Rosalind was thinking, trying to look at too many faces at once, don't a lot of people I know have Biblical names?

"No," Sarah Damian corrected Barney. "Matthew, Mark, Luke, and John were the *Evangelists.* The Apostles were the disciples," she said to Rosalind.

"Was Paul an Apostle?" Rosalind asked, looking speculatively at Paul Damian's profile.

"I knew it!" Sarah Damian leaped to her feet. Like déjà
vu, Rosalind saw Sarah's head whirl against the bookshelves
behind her, whirl this time to glare accusingly down at Will.
Will looked sideways up at her, startled. "You've got us all
set up like the end of a mystery novel, Will Eddy!" Sarah
ranted. "Where were *you*?" she suddenly screamed at Paul.
"Where were you, that New Year's Eve? Were you with
her?" She pointed an angry finger at Rosalind, then steered
the finger to Paul. "Did you kill him? Did you kill her poor
husband?"

Paul waved his hand in front of his face. "I never set eyes
on Rosalind's poor husband," he groaned. "I never even
knew his name. Will, tell her; please tell her." All eyes at the
table turned to Will.

"Sarah," said Will patiently, "Paul had an alibi. You didn't
have to give him one; you didn't have to lie. Actually, Paul
had rather an embarrassment of alibis," Will said, raising an
ironic eyebrow at Paul. Paul grinned and shrugged, as if to
say, Ah, what a bad boy I used to be.

"Whom was he with?" Sarah still stood over Will.

"Sarah, that's hardly relevant now. It's been seven years."

"Yeah," Paul said, "it's not relevant now, Sarah." He
slumped in his chair, looking all of his fifty-two years, Rosalind was a little sad to see. "For God's sake," Paul barked
suddenly at Sarah, "sit down!" Sarah sat down, looking vin-
dicated.

"What were the Apostles' names?" Rosalind asked in an
offhand way, as if she were just trying to smooth the awkward moment. Nobody said anything. She saw that glint in
Will's eyes. "Well, hell," she said, getting up fast, "I'm going
to look them up. What a bunch of dullards." She walked
breezily around the table, buoyant from excitement, imagin-
ing herself in an embroidered waistcoat. I'm going to miss

Percival's waistcoat, she thought irrelevantly. Dear God, a pinstripe! She could feel the people at the table watching her as she knelt behind Sarah Damian's chair and extracted A–BIB of the *Britannica Micropædia*. She fumbled through the pages, muddling the alphabet in her single-minded haste and having to recite it inanely to herself.

When she found the page, she stood up. She cradled the large volume in her arms and read aloud, as if she were teaching:

"APOSTLE (from Greek *apostolos*, "person sent"), generally understood to apply specifically to the twelve disciples chosen by Jesus. . . . The full list of the Twelve is given with some variation in Mark 3, Matt. 10, and Luke 6: Peter; James and John, the sons of Zebedee; Andrew; Philip; Bartholomew—"

"Stop!" Andy Grimshaw held up his hand as if he wanted to be excused from the table to go to the bathroom. "I did it. I killed Ben Roth." He dropped his head and stared at the table.

Every cell in Rosalind's body seemed to flinch, then to flow out and join an almost palpable uniformity of reaction among the other stunned spectators at the dining table. No one leaped to feet. Rather, there was first an impulse to change the subject so that Andy's unfortunate faux pas wouldn't hang in the air for too long. Then fuddlement: clearly, this wouldn't do. The faux pas was too . . . The next impulse, this one a thought, was: My God, Flo's pregnant! Then came the leaping to feet, as Sarah, Annabelle, and Cynnie all rushed to Flo's chair.

"I'm all right!" Flo feistily said, waving them off, her Bronx accent returning with a vengeance. "Leave me alone, already." She leaned across the table. "Andy," she said, "stop *crying.* Andy, why didn't you tell me?" She spoke as if they were alone, and Andy raised his head to look at her.

"I love you," he said.

"All the more reason," Flo said.

Rosalind felt her blood start to flow again. Carefully, she stooped to replace A–BIB of the *Britannica Micropædia,* and then stood up, fanned out both her hands, and eloquently told the table at large, "He can't have meant to."

Andy turned to look at her. His blue eyes were full of tears. "Roz, I shot him. I was taking him two dozen M 16 rifles, and I shot him with one of them. I killed him, Roz. I thought you'd know when I gave you the puzzle; I almost *hoped* you'd know when I gave you the puzzle."

The puzzle? Rosalind was thinking.

"Andy." Will's voice came out deadly calm. "I don't think you should say any more. You need a lawyer."

Panic contorted Andy's baby face. "Will, you're my lawyer!"

"I'm also with the D.A.'s office. Andy"—Will's voice cracked like a rifle—"don't say any more!"

"I shot Ben Roth with an M 16 rifle," Andy went doggedly on, "and a dumdum bullet, at approximately five A.M. on January first, 1971. Happy New Year."

"Andy, *shut up!*"

"You shut up, Will," Rosalind said. "Let him tell it."

"I can't shut up," Andy moaned. "I can't."

Will held up his hand. "All right," he said. "But you're going to tell it *right.* Come on," he said absently to the others at the table, "let's go in the living room. Unless some of you want to leave."

Nobody, apparently, wanted to leave. Everybody trooped down the five stairs from the dining room into the living room. Sarah Damian insisted on helping Flo. Kit's fire was still burning in the fireplace. Into the corner of the big couch that faced the fireplace, Sarah deposited Flo and sat down protectively close to her. Paul Damian—looking wide-eyed and alert, for a change—sat down next to his wife. Barney and Annabelle sat at the other end of the couch. Cynnie and Walter lounged on the floor before the fire, resting their elbows on the steel-and-glass coffee table.

"Sit down," Will told Andy, directing him to one of the Barcelona chairs that flanked the coffee table. Andy sat down, spreading his knees apart, resting his head back. He was breathing hard, almost panting. Across the table, Will pulled Rosalind down with him into the other Barcelona chair; he put his arm around her, as if she might fall off. "Andy," Will began, "in 1971, you were what? A college sophomore?" Andy nodded. "Nineteen years old?"

"Twenty," Andy said.

"Okay, twenty. Where'd you get two dozen M 16 rifles? Where'd you get dumdums?" There was a pause. The room was absolutely silent.

Finally Andy spoke. "I made the dumdums with a file. It's easy. Kit could do it. Even Joe could do it. I got the bullets and rifles from the FBI." Rosalind caught her breath. "I didn't know it was the FBI," Andy went on. "I got them from Matt DiLorenzo—Luke's brother. I figured out later that he was an undercover FBI agent assigned to Ben Roth ever since he was on the Ten Most Wanted List in March 1970. I think he was using that girl Muffy to get to Roth, and I know he was using me. That's why the investigation stopped, I'm sure. The FBI didn't want him involved."

"Andy," Will interjected, "tell it right. No speculations. Just what happened." (Just the facts, ma'am, Rosalind's mind commented inanely; she felt as if she were at a play.)

Will's even voice went on. "How'd you meet Matt Di-
Lorenzo?"

Andy closed his eyes a minute. He pushed his curly hair
off his forehead. "It was April, I think, in 1970. I was taking
Roz's Melville class. So was Luke. I got a C; Luke got an A,"
Andy added irrelevantly (or maybe not irrelevantly, Rosalind wildly thought. Maybe he killed Ben because I gave him
a C. Who the hell knows?) "One night, this guy came to my
room in Lacedaemon Hall. He leaned against the jamb and
smiled and said he was Luke's brother. He had a kind
of—oh, I don't know—charisma, I guess. He looked like
Luke—ah—Luke looked like a god! This guy was holding a
class list from your Melville class, Roz. 'Grimshaw, Andrew?'
he asked—"

Indignantly Rosalind broke in. "I was so proud of the en-
rollment in that Melville class, and now it turns out it was
full of spies!" As she heard it she couldn't believe she had
said it. Will patted her shoulder. "I'm sorry," she said. "I'm
sorry, Andy."

"Sorry!" Andy laughed a bitter laugh. "Roz, don't be nice
to me. I can take anything but that. Oh, Jesus Christ, you
have been so God damned nice to me! I thought for sure you
knew that day I turned up at your cottage. You looked at me
for such a long time. I hadn't slept in two weeks, just waiting
for the body to be found, and when I finally heard it on the
radio, I couldn't stay away, I just couldn't."

"I thought I'd met you before," Barney's gravelly voice
came from the couch. "The hitchhiker. Rozzy's student."

"And that day in the woods, I didn't mean to shoot you,
Will," Andy said. "The ground had finally thawed enough
for me to bury the God damned rifle I was stuck with, and
you and Roz startled me. The gun just went off. I love you
and Roz, Will; I wouldn't do anything to hurt either of you.
Oh, shit—"Andy started to cry again.

Will said, "Andy, we'll take up the question of your shoot-ing me later. Go back to Matt DiLorenzo coming to your room."

"Yeah. He said he was from Weatherman."

"You believed him?" Rosalind leaned forward to ask.

"Sure."

"Andy, that was pretty dumb," Will said.

"Caliban wasn't Columbia," Andy said. "Yeah, so shoot me, I believed him. I was excited." He looked into the fire. "He said did I know that my pretty teacher, Rosalind Chase, was in real life Ben Roth's wife. I was stunned. It was like destiny. You see"—his eyes went misty—"when I got out of high school, in Pittsburgh, I went right to work in a steel foundry. I was poor," he said. "My parents died when I was ten. Oh, that's not relevant!" he exclaimed disgustedly. "I'm not asking for pity or anything. I'm a *man*. I'm responsible for my own actions."

"You went to work in a steel foundry," Will gently prod-ded.

"Yes. It was hell, a literal hell. One day my second year there, Ben Roth came to speak to us—the workers. He was with SDS. Somebody played 'Joe Hill' on the harmonica." Rosalind started to cry; silently she started to cry; it wasn't fair. Will held on to her. She could hear words to "Joe Hill":

> And standing there as big as life,
>   and smiling with his eyes,
> Says Joe: what they can never kill
>   went on to organize. . . .

The world, her living room, fell away, and only the slow-gaited warbling harmonica went with her. She was a junior, and Ben was in his first year of graduate work in history. Among other ambling, milling students after Friday classes, they converged, smiling and dreamy-eyed, in the center of the Arts Quad at Cornell. It was spring. The forsythia was out. Kit was strapped to Rosalind's back. He'd been to class with her; he was eight months old and getting exceedingly heavy. "I'll take him now, Roz," Ben said, smiling with his eyes. He helped her unstrap the harness from across her breasts. His hand lingered. "What'd you learn today?" he asked, grinning at her as he fastened Kit on his back. Kit was laughing and pulling Ben's hair.

"D'you remember the six-inch chapter in *Moby Dick*?" Rosalind tilted her head to ask Ben. "Well, what do you suppose that *six-inch* chapter means?"

"You're kidding!"

"Let's face it, Roth. Your guy Melville's a dirty writer."

Ben laughed out with delight. She saw his profile slant against the smooth gold-gray of Goldwin Smith. "Six inches," Ben said then. "That ain't much. You'll do better than that, won't you, Kit." Ben joggled Kit on his back. Smiling at each other, Rosalind and Ben slowly followed the path to the statue of Ezra Cornell. Over the wall, they could see the distant hills, misty soft lime-green fading to lavender.

"What did *you* learn today?" Rosalind asked Ben. It was a ritual.

"Today I learned about Joe Hill and the copper bosses." Ben whistled a fragment of "Joe Hill." It hovered in the soft spring air. Kit laughed on Ben's back. "The Wobblies scattered Joe Hill's ashes all over the country. Labor, Roz; I like it. I might specialize. It must be my heritage."

"Your heritage? Ben, your father's a *dentist.*"

Ben laughed joyously. "Roz, I thought we agreed I must have been switched in my cradle." Ben began to whistle "Joe Hill" again. Ben's head and Kit's head slanted against the statue of Ezra Cornell and the distant hills. Ben's ambling, warbling whistle faded out. . . .

All right, Kit, Rosalind's mind dimly muttered; I mean, all right, *Ben.* Her body went vulnerable and loose, and she would have fallen sideways from the Barcelona chair were it not for Will's implacable, supporting arm.

I loved Ben, Rosalind thought then, with wonder. I loved him. I'll have to tell Kit all about him, now that he's growing up. . . . She came back into the world and felt Will's arm around her, heard Andy Grimshaw's voice again. "When I heard Ben Roth speak, I decided right there, right then, to get out of the foundry. I decided to go to college so *I* could talk like that. He was a spellbinder."

"He was," Rosalind said, hearing her voice come from far away. "Ben could hold a class in the palm of his hand." She felt Will shift on the chair next to her.

"I didn't know," he said. His voice was husky. He coughed. "I'm sorry, Andy," he said. "Go on. Matt Di-Lorenzo came to your room and asked about Roz."

"Well, I was stunned. It seemed the most unbelievable co-incidence. Then he said—oh, I can't believe this now—'Ben wants somebody to keep an eye on his wife, to protect her.' I thought I was *protecting* you, Roz, when I walked you from class. It was kind of fun—you know—I had a code name. 'Ben's into Christian symbolism,' Matt DiLorenzo said. 'Like Leonard Cohen and Dylan.' Matt DiLorenzo was 'the Evangelist.' I was to be 'the Apostle.' Every once in a while, he'd call and ask me if anything 'untoward' had happened—'untoward,' that's what he always said. Of course, nothing untoward ever did happen, or if it did, I didn't know about it, because all I dared do was walk you from class, to your car, your office, the Administration Building, wherever you were going, so I'd tell him, no, nothing untoward had happened yet. Over the summer I didn't hear from him, but just before registration in the fall, he called and said, 'Listen,

Apostle, you sign up for Chase's Homer-Dante course. I really need you now.' Well, I didn't want to, having gotten a C in Melville, but, well, I did."

"And you got an A," Rosalind said blankly.

"Yeah," Andy said. " 'Encrimsoned Odysseus.' " His voice broke. "I thought that line when I looked at Ben Roth dead. Oh, God, the blood . . ." Andy and Rosalind looked at each other for a long moment.

"Go on," she said.

"It wasn't until—oh, after the hunger strike, after Thanksgiving even, that I heard from 'the Evangelist' again. He came to my room, and he was mad. 'Chase has *moved*,' he said. 'Where's she gone to?' I didn't know. I explained that all I had was an old pickup truck, that I did carpentry and metal work to put myself through school, and I thought the pickup was too conspicuous to try to follow Roz in. DiLorenzo was still mad. 'Ben is not pleased,' he said. 'Tell Ben I'm sorry,' I said. I was getting sick of the whole thing by that time, and then suddenly DiLorenzo changed his tack. 'I've got another assignment for you,' he said. 'I hear you're good with your hands.' I said that, yes, I was; pretty good. 'Do you think you could make some dumdums out of five point fifty-six millimeter rounds, twenty-round clips?' he asked. I said sure. He got a big smile on his face, and said, 'Well, *great*. I told Ben I thought you might be able to help us out.' So," Andy went on, looking suddenly weary, "he said he had two dozen M 16 rifles for Ben. He'd give them to me, and I should hide them, and make a whole lot of dumdums, .22 caliber in twenty-round clips. Where the hell was I going to hide two dozen rifles? I wanted to know. 'In your pickup, dummy,' he said. 'I'll be in touch.'

"He brought me the rifles a few days before Christmas—Tuesday, it was—and told me to sit tight, not to leave my

room until he called. Well, finally, on Christmas Day, he
called me long-distance and gave me a message, a number to
call, and a number to tell the operator I was calling from.
The number I called was long-distance, and I've no idea
where to. I asked for Ben. I heard Ben Roth's voice come on
the phone. 'Hello, Caliban Apostle,' he said, laughing. 'I'm
calling for the Evangelist,' I said. 'I've got the hardware.'
'What kind of hardware?' he asked. 'Two dozen M 16's.' Ben
Roth whistled. 'Great!' he said. He called out to somebody
else, 'We got the M 16's—two dozen! Merry Christmas!'
Then I could hear a lot of excited voices and laughing. It
sounded like a party. Ben Roth's voice came back on the
phone. 'When?' he asked. 'The Evangelist says, here, four
o'clock in the morning, New Year's Day.' 'Where?' he wanted
to know. DiLorenzo hadn't said, and I was confused, but
Ben Roth said, 'Listen, I've only been in your town once, but
isn't there a cemetery you can see on a hill from that bouncing Philadelphia road?' Somebody got laughing in the background. 'Ben, you ghoul!' a girl said. 'The cemetery's a good
place,' I said. 'That'll be fine.' I was relieved. 'All right,' Ben
Roth said. 'Four o'clock, the Apostle, the cemetery, got it.'

"I called DiLorenzo back, and he was, of course, delighted," Andy said wryly. "He told me he'd come to my
room at midnight on New Year's Eve, and we'd go to the
cemetery together. He never showed up."

"He got married!" Rosalind indignantly interrupted. "He
was on his honeymoon. A motel in Niagara Falls, wasn't it,
Will? Oh, the bastard, the unspeakable bastard. You could
have gotten out of it right then, Andy. How did you dare go
without him?"

"What else was I going to do? Roz, I was twenty years old!
I'd sat around that spooky dorm all through Christmas vacation. The dining halls were closed; I had two dozen M 16

rifles and a lot of dumdums stashed in my pickup. I got in my pickup and drove to the cemetery. There was a Land-Rover waiting next to—Roz, it's very close to where you buried him—near the spruces."

Rosalind felt a rush of hot, stupid tears. "Andy, are you the one who plants geraniums on his grave every Memorial Day?"

"Yes," he said. He blushed.

"Oh, Andy!"

"Go on, Andy," Will said. His voice was hard.

"I got out of the pickup and went toward the Land-Rover. 'Who goes?' a voice said. 'The Apostle,' I said. Ben Roth poked his head out of the back of the Land-Rover. 'Welcome, Apostle,' he said. He was laughing. He looked around. 'Where's the Evangelist?' he said. 'I've been wanting to meet the Evangelist.' 'He didn't show,' I said, 'but it's okay. I've got the hardware.' Ben Roth got out of the Land-Rover, and I took him to the M 16's in the back of the pickup. He whistled." Andy whistled to demonstrate. "Then he patted me on the back and said, 'Come along, kid; I want you to meet Muffy.'

"We both climbed into the back of the Land-Rover, and a girl was sitting there. They had pillows and blankets and sleeping bags and a lantern, and it was warm. 'Where's the Evangelist?' the girl Muffy wanted to know, and Ben Roth said, 'You know the Evangelist, Muff; never around when you need him,' and she laughed and said, 'The Evangelist is the most fantastic *fuck*.' " Andy choked. "I'm sorry," he apologized, looking at the people on the couch. "That's the way she talked."

"Oh, for God's sake, Andy!" said Flo, exasperated.

"Continue with your story, young man," Annabelle said. "You're telling it beautifully. Isn't he, Barney? Barney, did I tell you I'm thinking of writing a play?"

"Shh!" Barney said.

"Well, we all laughed," Andy said. "Ben Roth was in really high spirits, you know, laughing, happy. 'It's a New Year,' he said. 'It's a New Morning. Let's celebrate. Muffy, pass the grass.' 'Around all those guns, Ben?' she asked. 'We're not having target practice, Muff,' he said, so Muffy brought out a Marlboro pack and gave us each a joint. They were fat and beautifully rolled—they looked just like regular cigarettes, and I was interested in how they made them, and Muffy said, 'Shit, we got a regular factory,' and she explained how they laced their grass with hash or acid, but that these were just grass, they wouldn't hurt me if I wasn't used to them. Well, it was dynamite grass. Right away, I was flying, and after a while we were all laughing, you know, silly, and it was fun. I'd never had so much fun in my life before, and—I can't believe this now—I asked them if I could go with them. They both laughed, but they were sort of flattered I think, and Ben said, 'We'll see about that, son,' and Muffy said, 'This dope—it's won more converts than Mao and Jesus combined.'

" 'Time for a toast,' Ben Roth said then. He raised his cigarette. 'Here's to monogamy,' he said. Muffy raised her cigarette, and she said, 'Here's to Ben Roth who last night' "—Andy swallowed—" 'raped a woman.' "

A jolt ran through Rosalind's body like an electrical shock.

"And Ben reached out as fast as lightning and smashed Muffy across the mouth. The air seemed to change. It was as if the magnetic field had reversed. I was scared; I wished I could evaporate, never have been there. I hoped it was a nightmare.

" 'Not rape,' Ben said in a tight voice. 'It wasn't *rape*.' Muffy's mouth was bleeding—she had this cold sore or something on her lip"—Andy touched his own lip—"but she didn't say anything, just sort of huddled up, and Ben Roth

said to me, all business now, 'Come on, kid, let's get this
show on the road. Move your ass, Muffy, we need you to
help carry,' and we all got out and went over to the pickup.
We transferred the M 16's from the pickup to the Land-
Rover, or rather Muffy did most of it, because Ben was interested in the rifle. He chose one and took a clip, and he
said, 'Show me how to load it. I'm left-handed, but I'm a
quick study.' "

Rosalind gasped. Then she huddled up next to Will, un-
abashedly fetal.

"Roz, do you want me to stop?" Andy asked. His eyes
looked glazed.

"No," she said. "It was just his being left-handed. I mean,
he *was*." She was crying. "Please go on."

"All right." Andy put his head back and looked at the
ceiling. "Muffy came back over to watch. It was awfully cold,
and we were all shivering. I could hear Muffy's teeth chat-
tering. Ben Roth sat on the tailgate of the pickup, and I
showed him how to load the M 16. They were a new gun
then, and they're complicated to load." Andy pantomimed
pulling a bolt back with his hand, and then snapped his
wrist. "While I was loading it, I said my conscience had been
troubling me about all the dumdums I'd made, that I knew
he wanted them so they couldn't be traced back to the rifles,
but he should bear in mind how a dumdum can blow a body
to bits; and then Ben Roth started to laugh.

" 'Conscience!' he said. 'That went out with monogamy,
didn't it, Muff?' She didn't say anything. 'Ain't talking, huh,
Muff?' he said then. 'Look at her,' he said to me. I looked at
her. 'You know my wife,' Ben said. 'She's beautiful—oh, isn't
Roz beautiful? My fair Rosalind. Look what I gave her up
for—this! *Look at her*.' Muffy started to cry. I felt awful. I
didn't know what to do. Muffy went away and got into the
Land-Rover. We watched her.

" 'You want to go with us, kid?' Ben asked me then. 'Show
me how you hold a rifle.' I held it as if to shoot. 'Ah, not
bad,' he said. 'Take the safety off.' I released the safety. Ben
Roth was sitting on the tailgate, rocking back and forth while
he talked. 'You want to go with us, son?' he asked me again.
'You know you can't go *back*. Your cells change. You don't
go home,' he said, 'from the Donner Pass. You don't want to
go with us; we won't *let* you go with us,' he said, 'you haven't
got the guts to shoot that thing, look at you, you're a little
shit; you're a *wimp*—'

"The gun must have gone off," Andy said, with a great,
shuddering sigh. "There was this sound of a gunshot. I'm
not saying I didn't pull the trigger, because of course I must
have and I probably even meant to. But it was so fucking
cold, and my hands were numb, and it just seemed like
something that had to happen, had already happened, the
gun going off, Ben Roth falling back, the whole middle of
him gradually bright red, and I remember thinking, gee,
those dumdums really do the job. I thought it was a nightmare I'd wake up from. Muffy came running from the
Land-Rover—she hollered Ben's name, and then she
climbed into the back of the pickup next to him and held his
head and felt his pulse, and then she tried to give mouth-to-
mouth, but of course it was no good; the middle of him was
gone."

Rosalind was huddled in Will's lap, sobbing, tears streaming on his chest. Will stroked her hair. "Go on, Andy," he
said. "Go on! Get it all over with!"

Andy heaved a deep sigh. "Well," he said, "we didn't know
what to do with him. Muffy was crying, and I said, 'We can't
leave him here in the cemetery; that is just too bizarre,' and
she agreed, and then she said, 'Wait a minute, I know just
the place. You can follow me,' she said. 'I'll drive slowly.' So
we got his body straightened out and put the tailgate up on

the pickup, and Muffy got a blanket from the Land-Rover and covered him with it. 'Follow me,' she said. 'And listen, don't *worry*. I'm not going to run away and leave you all alone with Ben's body.'

"So I followed the Land-Rover, and I sort of vaguely recognized the road, but I had no idea you lived out there, Roz. I had tried to find out where you lived for Matt Di-Lorenzo, and *nobody* knew."

Rosalind struggled out of Will's lap, to sit up. "How did Ben know?" she asked. "Cynnie, did you tell him?"

"Me?" Cynnie was offended. "I wouldn't have given Ben Roth the time of day."

"I told him," Annabelle said.

"You?"

"He telephoned me. The call was long-distance. Crackly." Annabelle cocked her head as if listening to the crackle. "I always liked Ben," she mused. "He was a charmer. It was the afternoon of New Year's Eve, and I was playing Gertrude in *Hamlet* that night, and I was napping. I always nap before a performance. Ben said, 'Annabelle, it's your prodigal son-in-law, do you know where Roz is now? I want to spend New Year's Eve with her and Kit.' I gave him directions. Was that the wrong thing to do?" she asked Barney.

"Of course not," Barney said. "I'd've told him too."

"I just wondered," Rosalind said. "Please go on," she said to Andy in an impersonal way. "I'm sorry I interrupted."

"That's all right," Andy said politely. He looked exhausted. "Muffy and I carried the body to the center of those marble ruins. He was heavy and he was already stiff—from the cold probably. I liked the place she'd chosen; it was like I'd imagine a tumbled Roman temple would look, and I kept thinking if only it weren't so cold, it'd be nice here, and then I said a prayer, to myself, not out loud, and Muffy knelt and kissed him, and we went back to the trucks. 'It wasn't your fault,' Muffy kept repeating to me, like a charm. 'It was his fault, and it was my fault—I went too far. Don't you blame yourself.' She patted my cheek. 'Okay?' she said. Then she said, 'I hope the pigs leave you alone. If they do, try to forget it'—forget it!" Andy groaned and covered his face. Then he took a deep breath and resumed. " 'No confessing, now,' Muffy warned me. 'You'll bring the roof down on a lot of people.' Then she smiled a sad little smile and said, 'So long, Apostle.' I started to tell her my name, but she said, 'Don't. If the pigs run me to earth, I might break. I mean, who the fuck knows?' Then she waved and got into the Land-Rover and turned it around and drove off. So did I, like a bat out of hell and then back into it.

"I was in hell for a month," Andy said, his head flopped back on the chair. "I was like Raskolnikov, wanting to confess all the time. I couldn't sleep; I didn't dare talk to anyone because I knew I might blurt it out any minute; but then the spring semester started, and I met Flo, and all at once, I had something to lose. . . ." He smiled mooningly over at Flo on the couch, and then he lowered his head and started to cry. "I'm a murderer, Flo."

"I love you," Flo said. "But please stop crying."

The story held them, round the fire, a long time. No one moved or spoke. Then Annabelle stirred and murmured, "Calm of mind, all passion spent."

"Oh, Annabelle!" Rosalind impatiently breathed. She pulled away from Will and stood up and walked to the fireplace. She wished that everyone would go away, but of course they wouldn't. She felt thrown down; she felt trampled, with all the wind knocked out of her. Her own seven-year-old mistakes whirled in her head, taunting her like

pre-Aeschylean Furies. Why hadn't she told Ben about Luke
and his big brother? Wouldn't Ben and Muffy then have
turned tail and run, leaving Andy with the M 16's? Wouldn't
that have served Andy right? Served him right enough,
she meant. To kill: what an appalling punishment! Ah, she
could feel bated breathing behind her, eyes on her from the
couch, the chairs, and the floor, waiting for her to say
something—to condemn, to forgive—but her inclinations
were locked somewhere between; and the fireplace, with its
glowing hot coals and desultory fits of flame, held her eyes.
Digging for her voice, she cleared her throat to speak, but
then Walter Pettinger's voice took over for her.

"Man," Walter said, "why didn't you *tell*? You know how
scared Roz was? Were you following her? Remember, Roz,
that night you came running in. . . ?"

Rosalind turned from the fire to Walter. She found her
voice, a slightly hoarse version of it. "I remember the chain
lock on Cynnie's door." She could see Walter's dark, deft
hands slide the chain across. "Everyone was scared," she
said, still looking at Walter so she wouldn't have to look at
Andy.

Cynnie, next to Walter, languidly wrapped her arms
around her knees. "Roz, that chain lock wasn't because of
Ben," she explained. "That chain lock was because of Walter." Cynnie turned one hand palm up. "You see, Walter has
this ghetto paranoia."

Walter sat up straight. "Paranoia! Woman, the first year I
was here I was almost lynched every time I went out the
front door!" Cynnie laughed and patted his shoulder. Rosalind's eyes edged stealthily away from them and, almost
without her volition, made their way to Andy, still on the
Barcelona chair across the coffee table from Will. Andy's
pale-blue eyes confronted hers. He had stopped crying,

thank heaven. Rosalind touched the suede pendant he had
made for her; she felt the house he had built surround her;
she wondered why on earth this talented craftsman (for
talented he certainly was) hadn't left town. Had he stayed
around all these years *to make it up to her?* The possibility ap-
palled her. Soberly, she pondered Andrew Grimshaw, the
Apostle. She was amazed at how jaundiced her eye had become. Even tear-stained, his baby face no longer struck her
as endearing or innocent. Rather, it was bland, a trifle an-
noying, his tears an affront, the pathos of his story's closure
almost . . . calculated: if tough Muffy forgave, we all should
forgive.

As if he could read her thoughts, Andy said, "I almost
killed both your husbands, Roz." She wanted to slap him.
Then she remembered, like a whimsical scene from a movie,
the silly, whey-faced Trilling girl—Bratty?—slapping Andy
in the colonnade long ago. Good for Bratty. If Rosalind
slapped him now, would he turn the other cheek? She had
no idea. Ah, to slap him would be as absurd, as presump-
tuous as to forgive him. She didn't know him. When had she
ever thought of him as anything but her adoring student?
No dramatic gesture was called for from her.

The relief she felt—relief from judgment, for wasn't judgment what she had arrogated to herself?—liberated her
from Andy's goading eyes and the palpable expectations of
the room. Let the groundlings remain unsatisfied. She could
look where she would look, and with some irritation she
looked around the room at all the dawdling dinner guests.
Hadn't they had enough of a show for one evening? There
were practical questions to settle, legal questions. Why the
hell didn't the irrelevant people leave? She turned and shot
Will an impatient look, feeling her hair swirl. Her pendant
bumped her sternum and turned over. She righted it. With

a smile at the corner of his mouth just for her, Will stood up, walked between her and Andy, and positioned himself at the bookcases near the front hall. Andy turned around to look at him, leaning his elbow on the back of his chair. Snow spattered against the high windows over the bookcases. A lot of snow. *"You don't go home,"* Rosalind heard Ben, *"from the Donner Pass."* She shivered.

"With me, Andy, you didn't even come close," said Will, his voice casual, but his body taut as wire. Rosalind could see in the set of his shoulders and the angles of his wrists. "Although Roz nearly killed me, getting to the hospital. You know how Roz drives," he said to the room at large.

From the couch Paul Damian gave a sudden bark of laughter. "I'll say!" he agreed, then looked guiltily sidelong at his wife.

"Speaking of driving," Sarah jumped up from the couch to exclaim, "Paul, we ought to be going!" Immediately the spellbound torpor dissolved, and eyes veered to the windows, where snow piled in gentle ellipses. Rosalind saw Annabelle raise an eyebrow at Will, and then Annabelle stood up, an implacable queen. "Cynnie," she said, "it's time you were going too. Come, Barney." Barney got up, and together they began to walk to the front hall and the coat closet. Walter took Cynnie by both hands and pulled her, protesting, up. Paul Damian stood up, looking bright-eyed and mettlesome: Percival Dane leaving the knotty denouement to others. He and Sarah and Cynnie and Walter moved slowly to the hall where Barney and Annabelle stood, already holding coats.

Rosalind sat down on the raised hearth, rested her wrists on her knees, and held her hands with fingers laced, as if she were praying. Will stood motionless at the bookcases. Andy stared into space from the Barcelona chair. Flo Grimshaw leaned her head back against the couch, then absently smoothed the soft olive smock over the mound of her belly, and neatly crossed her ankles, waiting. They all listened to Barney and Annabelle speed the departing guests.

"Beautiful lynx!" Annabelle effused to Cynnie, pushing her out the door.

"Drive carefully," Barney said, his voice hoarse. "That snow's really coming down." The door closed. Annabelle and Barney, murmuring, could be heard starting up Andy's hand-carved spiral staircase to the bedrooms.

"Barney, we're getting too old for stairs," Annabelle's voice floated plaintively into the living room. "Let's find a little cottage for just the two of us where I can write my play." Barney's gravelly laugh rolled.

"Up you go," he said.

As if that were his cue, Will went around the coffee table and sat down on the couch near Flo. Rosalind stood a minute, her hand on her jaw as if she had a toothache. "Would anyone like anything?" she asked politely. Heads shook. Rosalind sat down fast, cross-legged on the floor by the coffee table, her back to the dwindling fire, Andy to her left, Flo and Will across; she felt low to the ground and humble under the high, peaked cedar ceiling.

Flo smoothed her dark hair and slanted a silent, eloquent question at Will.

Will sighed, stretched out his legs, and put his hands in the pockets of his jeans. "Handled properly, it should be all right," he finally said to Flo. "It may take a while, but legally it should be all right." Rosalind moved a jug of hothouse daisies to the side and let her hands fall limp on the glass table like water spilled. Andy'll get off, she thought. Do I mind?

"How?" Flo asked Will. "It wasn't self-defense."

Will looked at the ceiling. Rosalind admired the way shadows shifted under his cheekbones. "Well, if they won't give us accidental death, and it comes to a charge, Flo," he said, "we can always barter Andy's testimony to get Matt DiLorenzo and the FBI. Everybody's doing it these days."

Andy turned to Will. "No!" he said. "I won't rat."

"Jesus, Andy—"

"I won't."

"You won't rat on the *FBI*?"

"I won't rat."

Will leaned forward, really angry, Rosalind was startled to see. Will never got angry. She could not remember him angry; but then she had never seen him in court, just as he had never seen her in the classroom. Will's temple bones stood out like earthworks. "Tell me," he asked Andy, "how much Matt DiLorenzo paid you. How much did you get for ratting on Roz? A couple of grand? Come on, Andy, the FBI has a budget for its *finks*. How much did you get?"

"I wouldn't have taken money! And I didn't know it was the FBI!" Andy glared at Will. His ears turned bright red. Rosalind and Flo exchanged worried looks, then both started to speak at once. Flo deferred to Rosalind.

"Do you feel okay, Flo?" Rosalind asked her. She was almost amused at how fast the homely question drew the men's eyes away from each other. "Would you like to lie down?"

"Listen," said Flo, "if I haven't lost Junior here by now"— she patted her stomach, and everyone looked at her stomach—"I'm not going to lose him." She turned her head to Andy. "One thing I'm wondering, Andy . . ." She raised her hand towards him and cupped it, as if to catch an answer. Andy reached out and took her hand in his. "You never answered Walter. After it . . . happened, were you *following*

Roz? I mean, Roz had this little boy, and you were following her? Why would you follow her?"

"Huh?" Andy snatched his hand away. "I wasn't following her!"

Rosalind let go a little rueful laugh. Can I forgive him for all those years of *not knowing*? she wondered. "Do you know?" she asked dryly, letting the question be general, "it was years before I'd let Kit go out alone. A Jewish mother, Ben would have called me." She heard Ben's Brooklyn inflection in her own voice. "Ben!" Her laugh came out a trifle strangled.

Flo's turn it was to smooth the rippling waters. "You're not a Jewish mother, Roz," Flo said. "*I'm* going to be a Jewish mother."

"I wasn't following Roz!" Andy repeated as if nothing had intervened since his last protest. "How could I have followed Roz? I didn't have time; I was obsessed with the *gun.* It was in the back of my pickup covered by old clothes and a tarp. My worst nightmare was that suddenly it'd disappear. Sometimes I'd sit in my room, and all I'd do would be look out the window at the pickup. Sometimes I'd have to go out and check to see if the gun was still there. I kept *wiping* it."

"With the safety off," Will said. Andy started.

"Oh, no, Will." They locked eyes.

"If the safety's on, you can't shoot someone accidentally."

"I didn't mean to shoot you, Will!" Andy leaned forward towards Will.

"Leave Andy alone," said Flo, turning angrily on Will.

Will was cool as rain. "The safety was just accidentally off for over a month," he stated flatly.

"Honest to God, Will, I don't think I even looked."

Will pressed. "You looked at the gun every day, you said."

"To see if it was *there,* not to see if the fucking safety was on!" Andy almost snarled. "All right, all right! I wanted to shoot you, Will. Shit, I didn't even know you. I wanted to shoot you right where I shot you, to get you out of there and to get you away from *Roz*; and I stood there thinking as hard as I could, Come on, Roz, move, Roz, and damned if she didn't." Andy put his elbows on his knees and buried his face in his hands.

Will took a deep, deep breath. "All right," he said. "I can live with that." Flo and Rosalind looked at him, amazed. He shrugged his hands out. "What can I tell you? I can live with that. I can live with Andy shooting me in the shoulder. Listen, what I did just now was personal. I wasn't rehearsing you or testing you. My injury won't come up. It doesn't affect the death of Ben Roth, and it doesn't affect the fact that I'm your lawyer. My injury went on the record as a hunting accident, and that's how it'll stay. The record," he said wryly, twirling his hand. "I just wanted to know, that's all."

Andy was looking at Will incredulously. "You son of a bitch, you set me up. You set me up for the whole thing. You set me up to confess. You called me on the phone and you laughed and you joked and you asked me to come watch a football game and eat dinner, and all the time it was for *that*. . . ."

They all looked at Will. Rosalind recollected her own sporadic sense that she was trapped in the last act of *Hamlet*; she heard Paul Damian's half-joking suspicion that the table was a setup for Percival Dane; she saw Sarah stand up and holler at Will: 'You've got us all set up like the end of a mystery novel, Will Eddy!' Had he done it? Had he known? Cynnie had set the table. Who had thought of asking Andy and Flo? Rosalind was pretty sure she had. How the hell . . . ? Mystified, she examined Will's unreadable expression, his eyes not cold but speculative, his red-gold head slightly tilted, his hands holding his knees as if he would either get up or say some more. "Will, how did you know Andy did it?" she asked.

"The puzzle." A loud stage whisper, like a prompter's cue, came from the spiral stairs. Not even daring to turn, Rosalind stared at the look of wise and sheepish resignation that came across Will's face.

"All right, Kit," Will called softly. "Come on down."

"Kit. Oh, Kit!" Rosalind struggled to her feet, her legs crossed Indian-fashion too long tangling; Kit caught her. She felt her tears flood his turtleneck. His turtleneck. "You didn't even get undressed!" She pulled back to reprove him. Kit and Will let go identical, ironical laughs.

"Well, Kit, as long as you're up, you might as well stay up. Sit down, you two." Will gestured wearily, rubbing his hand across his eyes in the process. In unison Rosalind and Kit sat down across the table from him. Andy and Flo looked at Kit with blank expressions, as if they'd never seen him before, and then Andy leaned forward.

"Roz, I thought you'd be the one to figure that out," he said.

"Figure *what* out?" Rosalind found her control of the stress and pitch of her voice loosening. She covered her mouth with her hand.

"The puzzle, Mom," Kit said sidelong, as if helping out a slightly backward classmate. "Tell her, Will."

Baffled, Rosalind looked from one to the other. Will ran his tongue in his cheek and tapped his fingers on his knees. "Roz," he said, "it's the damnedest thing. Do you remember the jigsaw puzzle Andy made us for Christmas?"

Rosalind nodded. She frowned, trying to picture it. Will said, "Roz, it looks like Calypso: a woodland scene with a

Roman temple crumbling, a hunter with a highly sophisticated rifle." Will turned to Andy. "I couldn't help thinking,
this is a really odd picture—what's a hunter doing with an M
16? Then, I said to myself, ah, it's just allegorical, a Vietnam
rifle to go with the mushroom-shaped clouds, just a general
sixties protest, you know—"

"Oh!" Picturing the puzzle, seeing how obvious, how plain,
how *glaring*—Rosalind could have kicked herself. "I'm the
expert on medieval allegory," she said woefully. "How could
I have missed it?"

"I must have done the puzzle a hundred times," Will went
on, "and every time I did, it felt like déjà vu. I'd get this
flash picture of Calypso, and then I'd see Andy there, and
when I let myself indulge what I thought was probably fan-
tasy, I figured he was subconsciously 'telling' "—Will
sketched quotation marks in the air—"that he knew who had
killed Ben Roth, and I was sure it was Matthew DiLorenzo,
despite his alibi—a bride's alibi, after all. What I couldn't
imagine was a kid Andy's age being able to cope with all that
sophisticated weaponry. I still can't see Andy doing it."

Quickly Will turned his head and gave Andy a probing
look. "Andy, it *wasn't* DiLorenzo, was it? I mean, you're not
taking the blame for him, are you? Or are you? Oh, I'd love
to get the FBI for the whole thing," he said sideways to
Rosalind and Kit.

Andy's exhausted, rather glazed face broke into a frown.
"Huh? What? What the hell, Will? *I* killed Ben Roth. Di-
Lorenzo wasn't even there."

"Wait!" Kit whispered hoarsely, lightly pounding a fist on
the glass table. Startled, they all looked at him. "Was there
really a question about Matt's alibi, Will?"

"Matt," Rosalind murmured. "Did you *know* him?"

"No, no, that's what Luke always called him," Kit said im-

patiently. Rosalind watched his face shift back through half
his life. "Matt taught Luke to play basketball," Kit said.
" 'Cause I didn't have a big brother, he'd be my big brother,
Luke said." Stupid tears started down Rosalind's cheeks
again; she saw Kit small and blond next to tall Luke, walking
trustfully towards the gym at the college.

"*I* was suspicious of the alibi, Kit," Will said, "but I was just
a lowly state trooper. The FBI investigators professed to
find it airtight. Let me see." Will tapped his forehead with
his index finger and consulted the ceiling for inspiration.
"The afternoon before New Year's Day Matthew and Teresa
DiLorenzo were seen at a motel in Niagara Falls, where they
had been for five days. The next afternoon, New Year's Day,
they were on an afternoon flight to Rome, where they stayed
for two weeks. The thing that didn't sit right with me was
that the plane flew out of *Washington*. DiLorenzo of course
lived in Washington, but only the bride's word held up the
gap between the two afternoons: she said they drove
together to Washington."

Rosalind felt herself shrug rather blankly, but Kit continued questioning Will. "Who found my father's body?" he
wanted to know. He and Will looked intently at each other,
as if they were alone.

"Ah." Will closed his eyes a minute. "The FBI. They got,
wait a minute, I'm trying to see the page—they kept trying
to keep the records from us. 'An anonymous telephone tip,
male caller, presumed to be a hunter.' Yeah."

"When did they get that telephone tip?" Kit pressed.

"Oh, Jesus, Kit, I don't know!" Will sighed deeply. "That
whole investigation was botched from start to finish, probably on purpose. They must have gotten it right before that
son of a bitch from the FBI arrived at the barracks here. He
was in a hurry. God, remember him, Roz? Well, he came in

huffing and puffing and *alone*. That's almost unheard of; the FBI always travels in pairs. He appropriated me as a makeshift partner, but he never let me say a word. He dragged me to pick up your mother, Kit, and then, to my complete amazement, to the body." Will snapped his fingers in the air. "That was the single cruelest act I have ever witnessed; that was the end of police work for me. God!" He let out his breath in a rasp. "Roz, you were terrific." Will and Rosalind held each other's eyes for a long moment.

"So they found the body right after Matt got back from Rome," Kit said, as if to himself. "Mom," he turned to ask her, "why was Luke at the cottage that day?"

Rosalind looked at him. "What day?"

"The day they found the *body*."

Andy broke in, as if out of a dream. "Luke was there that day? What was Luke doing there?"

Will said, "Didn't you invite him, Roz?" Everyone looked at Rosalind.

"No," she said slowly. "He came, um, to bring us a basketball." She looked around at the incredulous faces. "Well, he did bring a basketball. A Rawlings," she lamely concluded.

"Mom," Kit said, "that day was freezing cold."

"Um." Rosalind frowned. "I remember!" she said then. "He came to watch the Super Bowl in color." She distinctly remembered thinking that had been Luke's prime motive, for the earlier night he'd spent with her he'd also spent with the color TV.

"Roz—" Will began, but Kit broke in impatiently.

"Mom, he could have gone to a *bar*. Instead he hitched twelve miles in the freezing cold, carrying a basketball? Mom, you're not *thinking*."

Rosalind bit her lip. She looked at Will, who had his head tipped to one side as if he were listening for something.

"Roz," he said thoughtfully, "what did that bastard from the FBI say to Luke DiLorenzo when he saw him?"

Rosalind racked her brain. She could conjure the prissy rosebud mouth. "He told him he could go."

"Did he ask him his name?" Rosalind could almost feel Kit's brain racking next to hers.

"I don't know," Rosalind finally said.

"I don't think so," Kit said. "He told Luke he could go, and Luke said he didn't have a car, and the man said—excuse me—'Shit! Keep your mouth shut.' "

"That's right!" Will said.

"Then you threw the basketball to Luke and Luke threw it to me and I threw it to Mom, who missed—" Kit looked a sidelong reproach at Rosalind. "And then Luke and I played basketball all afternoon in the snow."

Andy Grimshaw was hitting his head with the heel of his hand as if he had water in his ear. "That is the weirdest thing I've ever heard," he said. "It doesn't make any sense."

"Well, I was glad Luke was there," Rosalind declared. "He took care of Kit."

Will had his face buried in his hands. "Could his brother have sent him there to *baby-sit*? Nah, that's crazy!" Speculatively he looked at Kit. "Did Luke do anything strange when you two were alone?"

"Did he make a phone call?" Flo, suddenly alert, wanted to know.

"There wasn't a phone," Rosalind, Will, and Kit all said together.

"We watched the game," Kit said, his eyes fixed on the past. "Luke went to the kitchen a few times and got stuff to eat. Potato chips. Sandwiches. I didn't think you'd mind, Mom—"

"Could he have planted something?" Andy wanted to know.

"I don't think they found anything," Rosalind said. "Did they, Will?"

"I don't think so," Will said.

"Maybe he took something," Flo suggested.

Rosalind and Kit looked at each other and shrugged. "I suppose he could have been looking for something," Rosalind said. "Will, maybe for that envelope I had sewn into the quilt. Kit, did he seem to be looking for something?"

Kit frowned. "No. As soon as you left, Luke said, 'Hey, let's build a fire.' Mom and I didn't usually have a fire till night, but I said okay, so we built a fire. We raced to see who could get it to light first. But then we just sat down and watched the game."

"You built a fire," Will said eagerly. "As soon as we left?"

"Yes," Kit affirmed.

Rosalind made an incredulous face. *"Smoke signals,* Will? This is too much! To signal what? We had already left."

"Roz!" Will's face lighted. "Honey, what arrived at the scene right after we did?"

"Cars," Rosalind remembered. "The press, an awful lot of press—"

"God damn it!" Will slapped his hand on his knee. "Even at the time," he said expansively, "even after you had thrown up all over me, I thought"—he raised a finger and jabbed it at her—"I really thought the words: *right on cue.* It couldn't have been better timed if it had been staged, and who got all the publicity? You did, Roz. Your face was in every newspaper in the country. In fact you got so damned much attention, the intentional bungling of the investigation got completely obscured. The press zeroed in on the revolutionary outlaw and his beautiful young wife, who had on her own a couple of famous parents—"

"And a couple of wildly disparate lovers," Rosalind wryly added.

"So, this is what had happened," Will continued. "Matt DiLorenzo got home from Rome and found that nothing had happened. Nothing." Andy started to protest. "Shut up, Andy! Let me finish," Will almost shouted. "So *Matt* phones in the tip to the FBI. *Matt* alerts the press and arranges a signal. And Luke DiLorenzo, probably on blind orders from his brother, lit a fire to make sure the press arrived at the scene the minute Rosalind was there to absorb all the attention. Nobody ever cared much who the murderer was. There was enough excitement, enough glamor. I mean, who killed Valerie Percy? Who killed Malcolm X? So many murders go unsolved, and *nobody cares*."

"But, but, Will—" Andy was starting to sputter.

"Andy," Will said, with a smile in his voice, "I don't think you did it. I don't think you killed Ben Roth."

"Oh!" Flo gasped.

Andy was doggedly shaking his head. "Will, I shot him. I know I did."

"You said you didn't remember pulling the trigger," Will pointed out. "I can hear you saying that. You 'must have,' you said."

"But Will!" Andy held his hands in fists in front of him. His voice went falsetto. "I was right in front of him! Ben Roth *died*!"

"Did you find your shell? Did you check the clip to see if a shot had been fired?"

"No," Andy mumbled, hanging his head, "I didn't check the clip. I did vaguely look around for a shell, I think, but—" Andy lifted his head and looked at Will like a little boy. "Will, I had never fired a gun before; I had held guns, and I had read up on how to load an M 16, but I had never fired one."

"You had never fired a gun?" Will was thunderstruck. "My God, I'm surprised you didn't kill me *and* Roz that day in the woods! Well, never mind." Will bounced his hands in front of him. "When you were with Ben, did you feel a kick?" Will slapped his own shoulder.

"Shit, I don't remember."

"Did you feel a kick when you shot at me?"

"Yes, I felt one then," Andy said. "It scared me. It hurt."

"Listen, have any of you ever seen films from the FBI Academy at Quantico?" Will asked everyone in general.

"They have dummy figures that jump out," Kit said, "when the agents are learning to shoot."

"They have to be crack shots, that's the point," Will said. "Matt DiLorenzo would have been able to hit Ben Roth from a hundred yards, even with a touchy rifle like the M 16; he could have been in the spruces; he could have been any-place. No, wait, Andy." Will put out a hand to shut Andy up. "He knew the time; he knew about the cemetery; he even knew you were so conscientious, you'd go on your own. If the bride Teresa's testimony is disregarded, say three and a half hours to Caliban from Niagara Falls, then either three and a half back and they drive to Washington together, or they simply meet in Washington, New Year's morning. He could have driven; she could have flown—"

"Under an assumed name," Rosalind added. She found she was laughing.

"Why would she *do* that?" Flo wondered. "Wouldn't she be suspicious?"

"She was too much in love to care," Rosalind decided. "She must have known he was with the FBI, and that would cover a lot of what we would consider suspicious. Matt could say"—Rosalind held her hands in a frame—" 'Teresa, honey, I've got some last-minute business to take care of before I

leave the Bureau, and I need your help.' This is the afternoon of New Year's Eve," Rosalind paused to narrate. " 'Tell
you what.' Matt says then, 'you fly down tomorrow, using an
assumed name; ah, come on, honey, that's *fun*; where's your
spirit of adventure? Meet me at my apartment on, oh, P
Street at noon. I'll be all packed by then. If you have any
time beforehand, take in Dali's *Last Supper* at the National
Gallery. Just think, we can compare it with Da Vinci's in
Milan!' "

Will and Kit got laughing. Flo looked totally absorbed in
Rosalind's reenactment. Andy was shaking his head as if to
clear it.

Will took up Rosalind's story. "So Teresa, this trusting girl,
agrees, and when she falls asleep—"

"After who knows what night of *magic*," Rosalind ironically
interjected.

"Matt, having waited till just after midnight, the New
Year, takes off in the car for Caliban, goes to the cemetery,
and *waits*. All he has to do is wait. Ben and Muffy arrive.
Andy arrives. Muffy, insulted, goes to sulk in the Land-
Rover. Andy shows Ben how to load an M 16. Matt Di-
Lorenzo shoots Ben Roth. In the hubbub that ensues, you
following Muffy—I mean, where were your eyes on that
ride, Andy? Weren't they fixed on the lights of the Land-
Rover? Weren't you terrified she'd leave you alone with the
body?" Reluctantly Andy nodded. "So," Will went on, "Matt
is able, probably with his lights off, to follow you to Calypso,
and when he's satisfied you two are disposing of the body, he
takes off for Washington. Matt killed him, Andy. I'm *positive*.
All these years, all these fucking years, you've been suffer-
ing for nothing."

Everyone looked around, amazed. Rosalind, still playing
Percival Dane in her head, was thinking, Opportunity, yes,

but what's the motive? "Of course," Will continued, "if you'd confessed, the FBI would have been pleased to let you take the blame. Christ! They could even rely on you not to 'rat.' DiLorenzo probably didn't even mean for you to think you'd shot Ben Roth. He was confident both you and Muffy would cover up, whether you'd been responsible or not. He had the two of you in a kind of thrall: Muffy from sex, you from romantic politics. You certainly weren't going to get *him* in trouble. Oh, Jesus, what a story! Neither of you had any idea then that he was with the FBI. He was 'the Evangelist.' In any testimony of yours or Muffy's, if it came to that, he'd become 'the missing Evangelist.' I mean, who's Muffy? Even today she's 'the missing Muffy,' and that's all she is."

Will's gray eyes gleamed on the stunned gathering. "Motive," Rosalind heard Kit mutter next to her. "Why did he want to kill my father? Why didn't he just arrest them?"

Will bit his thumb. "An arrest. Andy could have gotten off completely on grounds of entrapment. He was," Will explained round, "induced to commit a crime he would not have contemplated on his own."

"Weren't Ben and Muffy?" Rosalind wanted to know.

"Yes," Will said, "but there were a lot of other counts against Ben, and probably some against Muffy, once her identity was determined. Back in seventy-one, revolutionaries went to jail. Wiretapping and all that jazz. So DiLorenzo might have been disciplined for entrapment, but the arrest of Ben Roth would still have been a coup for him. It would have rounded off his career with the Bureau nicely." Will held out his hands and flexed them. "Roz, did Matt know Ben? Did he have any personal reason to hate him?"

"Matt and Ben had never met." Everyone remembered Andy's story at once, even Kit.

Rosalind turned to Kit. "Were you listening all the time? Did you hear everything? Aren't you *upset?*" She couldn't believe how poised and calm he was.

"I had to hide when Barney and Annabelle came up," Kit admitted. "I might have missed something then." Rosalind rolled her eyes at no one in particular.

"Why would Matt hate a man he had never seen?" Will was asking the ceiling. "The FBI was never named in any pejorative sense at the inquest or on the pages of the record. Matt and Luke DiLorenzo were never subpoenaed. The murder was attributed to 'person or persons unknown,' and this was generally interpreted to imply rival members of the Weather Underground, almost a gangland killing as the FBI would see it. For Matt DiLorenzo, Ben Roth, his elusive assignment, simply dissolved. But, damn it, there was no reason to have him dissolve. Ben Roth could not have hurt Matt DiLorenzo in any court in the land in 1971. Why the hell—"

"Ben Roth could have hurt Matthew at the cemetery," Flo suddenly volunteered. "Matthew was outnumbered there."

They all turned to look at Flo. Her dark hair was a mess by now; her knees were stolidly apart; her stomach seemed to have ballooned. "Flo's right," Will said. He started to smile. "And they had all the guns! You can load an M 16 fast, once you know how. Matt didn't know Andy couldn't shoot, and he sure as hell knew Ben and Muffy could —Weatherman trains harder than the FBI. Any law officer approaches even one Weatherman with extreme caution. I mean, some of them are absolutely fearless in combat. According to their behavior, Mao was a chicken, Ché was a wimp, the Panthers are overly cautious. Do you know something?" Will paused, as if he wanted an answer. Obediently they all shook their heads. Kit even said, "No."

"You know something?" Will repeated his question. "I

think Matt DiLorenzo shot Ben Roth because he was, plain
and simple, scared to die."

"Will's right." Flo's voice dropped into the bemused, startled silence.

It wasn't that real! Rosalind wanted to scream. Nobody
was going to die! But her hands stayed on the table, and her
voice died in her throat.

"What was it you said, Andy?" Flo shyly asked, turning to
him. "That you met me and all of a sudden you had something to lose?" Andy had tears on his face again; he lunged
over to Flo and tried to put his head on her breast, but her
belly was too big. Will moved over to give him room to sit
next to her. Andy put his head on Flo's shoulder. Flo spoke
over his head: "Matthew had just gotten married. He had
something to lose too. He panicked, just like Andy
panicked."

"He was a person," Rosalind mulled aloud. "You've
turned him into a person, Flo. Matt DiLorenzo was somebody's big brother, and he taught him to play basketball. It is
so hard to think of him as a person." Matt *killed* Ben, she
thought. He almost cut in two the body of the man who
fathered my son. He had me followed; he watched me, Rosalind's mind went on. He wanted his brother to make love
to me; *he* made love to poor Muffy. What would we call a
woman who did what he did? A whore. He was a whore and
an assassin. Who dragged at least two college boys into his
web. Who got married, yes, to the richest girl in Buffalo, and
maybe he loves her, who knows?

"We should tell," Rosalind said, almost without her volition. She looked at Kit.

"I think so too," Kit said in a voice barely audible.

"Ah," Will said, beaming on them, "we can ring down the
curtain on the FBI with this one."

Andy raised his sandy head from Flo's shoulder. "I won't rat," he said wearily, but emphatically. Will looked at him.

"Why not?"

"Rat on *Luke*? Luke has five children. Luke was the nicest guy you'd ever want to meet. Wasn't he?" Andy demanded of the startled Rosalind and Kit.

"Yes," they both admitted. Rosalind had a flash image of Luke against the fieldstone chimney and the daisy sheets; she could hear him so perfectly talk to the seven-year-old Kit.

"I loved Luke," Kit said, looking down at his hands folded on the table.

"For Christ's sake," Will said, looking at them all in amazement, "all *Luke* did was make a fire to alert the press. He probably didn't even know what he was doing it for. As a clue that helped us put it all together, it's important, but as evidence against him, it's laughable. Nothing is going to happen to Luke. It's Matt we're after, Matt and the God damned FBI. We can expose them." Will's voice went silky as he turned to Andy next to him. "Why won't you help me expose them?"

Andy sat up straight on the couch, leaned over, and with both fists pounded the glass coffee table. The jug of daisies rattled. "I don't want to *rat!*"

"Andy, we can't do it without you!" Hectic red stained Will's cheekbones. Will and Andy leaned at each other like dogs growling. Looking from Will to Andy, Andy to Will, alarmed at this hostility, this aggressive masculinity, this, well, *testosterone* in the air, Rosalind heard herself suddenly and wildly laugh.

"Flo," she got up on her knees to ask, "did I ever tell you that the day Andy introduced you to me in the colonnade inspired me to absolutely the corniest act of my life?"

Andy turned his head and looked at Rosalind as if she

were about to tell them all a bedtime story. "I proposed to Will," Rosalind declared. "But that wasn't the corny thing; the corny thing was the way I did it. That was pure corn. . . ."

· *Pure Corn*

March 1971

With a gesture of submission he bared his head and stood gravely, the square cap dangling in his hand.
  "Placetne, magistra?"
  "Placet."

                                          Dorothy L. Sayers, *Gaudy Night*

At two o'clock on a Thursday afternoon, fleeing her Shakespeare class but unable to shake her regular, straggling train of followers, Rosalind saw Andy Grimshaw in the colonnade. The wisteria leaves were just beginning to bud on the latticework between the brick pillars. With Andy was a short dark-haired girl in a plaid skirt. They were hand in hand, looking only at each other. "Andy!" Rosalind called out to him, arresting her forward motion, stopping short. "Andy!" Surrounded by a whirl of whispering, buzzing Shakespeare students, she gave him a big resounding kiss on the cheek.

"Roz," Andy said, looking dazed. "Roz, this is Flo." Rosalind and Flo smiled at each other. "We're in love," Andy dreamily said.

"How marvelous," Rosalind murmured. "Well, see you."

At the end of the colonnade, she cried, "Oh, I forgot something!" Before the dangling students could gather their wits and their bodies, she was running back through the colonnade. She cut across the lawn to the low brick wall above Hobbiton, vaulted over, ran up the road to the back-campus parking lot, got in her Firebird, drove out through the chain-link gates, and headed straight and mindless for the Interstate. She'd pushed the car past ninety before she heard the siren, saw the flashing red light in her rearview mirror. It had better be him, she thought, pulling over.

Will Eddy got out of the green and white State Police car. He wore a ridiculous Stetson hat with a chin strap. "Where's the fire, lady?" he cracked. He stood at her open window.

"Will you marry me?" she asked him. "Will, will you marry me?" She grimaced at the double *will*'s. "I know we haven't slept together, but how important is sex, really . . . anyhow. . . ." Her voice trailed off.

"How important?" He got laughing. He took off his Stetson, and she saw his red-gold hair flame against the pale blue of the sky. He bent his head through the window and kissed her mouth. He didn't touch her, just his mouth, and their lips clung, and her body grew warm from the center out, velvet darkness, liquid; and then she felt his tongue, and all the soft parts of her body seemed to flow towards his warmth, oh, it was unbelievable, would never do, not through a window on an interstate highway. . . .

He pulled his mouth away and asked, "Didn't you know?"

"Know?" She fluttered a hand. She was panting.

"My God, woman, what there was for us."

"Was?"

"Is."

"I'm the one who propositioned *you*," she said, laughing triumphantly. "God, Will, what luck, what incredible luck . . ."

"I feel so stupid," Rosalind murmured to Will, "that you and Kit both knew there was something significant about the puzzle, and I didn't. And Kit was the one to wonder why Luke was at the cottage that day. . . ."

"Well, honey, you did figure out Ben's code from a card in his wallet."

"That's right! D'you suppose Ben wouldn't work with anyone who didn't have a biblical name?"

"Like 'Muffy'?" Will asked ironically.

Rosalind snorted, and Will raised up on his elbows. He was inside her, and her body lifted to keep him there. For half an hour—ever since Will got back from driving Andy and Flo home through the snowstorm—they'd been making desultory love and also talking nonstop. Is Will the only man who can do this? Rosalind wondered. The only man with such damnable, indifferent control?

Sudden, involuntary tears spilled like cascades over the arch of her cheekbones into her ears and her sprawled, tangled hair. Abstractedly Will stroked into her long and slow, then poised himself therein, a complement. His body was as light as if he'd taught himself to levitate. "You are so beautiful," he said, "inside. Like silk. Silken."

"Stay," she said. "Stay in me all night."

He smiled, then looked at her thoughtfully. "Think it through, Roz. If you'd told Ben about Luke and his big brother, Ben would have realized the connection and gone anyway. He'd've been out for blood. I'm sure he and Muffy were carrying firearms of their own. Somebody would have been killed, maybe everybody. God, two dozen M 16's!" Will moved lightly and fast inside her as if to gather his too rapid thoughts. "They were a lot alike, Ben and Matt, both almost thirty, both mucking around with schoolboy codes and willing women and grown-up rifles. But Ben was out to commit suicide."

"What?"

Will stopped, propped himself on his elbows to look down at her face. "Come on, honey, give it the kind of scrutiny you'd give a *book*. Ben was inviting Andy to shoot him. And Andy might even have done it if Matt hadn't beaten him to it. Ben couldn't go back. Maybe if he hadn't seen you that one last time, he'd have survived—"

"Me?" She felt her body tense. "Hadn't seen *me*?"

"Easy. Easy." He stroked again, strong and soothing. "Ah, Roz, Ben knew then what he'd lost, what he'd so cavalierly thrown away. 'You don't go home from the Donner Pass.' Whew!"

"Will Eddy!" Rosalind pulled her knees back fast and with the soles of her feet kicked him away from her. Will fell over on his side, regarding her with mock reproach. Rosalind sat up, cross-legged and desperately literal, to protest the historical reference: "Some of the Donner Party did, or they went on to San Francisco, where they were heading anyway. One fool even opened a restaurant."

"A restaurant?" She saw Will swallow hard. "Did people *know*?"

"I think he used it in his advertising."

Will shook his head and laughed a little. "I suppose," he said wryly, "it's no worse than Haldeman and Ehrlichman."

"Tamsen Donner wouldn't go down from the Pass," Rosalind went on. "The rescue parties tried and tried to persuade her, but she wouldn't. She'd put on weight, eating the dead. Her husband was dying, and that gave her an excuse to stay. She died at Donner Lake. She was too intelligent to want to survive, Ben said. Ben was fascinated with Tamsen Donner."

"Ben?"

"Ben did a paper at Columbia on the Donner Party. I could almost see it when Andy was talking. I typed it for him—it was publishable, but he never got around to it. Ben was working on a doctorate in history, you know."

"I didn't know."

"Oh, Lordy, yes. He was good too—a wonderful teacher. At Columbia, Kit and I used to sneak into the back of his classrooms to listen to him."

"You should tell Kit."

"I'm going to. I'm really amazed at how well he's handled this." Rosalind bit her lip. "Will, I've been wondering why . . ." Her voice trailed off.

"Why what?"

"Why Muffy took Ben's body to Calypso. Did she want to get back at me, or did she know Ben would have liked it there? She mourned him, didn't she? I didn't, I didn't, I didn't." The tears started streaming again.

"Roz . . ."

"He did rape me," she said almost involuntarily.

"I thought so," Will said. "I was glad the FBI didn't push it. That was your motive, you know."

"Well, maybe it wasn't exactly rape," Rosalind discriminated, wanting to be fair, definitions of rape being so con-

troversial. "I didn't fight. I even tried to help him. I think I
tried. He hurt me though, and when it was over, like a silly,
romantic fool, I put the . . . indignity out of my mind. 'The
lovemaking'll get better now,' I thought. 'Now Ben is mine
again.' From where Muffy saw it," she mournfully admitted,
"it must have been a brutal, hard-core scene." As the details
of the scene rammed back, Rosalind let go a wild laugh. "I
was wearing yellow knee socks."

Will took hold of her shoulders and pushed her back. He
moved inside her again. She felt his heart beat against her.
She breathed with his rhythms. "The day I met you," he
said, "you were wearing red stockings."

"I was," she laughed. "I *was*."

"You had all that hair," he said. "I was dazzled. Then you
started screaming those incomprehensible Victorian curses
at me, and I fell in love. All the time, I couldn't take my eyes
off those long red legs. Oh, Jesus, Roz, you had them apart a
little, and when you yelled at me, you knocked them
together." He thrust into her three times: hard, staccato,
white-hot probes. She felt her breath catch. "All night?" he
asked her. "Are you sure?" Testingly, gingerly, she contracted a little. She was awfully ready, she discovered, all
poised vagility, ready to sail away. The palms of her hands
tingled at the thumb joints; her face was hot; her ears
thrummed.

"Are you sorry?" she asked him, holding off the symptoms
for one breathless, exquisite second. "Sorry I came ninety
miles an hour into your territory?"

"Roz . . ." Will moved into her deep, pulled back, went
deeper, started to thrust; oh, he knew how to handle her.
She could feel her resentment—of what? his power? his passion? his precision?—begin to alter as all that was kinetic
focused and pulled to where she and Will connected, and

then her resentment whirled away into the violent stasis of that spinning point. She lost the world, split apart, and every atom of her body vibrated with the skill of his love, her hands, the soles of her feet, her loosening, ranting thighs; but when she recovered, she still had hold of the thread of her question, as if it were a valuable, silken kite.

"Are you? Are you ever sorry?" Before her mind's eye, a dark-haired kindergarten teacher skipped like a harlequin.

Panting, his red-gold hair damp on his forehead, his gray eyes glittering with irony, Will, leaning on an elbow, regarded her. "The day I saw that Firebird the second time," he said, waving his hand in an eloquent arc, "the Interstate Highway became for me"—he paused for effect—"the road to Damascus!"

"The road to Damascus?" Rosalind sat up fast and glowered at him. This is too much, her mind protested. I've married two men who've tossed off that transcendent, beautiful image *flippantly,* like a cliché. "Will, that's not an appropriate image. That's awful—"

"Yeah, Damascus, New York. It's up the road a piece, lady, just over the state line. You go across the Zeugma River, turn left, and—"

Rosalind bashed him with a pillow. "Blasphemer!"

"Sticks and stones . . ."

Rosalind eyed him speculatively. "You know," she casually offered, "Andy could have done it after all, Will."

· *Coda*

"Some of the Donner Party Did . . ."

MARK RUDD SPEAKS
. . . my New York and Chicago charges were settled as of January
19, 1978; I have faced no federal charges since 1973, when the government refused to disclose its illegal burglaries, wiretaps, mail
searches, political sabotage, and torture directed against me and
others [thus] requiring dismissal of all charges.

These activities were part of a broad counterintelligence opera-
tion, which often included the planting of false rumors in order to
sow distrust within progressive and revolutionary movements. The
black movement especially has been targeted, as is commonly
known. From Martin Luther King to the Black Liberation Army,
many people have died or are still in prison due to Cointelpro.

Mark Rudd
c/o Gerald B. Lefcourt
Manhattan

New York magazine, "Letters," April 24, 1978